Books by Charles W. Bechtel

Novels

The Odor of Orchids
Book of Days
The Lady from Spain

The DREW NOLAN series

A Hole in the Water
Hell's Cold Furies
When the Ball Drops Foul
Running Before Thunder
And Then You Don't
A Hypocrisy of Oaths

Non- Fiction

On Second Thoughts, a collection of essays
Writing Tips, a guide to writing better sentences

Short Story collection

The Long and the short, collected short stories

Poetry collection

Sound Words Seen, collected poems

visit

www.charlesbechtel.com

the Lady from Spain

CHARLES W. BECHTEL

Ruk Books
Mesa, Arizona
2014

First edition

ISBN-13: 978-0692292846
ISBN-10: 0692292845

the Lady from Spain

CHARLES W. BECHTEL

Dedication

To my wife, **Manuela Iglesia y Serrano,**
for sharing her story,
and for casting shade on where I toil.

Spain

Memories unburied
return in present tense.

A Place to begin

Two in the afternoon, a Madrid courtyard again is quiet, too hot, and many sleep. Even the kept canary on the patio sleeps. Some around the courtyard have shuttered the windows to keep out the light. The light is too much, and it is not good. There is shade behind shutters, and if they are good shutters there is dark. It is a good place to lie. Some prefer the dark, others must keep to the shadows, where breath can be had, and, sometimes, even sleep.

When the sun goes down, even midsummer, well, that's a different story.

Take this one, for instance.

Though the evening is young, a man returns to a bed, having come away from a phonograph where he has restarted a song. Always the same song, something from Brazil, in Portuguese. The woman in the bed, having lit two cigarettes, keeps one in her lips, holds the second for him. Smoke climbs over her head. She does not care for the song.

He takes the cigarette, sits, and looks at the record cover propped at the foot of the phonograph cabinet. A girl, a woman, hard for him to tell, a woman on the cover is looking up, away and out, as though she watches a silver airplane winging north, perhaps to America. She is not laughing, not exactly, nor smiling, but she looks happy, excited for whoever rides in that plane.

The woman in the bed, she is a woman and he has no reason to think otherwise, fingers a tassel on a small pillow pulled onto her bare stomach.

They lie in the lull of interrupted conversation. It had not been the song's ending that interrupted them. He has asked a question. In the song playing, its bridge is without words, and they listen to the piano player picking out a part of the melody to vary.

When the piano fades and the singer reenters, she answers his question.

A girl.

Ahh. I have two girls, he says, over the lyric.

She knows that already. Does not care.

Why don't you take her, now that you can?

Why should I?

She's your future.

She's my past. The woman draws deeply on her cigarette. She is done, and stubs it into a tin ashtray. *One of them.*

What do you mean, one of them? Don't you only get one past?

You only get one past. My past is new.

How can your past be new?

Because that is what I want.

He hands her his cigarette to snuff. *I suppose with pasts so variable, we should see a gypsy. Have our fortunes told. They must change rapidly too, eh?*

No. The future is the same. Now shut up, Alejandro. I want to listen to this song.

Why do you call me Alejandro?

Because, she thinks, *you are all Alejandro.* It will become a joke she makes, which none of her men understand, when she learns English. *Men are all Alejandro and the same.*

Later, she lets him lie again over her. She admires the new bracelet.

This evening is one from the middle of the story.

There are others, of course.

MORA

Nothing worth keeping that cannot survive its loss, Mora reads, though in her language: *Nada digno de perdurar que no pueden sobrevivir a su pérdida,* which sends the book flying to the floor. *¡Fah!* Hits against her private nightstand, the candle shuddering, attracting her attention, and enmity. She snuffs it with her fingers.

The Little One already in bed asleep, pink with perspiration, mewls and twists, her thumb in her mouth. *Ugh.* The room is close as a closet; the air, she supposes, sweeter, cooler, at the glassless window.

She sweeps from the bed, running her hands underneath her long black hair, lifting it away from her neck. Her hair is fine and dark. It spills through her fingers to her shoulders, a black cloud overtaking a snowy mountain. She has never seen a mountain. *Perhaps, one day — and soon!* — and from a lacquered coach pulled by black Arabians, four — *sí, quatro* — the flesh of each gleaming, polished coal eyes, each dressed with red pompons and tassels the color of fire. *That would do,* she thinks, picking the dry wood of her shutter. *That would certainly do.*

The shared courtyard of the Sevillano barrio is near empty. Only a dog licks itself within a circlet of electric light. Quiet lies everywhere in the square, and the moon not yet risen. Stars she can barely see without pressing herself too far through that window. No love of stars, no. Too far, too cold, worse than diamonds on the fat fingers of women she passes but cannot know. For Mora? *The moon.* It rules her expectations now, a close friend pregnant with an exciting idea.

He will come. Would he? He must! She strains to hear, but falling terrifies her, and she allows only her face to reach into the night air. The silence is good; she will hear his footsteps. *Or had he already come?* Had he already dropped pebbles from the roof? Has she missed them rattling onto the cobbles? *¡Imposible!*

My little monkey, he had called her when she showed him how easy a climb was to the roof. *Mi pequeño mono.* He is her little monkey, once he had learned to climb the rainspout. As fast as Doña Oroszcos' capuchin up a curtain. But not in his uniform. So handsome in his uniform, La Guardia Civil, with their little monkey hats. He would never climb with his hat, even though she had asked him, demanded, pleaded short of begging. She would not beg. She would never beg. Never as a woman. But she teased like a little girl. *Wear your funny hat,* so that she could take it and put it on her own head. She dances for him, until he catches her, when she has his hat. She claps her hands above that hat — quietly of course, to be caught was the end of dancing with a little monkey hat. To silence and absent music she curls like a gypsy, Carmen before Don José. Perhaps one day on the flagstones of the *Patio de los Naranjos?*

He did not need seducing.

Will he come? He has to come! There is something to say, something to tell.

There is no moon, but there was a moon, and it had brought her an exciting idea, and he will dance to hear what she has to say. *If only he comes.*

But the courtyard is silent. No breeze in the hot night air. There is nobody any longer in Seville. Nobody living. Nobody worth living. All dead, she wishes them, all of them, sleeping as though dead, all of them. *Somewhere. Somewhere where they take them away and make them dead.*

Mora rises from her crouch at the window to fetch the book flung down. It had fallen open to the page it always opens to, for how many nights has she fallen asleep with her finger crooked between the always same two pages? All of them, since he had given her the poems. She has broken the book's spine on Lorca's poem, *Primer Anivesario,* the First Anniversary. It is coming, their first anniversary, the august August day a year from when she had first fed him her eyes and showed, with a snap of her fan, that he must look into her eyes forever.

She has no need to read the page with her eyes; her mind can do that, and does in the pitch black of the candleless room.

La niña va por mi frente.
¡Oh, qué antiguo sentimiento!
Girl so much on my mind, Oh the ancient sentiments…

Mora slides to the cool tile floor, curls her legs, presses herself against the edge of the bed, lays back her head, to whisper the poet's words to the close bedroom air, *«¿De qué me sirve, pregunto, la tinta, el papel y el verso?»*

Will you serve me, ink, paper and verses? She hears the clotted, snotty breathing of the Little One. *Ugh!* She would write her own verses, hopeless in every hoping phrase, and press them into his hand. Then he would come, and she would be able to share her secret now only shared with the moon, and he would dance. Of course he would dance. Like a fiend he would dance, a demon in his gleaming Guardia Civil hat! Until he could no longer breathe air, would only breathe her, drown in her perfume, so feverish the buttons would fly from his uniform and kisses would rush from his lips onto hers, onto her neck and breasts, and to her belly, her moon rounding belly…

Carne tuya me parece,
Rojo lirio, junco fresco.
Morena de la luna llena.
¿Qué quieres de mi deseo?

He will, he will, he must. She strains to hear the pebbles rattle from the roof. For without him, now, everything is lost.

La Madre, Señora Dolores Soledad y Vega

First, bolt the door, then all the windows and shutters. Then check again.

Her hand finds the stove, cool now at last, then the door against which she presses her one good ear. *Nothing. Silent.* Not even a heat-defeated dog scraping along the wall. Her worry, nonetheless, remains. It has become her old friend, her bed companion, her empty bed, empty eight years.

She feels through the dark. Each rent in the wallpaper, each chip in the plaster, each crack in the furniture she knows. Her fingers roll across a candle holder, the stub nearly worthless. No need for a candle, no allowance for a light bulb. The candle itself an expense. *Thank the Divine*, she says, kissing a knuckle.

The holder's brass cup is splattered with wax. She moves her thumb across the rim, the wax beads smooth and cool. *Tomorrow*, she says, *I will collect you tomorrow*. She counts each droplet. She counts each a child in her worries... *so many gone, too many gone, too many yet to go.* Maria, married. Alfonso, dead, his round face frozen at two. Diego, upon whose face she never looked, stillborn and lifted away forever. Isabella, where? She shudders at the possibilities. Vincenzo, mean. Josué, the face like a turd, his father's face, dead as his father. Nachito, somewhere on water, somewhere not safe. Mora, doomed by beauty, ruined by it already.

And the little German, *la rubia*, Luna, doomed by yellow hair, doomed to worship a sister who despises her yellow hair.

She reaches the front door, already locked, checks it again. Then she goes into the sitting room, lays her hand upon where she knows the cot will be, takes a seat, draws a knitted blanket over her legs even though the air is hot, close, still. She is cold. *I am always cold*, she often says to a daughter.

She sits upright, alert to knocks on her door.

There is no knock at the door.

On a square lacquered table rests a rosary. She has learned to use it. With a hard, yellowed thumb nail, she moves over each bead.

«*Dios te salve, María, llena eres de gracia. El Señor es contigo. Bendita tú eres entre todas las mujeres, y bendito es el fruto de tu vientre...*»

She has learned this, too. It gives her invisibility, she believes.

Alejandro Senna

Stopping before a dark glass fronting a carneceria, Senna measures himself by the parts of his uniform. The light from a distant street lamp glints off his cap, sparks dance on his buttons. He tugs down the corners of his jacket, *better*. But nothing helps his shadowed face, a tired face, a young face working streets through the night.

Soon, he turns for a profile. *Someday*, he repeats, *they will give him the day to walk, and the best parade, the walk beside the Guadalquivir. And he will meet American tourists. He will be a statue among beasts, in his uniform, them in heavy suits and Parisian dresses.*

The streets are more quiet than they are dark, and they are always quiet. *The curfew, if not for the curfew, well…* he knows the Spanish heart and its disregards when shadows may be had. He once had the same heart, before. Before the buttons and the cap.

All know where he walks. If there will be any noises, they will not be where he's to hear them. In the barrio, the poor are afraid. And fear makes one quiet, and quiet lets one believe one is invisible.

He tugs down his jacket again into a perfect plane, touches his cap, and walks on. He lets his heels click against the sidewalk, a warning to those who would use the shadows. *Remain quiet, stay behind doors and closed shutters.* He is tired, and he does not want excitement.

He could have excitement, and he thinks of the blue perfumed note in his pocket, *Venid a mí a medianoche* scratched under a Lorca poem. Those last words were her signature, in case another found her note. He tilts his head, *Let them find it. Let someone else have her. She grasps too much.*

But, then, tilting his head toward the other shoulder, *She is beautiful. And soft, and willing. No, she makes love to clothes, not to me. Still, she is beautiful, and she is soft, and pressing against her does change the world.*

But she has a dangerous tongue, and danger feeds her eyes. I must stop, I will stop. Must not go.

Senna — long in the leg and elegant in his manner; one a legacy of his father, the other the demand of his mother — chews his cheek while imagining himself presenting Mora. With spit, *merde en la boca,* she would mouth *Too dark.* He shakes his head. *But how fine a thing would that be! if it would free me forever from the vineyard...* Would she let him keep his uniform? No. Banished at once. *¡Imposible, nunca nunca nunca!* She will stamp her hidden foot and command the second son to climb onto her lap.

He would beg, and would insist if he were more man and less a son, to *Let him inherit.*

¡No! She would shout. And insist. *¡No!* Everything stinking of grape must, and will, go to his hands.

And then she would call for a glass of wine, perhaps her third.

He walks on through the night shades. *I would rather march on Morocco from Algeciras than walk another row of dirt!* There would be more, more too much insufferable talk of duty and responsibility, a yoke dropped on his neck at the creation of Time and carried since.

You would not be lucky with that one. She will step on your head and bury it. Doña Senna would remind him, again, *You are lucky for the dirt, lucky for the grapes. Put your love there. And your service. And your duty.*

He had duty and service enough for his uniform, thank you very much.

A KNOCK ON THE DOOR

No sound forewarns with more terror than does a rap on the door after midnight. Whoever knocks in a black hour never comes with good news.

And when the knock is suspected, predicted — there have been rumors, weighted whispers, warnings, and there have been reports by others that, at the edge of the neighborhood, already some had heard such a knock — the sound enlarges, takes monstrous shape: a gargantuan specter, a protean haunt, a massive golem, a towering creature made of shadow and evil, and it knows your name.

October, the seventeenth day, 1939, a quarter past the second hour, one such knock rings on a door. Eight men wait behind the one who knocks, a varied lot: one thick-necked butcher and his dull son; the third, a twisted stick known as a junior member of the town council; two who dragged a third from his sherry and who hold him erect by strong grips on each arm; the seventh, a young dandy from the *Guardia Civil*, sharp in his coat and tricorn hat, but uncomfortable in its newness; and the last, someone never seen before and never seen again, his black uniform as foreign as his blonde hair and thick lips, a German. Austrian? *Alemana.*

Most — though not the drunk, who can barely bring into focus the tightly laced boots of the one empowered to gather them all together — most in that waggering lot keep their attentions fixed above some other's head, or on their clasped hands. One coughs, another blows into his fingers even though the air is not chill. At the German's snapping bark, the most forward of them, the butcher, pounds that door again, harder.

Inside, three generations sleep, having been asleep for hours. The eldest of them, the one who had turned off the last light and climbed a narrow stairs to his bedroom, his ears attuned to how each in their beds went to sleep, is first to waken. He knows the sound, knows it in his historic bones, knows why it has come. They have come for him, and his sons.

He comes awake, but cannot move. Cannot. But when the second rapping finishes, he hears someone stirring, and he slides his hand toward his wife. Then he hears the shout.

Raus!

It was the last night he would ever be. It was the last night his eldest son would be. It was the last night that any of the women struggling out of sleep would ever be known by the name — or the history — by which they had always been known.

And it was the last night any of them left to live ever went to sleep without imagining something to fear.

A MAN, A MOTHER, A GIRL, A VISITOR

For good reason, Mora's young man fingering his tricorn hat turns the stomach of Señora Dolores. When such a cap is seen, whether as she returns from the market, or if bent under the *picante* sun to collect snails — *caricoles* — to sell, even during a careful stroll among the fancy dressed at a fair, Señora Dolores slips into shadow to wait its disappearance, perspiring no matter the weather, her breathing fast, heart faster, each beat that pounds in her ears expands a hope she has, that she will not be seen, into a prayer sent heavenward.

Yet, there, held upon the knee of a young man, one such cap sits. And that idiot Mora beams as though she is in the company of a saint, that glossy black cap his golden corona.

We must have our demands, she says, but thinks, *What's the use? Bastards. All of you, every damn one, bastards. And now us, with another bastard coming.*

The man, young, and yes, handsome, dips his head, acknowledging what she has said. His smile is small, frozen, assured of his duty and twice assured happily that he will never be permitted to endure what the woman demands. He shifts his weight toward his left where his mother, enthroned, sits as though carven.

Mora? Not once does he look at her. It is no longer her that he thinks of. No longer, now that he has seen the sister. As a child will, the blonde haired child hides, but is seen when she peeks. And the one who sees her is the man with the hat.

From where has such a radiant, golden child come? Where has she been kept?

Señora Senna, indifferent to the presence of whomever would disturb her afternoon, wears no smile. She has not once turned her head toward the woman standing amidst them all, nor set her eyes on the frilly *puta* then glowing with a woman's belief that she carries in her a trump card. She does not look, but she sees everything.

La rubia, the sister Luna, brought along after an hour of crying, lurks in the foyer, her thumb in her mouth. She presses against the arch between the rooms. She has risen on her toes, for a better look over the potted aspidistra at the man who will take away Mora. *He'll take me, me, and I won't ever have to see you again,* her sister had said. She had made Luna cry. On her toes, however, is tiring, and she drops down, *thump,* on her heels. The man's head turns, his eyes find her. As does his widening smile. She blushes, ducks behind the aspidistra, but not so much he cannot see — as she wishes — that she is in her best pink dress.

I don't care what you wear, Rat. He's not coming to see you. It's for me. To marry me.

The woman in black says to Señora Dolores, *How do we know that this?* Mora reddens. *How do we know that this* her lace-gloved hand rises, a boney finger extended *doesn't carry the bastard of any host of men? We have our own demands, and we will do nothing about yours.*

It is as Señora Dolores has expected, and had explained to her refusing child. *How, indeed. If,* she wonders again, *the stupid child...*

Mora has an answer, and moves to give it, but she receives a slap on the mouth. Shocked at what her mother has done, it does not stop her tongue. *You will let her call me a whore?* Then she stands, turns to the man standing, who has drained of color. *And you? You prefer I carry for you a bastard?*

She is red, her mother white. The visitors both are gray as stone.

«Salé» she hears. *Go.*

Corporal Alejandro Senna then rises, extends a hand to his mother, who dismisses the offer with a wave.

Luna, familiar with the sound of a hand striking a cheek, yet still surprised, steps into view of them all. Settling his glossy hat on his head and fitting it to his sense of perfection, Alejandro Senna watches the child for a long stretch. As do others, but his attention is different. His mother sees his smile, and darkens.

Doña Senna says to no one, but to all, *«Rubia, y eso explica lo que creo.»* She grabs at her son's coattail, tugs and shakes it. He continues smiling and Luna blushes. She does not tuck herself back from sight.

Mora, too, sees, and she condemns herself even further in the opinión of Doña Senna by the string of words she screams.

It does not matter, Doña Senna decides, still holding her son's coat tail. *Let them find their way to the door.*

ON A FOLLOWING EVENING, AND ON AN AFTERNOON COMING NOT LONG AFTER THAT

A different moon, the same moonlight. A different girl, a very different girl. Even the room has changed. The Runt no longer shares her bed. Mora, though, still looks out a yellow square into a dark blue night, her hair as brushed but clinging in strands to her perspiring neck. She would push her face to the shores of America, but even there, there would be no cooling air to meet her.

She has just again read the line, *Nothing worth keeping that cannot survive its loss.* She knows the lie for what it is. *Nothing lost was worth keeping.* What she knows, as she rests both elbows on the sill, dropping her chin into a cupped hand, is that what never will become lost is her beauty. *Even,* she rests a hand on the swelling, *this has done nothing to it.* Had she not that very day heard someone say, *Ever more beautiful, Señora?* Of course, the cow did not know her error. *Señora indeed.* Mora throws her hair brush into the courtyard where it clatters about like an old wooden shoe kicked across the tiles. *Fah.*

She has done this before. She spits into the dark, listens, then rises. A favorite hairbrush, after all.

Mora pleads and pleads, day after day, and finally she is allowed a visit to the market. But only during siesta, an hour before her courtyard will fill again.

Her feet have begun to hurt, and she despises her mother.

On one arm hangs a soft basket, and in the basket rests a *cartucho* holding a fish along with two brown eggs, and four figs. The figs she begged to have, an indulgence. *But it's the season,* as though that meant anything, hardly enough a reason.

But anything repeated often becomes reason enough.

Once or twice she catches an eye that has caught her passing by, an eye whose shape and definition she recognizes but disdains. *What do they know of love?* is always her response.

She is tired, though she can see no place to sit. The *churro* window is closed, and where men can sit they do, a few, drinking beer in glasses. She would like a beer.

Beyond the arch at the street, the August sun pounds every surface. Even within the comfort of the shaded market, such light stings her eyes and she starts to look away. But then *he* steps in.

She does not see him so much as knows it is him. The tap of his heavy shoes on the floor. The erect carriage. And the tricorn square and officious on his head. She does not look away.

His eyes dance over the produce. *He must find me,* she prays, but he continues to sweep his gaze from one side of the dusky market to the other. *He must see me.* And then he does, or appears to have, for his eyes stop, but only momentarily. Then, Mora sees, he looks away.

The figs are in her hand, two of them, and her arm rises, then, cocked, flung forward. The two figs land at his feet, and all in the market turn, faces gone to stone, eyes hard as coals on the man from the Guardia Civil, each mouth wordless, each body wishing itself invisible.

Mora hears someone whisper, *imposible.* Not impossible, *bah!* She has done it.

The tricorned man steps farther into the shaded market toward her figs, eyes down and fixed upon them, one broken and split, its ruby guts revealed. With his toe he flicks it toward a corner. The other he picks up, bites, enjoyment spreading over his face.

He smiles, she can see that, *and at her,* and touches his cap. *He touched his cap!*

¡Cabron! rattles the tiles and glass. Her mother's grip comes down on her basket-arm.

Not one more word.

The man in the fearsome uniform continues to smile, turns about on his heel, and goes.

A CHILD BORN UNWANTED

Take it, take it, take it! Mora has nothing left. Her screams slide into whispers, her eyes half close. She hears someone, her mother? Maria? someone, someone saying, *A girl.* She cannot care. *Take it, take it, take it.*

Later, in another room: Luna, each hand on a drawer knob, looks down at a mewling baby. All red except for the black hair. She wants to kiss the flush skin on the infant's shoulder, likes how soft it is under her finger. She does not like the hair. She wants it yellow, as her own is yellow.

Behind her, the eldest sister Maria folds white cloths into squares, settling each into a cardboard hatbox.

Tia Maria. Luna likes the sound. *Yes. Sounds old.* She does not like it when they say she must now be called *Tia Luna.* No, does not like that at all.

Luna reaches out for the baby, but Maria warns. *No.*

Later: Maria buttons her blouse and smooths down the damp bodice. Feeding the baby makes her sad. Luna asks, *Why?* Maria looks on the girl's face for a while, saying nothing. But her lips are tightened. The baby, returned to the bureau drawer, mewls louder, and it diverts all attention.

You wouldn't understand.

Luna frowns. They always say to her she doesn't understand, she won't understand, she can't understand, that she is too young to understand, that someday she will understand but they never tell her when day that will be. She turns her attention again on the baby, the infant ready to glide into sleep. She prods its chest with a finger. *If I don't understand, then you don't understand.* She thinks this to the baby, sending her thoughts from her forehead down into the child fighting to free a hand from the blanket. *You'll never understand anything before I do.*

Luna's mother comes into the room, a quick look at her youngest, one at the struggling infant, and then, fixing on Maria, Señora Dolores says, *They will take her. Tomorrow. They will baptize her. Nothing we can do.*

I will do it, Maria's eyes redden and get wet. *Me, and Peter. He will stand for her too. He knows what it is. After that, we'll do it.*

You won't have to keep going there. They have others.

Maria nods, still sad. *They have so many to nurse. I want to. And, I want to.*

Luna leans down to think more words at the child, then she kisses the baby on the shoulder. Its hand comes free and finds her yellow hair, holds it, does not let go even when Luna pulls away. Luna does not mind, but she does not like not being able to stand straight. Her mother, she knows, will not like it either and will strike her across the back.

But her mother does not hit her. She hears her mother say, *Christened. The Most Divine, help us all.*

Luna does not know what that means, either.

But she is right, will be right. The child will not understand before her. She will not understand for a long, long time.

EACH ANSWER A LIE, ALL ACCEPTED IN THE NAME OF THE LORD

The celebrant asks the witnesses, *What name do you give this child?* The answer is a lie. Maria studies the dark child asleep in the priest's arms, and thinks, *Miralea. She will be Miralea. She must be and will always remain Miralea.* But she says, *Lucia. Lucia Maria... Soledad y Vega.* It is a lie, but it is a necessary lie.

The priest and the celebrant choose to look at the font of holy water between them and the liar. The lie is acceptable. For the next question asked is, *What do you ask of God for... Lucia Maria?*

And here is where the difficulty lies, and will lie. The question is meant for parents to answer. But there are no parents. There are only those present who have come to give a bastard to the Church, and those also present who will take a bastard away.

But Peter, Maria's bent and sad husband, gives the answer. For him, it is not a lie. For him, it is custom, and to him Maria defers all that's to be performed. *Entrance into the Church.* The priest nods.

You have asked to have your child baptized. This, too, is a lie, but a necessary lie. *In doing so you are accepting the responsibility of training her in the practice of the faith. It will be your duty, yours Señor, and* with a knowing pause, in a voice that has no guards against its prejudices, *yours as well, Señora, to bring her up to keep God's commandments as Christ* a swift, dark look from the celebrant toward the sad woman in black, *as Christ taught us, by loving God and our neighbor. Do you clearly understand what you are undertaking?*

Peter looks at Maria, and she at her husband. The celebrant and the priest continue with eyes turned toward to the baptismal water.

Claro.

What? The priest's scowl deepens. There are formalities to be met. But he has asked too loudly, and the child in his arms opens her eyes.

Peter, in a clear voice, says, *We do.*

When the priest asks his next question, *Are you ready to help the parents of this child in their duty as Christian parents?* the celebrant smiles, but tries to hide it. The priest waits for the answer.

Peter says *I do.* Maria says nothing. Peter says, *We do.*

Lucia Maria, the Christian community welcomes you with great joy. In its name I claim you for Christ our Savior by the sign of his cross. I now trace the cross on your forehead, and invite your parents, your godparents, to do the same.

He signs the child on the forehead, in silence. Then he invites the two to do the same. Only bent Peter reaches across.

The priest turns. He and the celebrant have already discussed and concluded that what remains is to be dispatched later. *It will be done, but in due time,* the priest assures the couple, *though later.*

No one except the priest knows if the Liturgy of the Word had been spoken over Lucia Maria. The priest never says, and the family never asks.

EXPLANATIONS

In Seville, the heart of Most Catholic Spain, children frequently are born to people unfit, unable, or unwilling to continue as parents. Since medieval ages the custom of the Church has been to look upon an illegitimate child with a humane eye, for each is a product of God's love and the result of his injunction. Or so they believe. As there has only been one divine birth recognized by the Church, it follows that every child has a mother and a father, no matter how vigorous a man's claim may be against his paternality. Sanctification by vows of marriage remain preferred, but failure to secure that sanctification is not viewed as the fault of the child any more than an orange is blamed for the twists in the branch from which it has grown.

The Spanish Church accepts a child as its ward, no questions asked, no condemnations applied. Unlike what is the rule in more secular nations, in Spain the Church expects, demands, and gets, continuing support from the family if not the natural parents, when a child is brought by family and not found abandoned in a doorway, which sometimes happens. A father remains a father, so long as it is understood and accepted that he is the father. Denying a mother's claim against him is rarely sufficient to void his paternity. Usually. But there are exceptions.

They are few.

One is the unquestionable occupation of the mother. If she is a whore, fatherhood may be impossible to determine. If not a whore, then her liaisons must be documented. To name Mora as a whore was impossible; to provide the name of another suitor had its equal difficulties.

To what extent the wine-grower Doña Senna had to go, to find men willing to lie to the Catholic Church about having lain with Mora, is not documented, but her pressures, and her treasury, must have been extensively applied. Her brother had forced a son to testify, as did several from the field upon whom Mora had never laid eyes.

The only consequence from that parade of lies, so far as the Sennas were concerned, was that it removed them from any and all responsibility toward the infant Lucia. Any, and all.

As gone into the shadows of history as her true given name was to become, so vanished the name that even a bastard has the right to claim.

A DREAM

Not an uncommon visitation, but a fever again has Mora. She rests, but fitfully, the evening full of heat. A dampened pillow has become her only bed companion.

On this night, or rather dark morning, she has a dream. Much of her dream rises from a recollection of a magazine article that she had glanced through earlier in the day, when she stopped at a street vendor selling the old and unused. On the magazine's cover had been a gypsy dancing her gypsy dance, the bare-legged woman caught mid twirl with an expression of mad fire on her face. But that was merely its cover. Inside had been an article about fabric making, not the industry but the craft.

In one picture, a woman worked a loom, her right hand poised to thrust a shuttlecock between the warp threads.

This is what Mora dreams.

She lies inside a shuttlecock. A giant woman in mourning clothes bends above her. The threads between the woman and Mora are perpendicular bars of black iron and bright horizontal threads of a spider's web. As they would to one imprisoned in a shuttle, the warp and weft fly over her head swiftly, never allowing Mora to fix on any given thread. She struggles to free her arms, but the sides of the wooden shuttle pin her into place as would the sides of a coffin.

Back and forth, the speed increasing. The dark woman over her is intent only at her task. Nothing says she has a care that Mora is trapped inside the shuttlecock. Mora knows that only Mora cares about Mora.

She wants to scream, but she cannot breathe enough to scream. Then, as sometimes happens in dreams, there is a knife in her hand, which sometimes is a knife and sometimes an arm of a man. She stares at the knife, but when it is a man's arm she feels a need to cry. She will not cry. And then it is again a knife.

With it she reaches up, her arm stretching and aching with the need to reach. The strings are cut.

Then she becomes the woman weaving, but she is not wearing a dark shroud of mourning. It is a mantilla falling at the sides of her head, the comb in her hair so heavy it forces her head forward and down. The mantilla is colorful, brilliant with rosettes of red and yellow, leaves of greens and blues. There is spread across her bent back the wide carriage of a peacock, something she cannot see but knows is there.

The shuttlecock in her hand is sometimes a knife, sometimes a shuttle.

She weaves and weaves. She cannot stop, and the panel of cloth grows. But the pattern of what she makes does not emerge. All she knows is that the fabric sometimes shivers like silver and is hard to see.

Before she awakens, she hands the shuttlecock to a strange man, and he hands her back a wallet. Then she wakes.

GYPSIES AND SEMANA SANTA

The Easter crowd is thick, a swarm, which is good for it helps keep Mora warm, but too many are drunk. There are men in suits, most of them wearing small brimmed hats pushed up and away from their wet, glittering eyes. The women wear either black crepe or colorful cotton dresses, and jewelry. Some of the jewelry are thick-chained necklaces of gold, the ropes suspending between amplified and wrinkled breasts an amulet reflecting the *dolorosa* of the Passion.

Many bear an image of a mother who has lost a son.

None bear an image of any mother who has lost a daughter.

It is the cool, blue evening of Holy Thursday in Seville, and Mora has again her fine shape. There is no loose pendant on chains of gold against her breasts. There is only lace, and her dress is yellow cotton. Across her shoulders rests a fine black shawl with flower rosettes embroidered in brilliant colors.

She stands with her arms folded, though she has been commanded to hold tightly to her sister's hand. The Runt tugs where she keeps a grip on the skirt, though several times Mora has batted Luna's hand away.

From a short distance off comes the brass flourish of cornets. The procession which they await is coming, but it is not so near as to be seen. The penitents' dance is a slow shuffle with many stops. Mora is impatient, but not for a view of the penitents nor for an appearance of the gilded float bearing the wooden image of *La Macarena*. Not for that at all.

She keeps her eyes locked onto an iron fronted balcony above the narrow street. The twin, heavily curtained doors, a rich expanse of green velvet, are closed, but she knows what is happening on the other side of them. Laughter, abundant fruit and pastries, women in antique costume and carefully pinned and lacquered hair, magnificent mantillas draped over tortoise shell combs at the back of the head, perhaps a knot of uniformed men, maybe even some foreign, invited for the spectacle. But, she knows, a particular someone, a young proud man, is not among them. He is a proud young man walking before *La Macarena* for her protection.

Because of him, Mora waits. He will arrive with his head high and neck stiff, his tricorn cap glittering with lights from the many candles carried by the slow moving *nazarenos* before him, one flickering light atop the long staff of each.

Because of him, but not for him, she bides. The procession will stop under the iron balcony, the doors will open and out from the doors shall step a well-paid singer. Then will follow behind him la Doña Senna.

The evening is cold, colder than predicted, colder even than what Señora Dolores claimed it would be. She had frowned at what Mora has chosen to wear. The cobbles rob Mora's slippered feet of warmth. Though the Runt has heavier shoes, she complains by the hour, several times asking, then pleading, then begging, for her sister to explain why she cannot go to the corner to see the Virgin. Mora has not answered with anything more than *Be quiet*, and *Be glad I let you come*.

The arrival of the golden spectacle requires a slow turn at the tight corner, difficult for the hundred men carrying the ton on their shoulders. The jeweled statuette of the wooden Virgin, *la Macarena*, gently rocks, sways, until they set her down. Her supplicating hands are turned palm upwards. *Why, why, why have you had to kill my son?* There is again alarms of the cornets, and the crowd falls silent.

The twin curtained doors open.

Mora is unaware that a small, brown and barefoot woman has come up behind her, a basket in both hands full of rosemary bundles tied with ribbons, *para buona fortuna*. Mora steps backward. She wants a clear space before and around her. But her heel finds the gypsy's toes, and the woman, with a sharp scream, shoves Mora away. It is then that something Mora hides comes to light, a little tart blood orange she had pulled from a tree in a courtyard she and her sister had passed through. It falls from Mora's hand.

The gypsy woman, angry, stomps the fruit, the dark pulp pushing through a rupture. Mora, stunned, then slaps at the woman's basket, spilling several of the fragrant bundles.

Not one screamed word is understood by either Mora or Luna, who tucks herself behind her sister in fear, but the meaning of each is clear. Without a regard for any of the strung-together insults, Mora bends to scoop up her ruined fruit. She takes one posie from the ground as well, which she gives to her sister. The gypsy's hand comes out, demanding her payment for the token, but Mora turns away.

The singer on the balcony has begun his paid lament.

He sings a vibrating chant of deep sorrow, each note flowing out and over an outthrust hand as though his heartfelt pains were wáter spilling from a gutter pipe. Doña Senna, who has pulled into everyone's view her second son, who then rests his head against her hip, beams at the sorrowful singer.

Doña Senna sweeps a smile from one far edge of the milling crowd to the distant other. His song is her gift to them, her expensive gift to the undeserving, pitiable poor.

Mora raises the split orange to her mouth. It is bitter, though ripe. *Maybe,* she begins smiling, *she will enjoy this.* She sees Doña Senna settle her smile on the approaching shoulder-borne barge, or rather at her eldest walking head up at the barge's prow. She sees the woman's smile is stiff. *So much the better.* Mora cocks her arm, aiming the throw to sail over the heads of the nazarenos.

But it does not launch. A man's fingers grab and stop her wrist. The fruit, dislodged, strikes a stranger's back and tumbles down.

Mora flashes her dark eyes at the one who has ruined her moment. The man does not let go. Mora digs the nails of her other hand into the man's grip, her fingers a cat's, the lacquered nails gouging streaks. He does not let go.

Beside him the bare-footed gypsy dances. Mora hears a woman behind her say, *Gitanos. Steal you blind you let them* and she spits into the man's face. *They shouldn't be allowed here,* the woman's companion says. *None of them, no matter how pretty they make themselves up.*

The singer finishes. The cornets blare, there is a cheer, and the collective *hunh* of men lifting a ton back onto their bleeding shoulders, and the man still does not let go.

Would you like to see me dance? It's just there, the man says, pointing her gripped hand toward a bright opening to a long alley.

Why not, she thinks. *Why not?* She tells Luna to go watch the procession at the corner. The child cries as Mora leaves, but with a sharp eye and a snap of fingers, Mora ends that.

ROTA

An American in uniform tilts back from the smoke clouding the table and glasses, one foot up on a support rail to the chair of another American in a similar uniform. He pays little attention to the others, watching a woman dance on stage. He likes how smooth and muscular her legs appear under the swirling skirt, kicking out from many frilled slips.

Ya gotta love gypsy music, dontcha, Ned?

The woman on stage claps her hands, a violent wave shuddering up her calf at the hard stomp of her feet on the wood. Behind her, fingers fly up and down the strings of a blonde-faced guitar, the man's face in no way matching the fury of the sound.

Flamenco, a women says from the opposite side of their table, bobbing her blonde head in agreement with herself, satisfied she has exhibited the depth to her worldly knowledge.

I love gypsies, says second the woman. *Y'ever seen anything like?*

Last night, says Ned.

Two nights running?

Ned's friend says to the women, *Three nights. It's how I know here. He's the one found it. The dancer's pretty good, ain't she? Besides, I hear gypsies,* he leans closer to the blonde and her friend, *are easy.*

The blonde laughs. The other woman, caught by the man's guffaw mid-sip, darts her eyes from one face to the next. She has missed something, and doesn't like it.

The blonde asks Ned, *You got a thing, Honey?*

Ned ignores her question.

I bet he does, she says to the man still laughing. *He sure ain't paying us no attention.*

What I'm paying for is your drinks you're enjoying.

And maybe other things, the laughing man says, brow lifting. *But seriously, Ned. Do you got a thing, like the lady's askin'? Three nights running.*

It sounds like a question, but not one worth answering.

The blonde asks, *Maybe he knows her. You know her? I mean, when she's not dancing?*

Not yet. Ned lets the chair he has rocked backwards slam down into place.

AN ORPHAN'S HOLE

The holes in the wall are arranged in the same manner as crypts into which the dead are placed, though instead of cemented fronts these have small panels of wood that sometimes keep the rain out and the heat in. However, there is rarely rain, and often heat.

An orphan to each, an orphan saved. Or, as the sisters insist, they ought to be.

The orphan's holes pockmark and scar the wall opposite where Maria rocks, another woman's child sucking at her nipple. Another bundled and half-fed child, the one she had come to nurse, lies asleep in a box behind her skirt where there is shade.

This new one hurts, chews, sucking as though starved, and she probably has been. There are three other women, wet nurses, feeding the abandoned, but they sit apart from each other. They have not come to chat, they do not share gossip, for they are in the shadow of a holy place, and theirs is a holy duty. Theirs, though not Maria's.

One of the women has finished, both teats drained, and as she waits for a sister to take her infants inside, she rubs where the child has made her sore. She, too, studies the holes in the wall. Maria wonders whether, the woman perhaps an unfortunate herself, she contemplates her own days in such a hole.

The third woman pulls from her pocket an orange, peels it, and let the curls slip to the ground beside her feet. A dove comes close, to peck the pith.

The sun creeps onto Maria's foot, and the light bites her instep with the passion of fire ants. She kicks her foot and stops the feeding, to shove herself more into the shade.

If there is a holiness in her duty, it is in doing right what another who should will not do at all, but the goodness one does for an innocent does little to alter the flavors of bitterness.

However, before she is done, three women in swirling habits approach like officious penguins.

It is a stern and unkind face that looks on her without patience. Maria pulls the new child free. She hasn't time to button the front of her dress before the tallest nun lifts the child from her, a glance at Maria's flesh.

Maria thinks about the woman's frown during her long return to the barrio.

LA COCINA DE TRES GITANAS

The air is foul with smoke and sweat, but also full of hoots, claps, shouts and the music verging on an anarchy of sounds. All is awhirl and dizzying. Everything is bright, for candles blaze along both whitewashed walls of the alley, and lights spring from the many glasses, whether full, half emptied or awaiting a filling.

In every glass, especially in those nursed by wide-eyed Americans clutching their purchases at a table near the stage, is sherry. Dogs sleep or chew under a number of tables, and along the one edge of the alley wall that does not rise straight up to a third, fourth or even fifth floor, cats lick paws, stare down at the throng, or look into the crazed wraiths of the spirit world that only cats can see.

Mora finds herself at home, at last.

This she knows and she begins to smile, and smiling is not something she often feels worth the practice.

At the entrance she stops the woman who had cursed at her, by settling a hot hand on the woman's shoulder. In her other hand she holds a coin purse. The gypsy stops, a guarded curiosity on her brow. Mora gathers from the opened purse a number of pesos, which she then holds forward for the woman. *For the rosemary.*

The coins vanish.

The dark-eyed man who had asked her to the dance touches her lightly on the back, urging her to press farther into the crowd. He guides Mora with a murmur, sometimes with fingers against her covered arm, to a crowded table. An old woman seated there snaps her fingers, barks commands that Mora cannot understand, and five young children stand and make way.

Mora watches the musicians. Many young, a number older, a few very old, arc their bodies and raise their hands in gestures essential to the traditional dance. Mora feels herself pulled toward them, but the old woman at the table claps her hands once and points to a chair.

The man, noting how Mora bends and cranes for a glimpse, shouts to those who block her view and they part, revealing to Mora a woman curling herself about an erect and rigid partner in tight clothes. There, to the rhythms of outlawed music, writhes her inspiration, her future, in a red dress, a flaming mantilla, and shining black shoes. He bows to Mora, then pushes past the boys, to replace an elegant dancing boy with moves of a man.

Something that has never before occurred — even when the despised Alejandro had slipped his hand over her never before touched breast — happens to Mora. She blushes. Her face turns warm, her throat perspiring, and something other, something lower, older and inside, ripples with electric current.

The man who has asked her to dance is not stupid.

And it is several hours before she remembers Luna.

SCREAMS, SHOUTS, AND A GOOD RIDDANCE

Luna has fallen asleep against a stuccoed wall, and had she been awake, she would also be hungry, cold, bewildered and scared. But she sleeps until a gentle hand of a tall figure in a silk robe, the pointed hood tucked under his arm, his bloodied toes a bare inch forward of the hem, brushes her cheek and prods her chin. *Señorita? Chica?*. The Virgin has long since disappeared, and everywhere is empty and quiet.

Luna had waited against a ledge to a café, but the owner chased her off. She did not go far, for she did not want to lose sight of the bright alley into which her sister vanished. She found a buttress against which she first leaned, then slumped, then crumbled against its bottom.

Later: *Look at you! Look at both of you! Look at her!* Señora Dolores screams, swinging a broad leather belt. It catches the corner of a frame photograph on the wall, a country landscape of Navarre that crashes and shatters. She wheels the belt again, and this time catches Mora both on the cheek, ripping a bloody trail, and a length of her long dark hair. And there it lodges, the mother pulling a daughter closer, a daughter fighting herself farther away.

That's how it goes for two days, until the Señora, busy stirring a porridge of oatmeal and mango, sees her youngest approach. Luna, asleep though she stands, removes her thumb from her mouth to ask, *¿Dónde está mi hermana?*

Señora Dolores will not know where Mora has gone, not for a long time, a very long time.

José Greco

Mora dances until her slippers shred, and then she pulls them off and flips them away to dance barefoot. And then she dances until her feet bleed.

She dances in alleys.

She dances on corners, where passers-by drop coins into her new friend's hat.

She dances in bars, on sanded floors, on hardwood pallets laid down just for her.

She dances before a campfire, mashing stolen fruits into her mouth, the juice coloring her lips to that of a bruise. Even the women who hate her clap.

She dances under stone arches in Baena.

She dances through the night for the olive pickers of Jaen.

She dances outside of the sherry makers in Jerez de la Frontera.

She dances down *La Ramblas* of Barcelona, for Americans in Cadiz, the British in Cordoba, Germans in Malaga.

She dances atop the broad steps of the Prado in Madrid, two guitars fighting as jealous lovers.

She dances at *La Feria* in Seville, inside the tents to which none she knows will ever attend, before long tables filled with families, and later single men.

She dances, she dances, she dances.

In the heat of the afternoon, the cooling hour before the sun sets and — most often — into the night, past when shutters begin closing, lights go out, doors are locked and the sherry put away, Mora dances.

One early morning in Madrid, as she and her latest accompanist and lover return to a small room in a small hotel, she discovers a cinema crew in action. She begins to dance, no music, a hundred yards from where the director orders crew into place. Because of a snap of her fingers, her man slides his guitar from his back and begins.

The director barks at them over his shoulder, but the fingers do not stop strumming, and Mora's feet do not cease sweeping over the stone. One of the cinema crew, himself in love with the neck of a guitar, absents himself from the filming. They had set the lights and he has nothing to do but wait. He follows the flamenco music to where Mora dances. She does not dance alone, but for the crew member watching she may as well have been. He has never seen such a thing, and when Mora stops for water from a *bucaro* sweating itself cold, he dashes back and interrupts the director, who is slumped in his portable chair. The light setter's enthusiasm is vigorous, and the director motions a cameraman to pick up his always-ready Bell-and-Howell 8mm and follow.

Mora spots them filming and dances on. But nothing comes of it.

In Fuengirola, the plates of the *meriende* cleared away and the evening strolls beginning, Mora on a fallen column dances before a little crowd, when an even smaller party of noisy, festive drinkers come into the courtyard, disturbing the guitarist.

She stops dancing.

The crowd, seeing where she levels her angry glare, ripples with whispers, *Him! Señor Greco. It's Señor Greco.*

Central among the party walks a straight and angular gentleman in a shimmering sharkskin suit. His face is all assurance, confident, the lines scoring his cheeks and brow earned by stern concentration and a dedication to the perfect placement of his hand-tooled leather shoes. Even where his knees crease his trousers, the folds obey the poetry of flamenco.

The King of the Gypsies, the most famous of them all.

The gentleman catches the eye of the man with a guitar, and with a slight gesture of one hand he implores everyone, *Resume.*

There is music, a crash of guitar strings that rattle like the chains in a dungeon, and Mora strikes a profile. Before she lifts her foot, a *clap clap* rings out. José Greco's hands are over his head. Again, *clap clap.* And Mora begins.

Ho, ho and *hah!* Cries and trills, the clapping of hands, everyone's hands clapping. She spins, twists aside her skirt, the leg revealed to the hip, angles and curves locked into a single beat and changed to another curve and angle in the blink of an eye. Men down in the dirt stamp their own flamenco, the women gliding around them more intimate than if bedded.

And then it ends. Mora swallows deep litres of air, her breasts lifting like swells on a stormy sea, But her leg remains thrust forward, an arm curls over her head, the long rope of her braided hair coiling around her glistening neck, eyes as if tied onto Greco's own.

The King of Gypsies cocks his head to one side, a slight movement. Then he speaks to the woman beside him, *She has excellent feet, and a good leg. But the technique.* Like an ember given air, Mora's eyes burst into flames. And they roar when the woman adds, *It'll never get her off the streets.*

When the crowd is gone, when the party moves off to wherever the party must be, when the guitar is settled underneath a cot in her gypsy's wagon, when the camp fire is stoked and the aromas of food fill the air, what remains are a woman's words.

Mora, more tired of the snores beside her than she has ever felt before, does not want them to remain. Not the snores, and not the words.

The hours before sunrise have crisped the dirt, but her bare toes suffer nothing. She feels a tug at her skirt as the hem has caught on a step, against which she pulls until the fabric rips. She is not bothered, and vanishes.

THE DREAM

This is what Maria wishes was a dream:

She is almost asleep, almost, floating in that place between remembering earlier thoughts, guiding them back into her consideration with logic and dispassion, consciousness and thoughtfulness, to that place where life seems both odd and right, the place where the dead live and the living are elsewhere. Maria lies in the sweet place, full of calm that bears aloft a body towards sleep and the black empty.

Maria does not sleep alone. There are her brothers on the other side of the room. And with her knees as always driving into her back, Mora — well past that almost asleep stretch of time, mewling like a kitten. She is a kitten, dark haired with slit-closed eyes. She is forgivable, a little child among children and most beautiful.

Then arrives a knock on the door, followed by slippered shuffling, the creak of stairs.

Then it is daylight and her mother talks on about cockroaches. Mora asks after Papa and her abuelo, and her mother — draining of all colors though there is blood red in her eyes where there should be white — says with a dry croak, *cockroaches have them.*

Then it is dark, it is night again, and cockroaches bang on the door. They kick until they smash it open, and they run to the shutters where they twist them from the hinges, to fling them out into the night air to the street, wood crashing into a thousand sharp and flying splinters, into murderous needles and lances. There are hordes of cockroaches, everywhere cockroaches. They pull down her mother by her legs, and Isabella, arms and legs too, and their night shirts ripped away.

The cockroaches have a hundred arms, and in their hundred hands are knives, and they rush about everywhere, crawling over her screaming mother, climbing into Isabella's mouth, then inching over Maria's arms and up her legs and between her legs, biting her breast, many thick black endless cockroaches. Some wear uniforms with many buttons, some with a butcher's bloody apron pulled askew, some wear hats.

They drop from the walls, from the ceiling, thick cockroach waves pouring through the door, viscous as coal oil, determined as fire ants, thousands climbing over her legs and into her belly, crushing her, crushing the breath out of her, crushing the screams. They pull her hair, stuff foul rags in her mouth, crushing her hands under their knees, tugging apart her knees, cockroaches cockroaches cockroaches cockroaches cockroaches.

This is what Maria wishes was a dream, instead of a memory.

CHILDREN IN THE STREET

The first day that the child Lucia goes to the street to beg in the company of a Catholic sister is her second day in Church care:

A rock-faced nun waits with obligated patience for Maria to finish buttoning her blouse, the rough edges of several pesetas biting into her boney palm.

Has the child been changed?

Maria nods toward a rag by the hem of her skirt.

The nun reaches to lift Lucia into her arms, first thrusting forward the money. Maria stares at the coins. Had Maria a better understanding of Catholic myths, she would have smacked them away, but instead she drops her head, which she then shakes side-to-side.

The nun walks away, happier to return the coins to the Mother Church, astonished that anyone, especially a poor soul, would decline money. *And surely,* she says to the Mother Superior as she drops each coin singly into a wooden box, *that one must be a Jew. That nose!*

Perhaps, the Mother Superior says, putting the box under lock and key, *That is the only way her conscience will let her pay for a whore's child.*

The child, settled into yet another pair of arms, continues to sleep. Around the skirts of a second nun stand three other orphans, each female, all obedient, everyone silent as a gravestone, though each wants a peek at the newcomer. The second nun knows this, but the satisfaction of curiosities is not her concern, ever.

With the child in her arms, she herds the three others through the high arch of the *Puerta de la Macarena.* Once out on the sun-brightened street she hands Lucia to the eldest and instructs the child to stand at the curb, to urge closer any who may think it acceptable to pass by without giving alms. Then she steps into the shade of the arch. Snapping her fingers, she commands them to begin crying, *¡Para los pobres y los pequeños bebés!*

For the poor and little infants!

A lanky merchant smoking an American cigarette, knowing their tricks, pushes past the child nearest the curb. The second eldest, a pretty girl with pale gray eyes, grabs his coattail but he does not stop. Instead he drags her for a step, the littlest rushing to throw herself about his leg. Their faces turn up, eyes blinking against the morning sun already biting their cheeks. He flicks his cigarette at the dirty orphan holding the child, smacks away the hand that he is certain soils his suit. But the little one clings tight.

There is no charity in what he says to the sister in the shade, who snaps and draws her finger along her throat. The child releases the man, who kicks at her once she has come free.

In a moment there will come another. There always comes another.

THE VISITATION

Whether this is how it happened or not cannot be determined with precision, because those who would tell the truth cannot, and those who could tell the truth must lie.

The butcher shifts his weight from foot to foot, then, pointing at the German in a black uniform, says to the oldest man, *He wants you to drop to your knees.*

Why?

I don't know. Just do it. Please?

The soldier in black frowns at the butcher's trailing words, *Por favor.* He knows enough Spanish. *Now!* he says, though not one understands *Jetzt!*

No one understands any German, and they watch him to catch meaning. They only know inflection, and the old man does as the butcher has asked. His wife, terrified into silence, stifles her cry but not tears.

Josué, the butcher points to the man's eldest son and sighs, *you too.*

The butcher, facing no one, speaks as if a dwarf at his side waits for his instructions. There is no dwarf, and Josué demands, *Look at me.*

The butcher will not.

What is this, Nacho? We stole figs and oranges at the market together. And you do this?

The German steps forward as he lifts from his pocket a black, leather-covered bar of lead.

Que? the butcher asks.

Josué opens his mouth, but there is no time for him to speak. The German strikes him above the ear and Josué falls. The German kicks him, then gestures with his empty hand to those surrounding him, and the uninvited Spaniards stand gape-mouthed and dumb. The German points at the nearest woman, Josué's new bride, who had cried out when her husband fell. She has come downstairs in only a bedsheet, and in it she trembles. He turns the pointing finger up towards the second floor and says, *Nehmen Sie sie nach oben, und zu tun, was du willst.*

The butcher nods, doesn't understand but understands. With a heavy head and a mouth without a smile he tells his comrades, in words barely audible, what the German has asked. The men remain gaunt and stupid, but one of them — after working through the command, his eyes running up and down the sheet covering Josué's bride, every now and then flicking to the younger daughters of the condemned man but back again to the bride — says, *He said take them,* and he grabs.

So long as there is someone to lead them into Hell, men will follow. And they do, dragging even the heart of a beautiful child.

PLANS, AND THE EFFECT OF EVENTS

It often happens. Mora takes her place on the bus beside a man, someone's husband, who has deduced that the presence of her beauty is inevitably his invitation. He asks continuous questions, some she answers with a nod, most she answers with no answer at all, her attention fixed on the rolling hills carpeted with olive trees.

On a day in a year then well ahead, riding again through those groves but with an American Navy man who has been invited to sit beside her by more than her beauty, she will hear in English, *God I'd love to own my own grove like that one there. Wouldn't you, Hon?* And she will feel in that future year the same revulsion she suffers there beside an unknown someone's husband: the deep black horror of each tree, limb, branch and leaf, for she has broken her back and arms and knuckles in those groves to snatch out of them a thousand thousand nut-sized eggs needed to fill a woven basket for which she had been handed a barely worthwhile but too necessary shower of coins. Unlike on that future ride, when she will have a large cold diamond on her finger to offer some salvation, some consolation, a brilliant rock that will say there is eventually some reward, all she feels beside someone's husband is indifference.

The man smells of garlic, as have all on other buses who have presumed an invitation, and the sweet reminder of rot from his having taken more than one glass of sherry before coming aboard. He finally reaches that one question, makes that inevitable suggestion she knows always will arrive, a suggestion that has long ceased making her skin crawl but which nevertheless has her reach for his hand, settle hers atop it, to sink her lacquered fingernails into his browned and mottled skin.

But this one is not like the others who have felt the same bite. This one, perhaps from not moderating himself at the sherry bar, does not accept Mora's message. Quick as a cobra at a rat, his free hand comes around and strikes her near eye.

Mora is caught surprised, but not unprepared. The gypsies taught her more than dancing and how to cook over a camp fire.

It is a small blade, no more than a finger in length, but enough to drive through the meat of a man's thigh, enough to inflame him even more, but in a way to make him stand and scream.

Mora slips the knife back out of sight, donning an expression as one dumbfounded by his behavior. Though some nearby had seen the man's fist swing through the air, none have seen the blade slicing into his leg, and all — including the driver peering up at the screaming man in the center aisle — wonder what madness has sent him into the aisle to curse a beautiful woman, and to fear what he may do next.

What he does is lurch and grab something to hold because, on the empty road from Baena with few cars about, the driver stomps the brakes and swings his bus off the blacktop. In a hiss of air the door opens and the driver rushes the man. He does not hesitate, and soon the wounded man flies into the dry dirt at the roadside, dust rising in a small cloud around him.

With a determined movement, the driver drops into his seat and closes the door, upon which the banished man begins to pound with unremitting fury. The driver, no interest in debate, turns his attention to Mora, still with the placid countenance. Mora bears neither a smile nor a wrinkle on her a brow, having decided there will be like consequence for her if she expresses anything at all. The driver glares an unheeded warning, then returns to the road.

Mora has plans, and they include men, a number of men, stupid men, but not any who would smell of garlic and sherry.

CHIPPIONA ON THE ATLANTIC

Had they all been from a different family with different circumstances behind them, perhaps they may have begun singing. It is what happy people do in a car with a good radio that wends from Seville to the seaside. A familiar song begins, one of them begins a quiet murmuring to herself of the familiar lyric, when a sister hears and joins in, so that by the time the chorus is reached a consensus is reached, and they all send their voices to create a harmony that only a family of voices can manage.

Had they been a different family with different circumstances behind them, those in the unfamiliar car may have been singing. But Mora's family has learned that nothing said is everything said, and so they ride toward the Atlantic in relative quiet. Relative, because each one in the car sings along with the song then on the radio to his or herself.

The younger male — whom everyone called Nachito for no better reason than he had once, for weeks on end, insisted everyone call him that — sits between his mother, Señora Dolores, and the man driving, a man he does not like for no better reason than his mother does like him. He keeps his eyes locked onto the wavering horizon which has, in various moments, been flooded with grapevines in neat rows, or endless waves of yellow-headed sunflowers, or sometimes little more than brown flat dirt. What he looks for is his first glimpse of eternal blue, a substance and vastness that will one day claim his feet and remove him forever from the evidence of his past, but never the memory of it.

In the seat behind him, crushed together in a tolerated formation, is, against the driver-side door, Mora, who sometimes faces the countryside, and sometimes the back of the head on the man with slick hair, where there is hair. Beside her, asleep, rests Luna, her mouth open and head against her eldest sister, Maria.

Maria herself watches nothing, preferring what she can recall of a young man, Peter, who appeared often at her door with the same look in his eyes, the one that says he shall claim her as his own, fill her days with his needs and desires, who will ease the recurrence of a dream of cockroaches.

And against the opposite rear door of the big car, her head against the glass even though as the man driving rides over bumps that lift and drop her forehead painfully, rests Isabella, newly, secretly, in love with a Jew proclaimed God. She is in love with salvation. She follows the song — words in English that she does not understand although there are a few that suggest she might guess them to be about eternal unending love — with her own words about her own love for Jesú.

And last among the riders is Señora Dolores, glad for respite from the heat turning every street of the capitol into a sizzling illusion, though it had meant accepting an offer, a repeated offer, from a man not her husband, a man never dissuaded from paying her attentions despite her dour expression and unchanging black crepe.

They arrive. Nachito able to see ahead through the separation of two buildings his continent of water; Luna shoved awake by Mora, perspiring where she had been pressed by the thigh of sister; Isabella singing of her love in a manner that no one should hear.

They park, four doors opening and the car emptying with varied efforts, Mora's most vigorous, Maria's the least.

The man's name is Karl, and he is not a Spaniard, nor will he ever be. *No*, he had said, when asked by Maria in a low and careful voice, *I never served in Spain. Africa. I was shot, once, though. By an American.* About that she did not care.

Even a potential cockroach is one cockroach too much.

Luna, forced to remain in Mora's grip, tugs them all toward a stretch of sand fronting a harbor made of deadly sharp rocks, each stone well-placed to trap a fish unlucky enough to fail gliding over them while the tide is high. Just before the last street that they have to cross, Señora Dolores barks them all to a halt. She tells her children, *Give thanks to Karl, for providing the day.* All do, to some degree — Mora least with a mere *gracias*, Luna and Nachito most with *sí, sí, mucho mas, mucho mucho mas* — except Isabella, who kisses his hand and gives a whispered blessing, both of which embarrass more than the man.

All take hands, though Karl, reaching for Señora Dolores, thinks better of his action and offers an arm, and all cross the final street.

To reach the beach they round a concrete café, and when they do they hear a shriek from a strange woman, then a man's bellow. At Maria's feet, a man stumbling away from the woman falls, clutching his side just above his waistline. Maria, Karl, Mora and Señora Dolores see there is blood running over the man's fingers. Isabella at the far end, sees nothing, but hears the sudden gasp of her mother. Maria, holding Luna by the hand, tugs the girl to behind her skirt. Despite the child's efforts, she keeps her sister from seeing. Seeking a closer look at what has happened to him, Mora bends just as the crazed woman lunges with her knife.

Karl kicks Mora away and over the wounded man, who writhes face down in the sand. Grabbing for the upraised knife, their German host suffers the blade sliding across the meat of his palm. Despite the wound he grips the enraged woman's wrist, twisting until she cries out and drops to her knees.

Mora is furious to be so treated by a cockroach and begins screaming many of the words she'd heard used by neighbors and other children during the war. Señora Dolores kicks and slaps at her to make her stop, but Mora has words for her as well, words that cause the old woman to reach down for a fistful of black hair. She pulls her daughter to her feet and slaps her mouth.

So much at once, too much together. Isabella stands frozen in place. Maria, seeing how Karl bleeds, pulls a cloth napkin from a basket on her arm. Señora Dolores, her benefactor so hurt, pulls harder on Mora, who swings a wild foot she in truth does not mean to land.

Another man comes to help, snatching at the angry woman's flailing free arm. Karl does not let go of the knife hand still trying to slash, blood curling into his shirt sleeve, and decides the only tactic left to halt her is to smash into her jaw with his free hand.

The woman crumples onto the man she has stabbed, him gray and his eyes closed.

Mora pulls free from her mother's grasp, steps backward. She takes another step away, then turns, running to the sea.

Slowing, stopping, she slips off her shoes and peels her stockings from her legs, to walk and wash off the sweat and sand. Never looks back, not even when Luna, flushed and panting, catches up to her.

A CHILD IN THE STREET

Mora insists, and Maria objects. The younger addresses Señora Dolores, *Do you think I wouldn't be curious? At least a little?*

Curious? In six years, you've not asked one question about her. We, we, I, I was always the one going. No. She should never have even once see what her mother is. Has become.

And what have I become, dear sister, that I wasn't made into years ago?

Maria, enough. Mora... Señora Dolores does not ever again wish to fight what needs not be fought. She sees the determination her daughters, but does not feel there is as much reason in Mora's complaint as there is in Maria's expectation. *She is just a child, and you have never...*

Do you think I feel so little?

Maria laughs, and spits drily at the floor between them.

Regardless of what the two women may decide, Mora knows she will be taken to her daughter. She knows her success with them never depends on their deciding. Getting from others what she wants has depends depended on refusing to allow anything other than what she wants.

It is not strength of will but the consistency of an implacable nature.

To see her daughter after five years has never been her desired event, but she has always carried a preceding desire, which is to strike before getting struck, and there has only been one, just one, who stuck her down. *The child,* she has often thought, *will one day be useful.*

She has an implacable nature, and shouts down every one of her sister's utterances.

Maria, too, refuses to hear any of her wretched sister's words, especially if to hear any one word could bring Mora a pleasure she long ago decided was not worthwhile. She turns her head left, then right, closing her eyes.

The women, though, are not alone in this argument. Peter on a chair in the corner asks Mora, *Where have you been, what have you been doing?* He knows as well as does his wife that whatever Mora will say will be fabrication. *Busy,* she says, then, to her sister, *¡Cállate!* Then to her mother, the black look in her eyes blacker, *Bien, lo haré.*

Peter shrugs. Nothing to be gained by furthering this inquiry, for he does not care for anything that Mora would say. To him, this arguing is a small trickle of gutter water, and to change its course only requires a foot set against the flow. But his wife's has been a family of women for a long time, and he is irrelevant. A thing he knows but does never admit.

Mora says she again she will go to the orphanage. Peter, knowing how much it will cost him later, says they will all go.

It is early, siesta three hours off, and the streets are full of walkers and cars. Several times Maria offers greetings to those passing by. Once, Peter stops to converse with an old man waiting at a chessboard, and for a moment the small moving crowd pauses, but a well dressed woman stamps her foot and most of them move on. The family is nearly out of sight when Maria stops and calls. He laughs, the old man laughs, he scrunches his shoulders and turns his palm upwards.

Before the Basilica, they see the woman with children as they always are except Sundays: a black-cloaked woman leaning against the stones of the cathedral like a dead raven watching over a few filthy girls dressed in wrong-sized castoffs and patched shifts. Mora sees among the children begging a bow-legged runt whose demeanor and attentions to the other children qualify her by both height and weight, but without any quality that Mora would claim for herself. She sees the girl has been shorn to the scalp. *Lice, undoubtedly. Perhaps fleas as well.*

Maria's shoulders droop at the sight. She had hopes that her sister would see her daughter's black mane washed and given a comb, for it has rivaled the mother's, and that would have been delicious.

It is Peter who asks what Maria has expected would come from her sister. *Which one is she?*

And it is Mora who answers him, as she fetches a packet of America cigarettes from a silk purse. *The bald one.*

Of course it is.

Mora watches the child push herself in front of this man, that woman, sometimes dragging a foot as though crippled by some foul disease or malady of birth. Most stop to hand over what loose coins lay in their pockets.

Well, now what?
She should learn to dance.
Why?
It would be more profitable.

Peter, shifting the baby he carries to his mother-in-law, accepts a cigarette from Mora.

Luna, at an age to feel that whatever her elders do must be stupid and annoying, says, *We came to see that?*

Verdad.

It's hot. I'm sleepy. I'm hungry. What are they doing?

Maria says, *What they can* at the same time Mora says, *Not enough.*

Whether because the exotic scent of the American cigarette reaches her or because the child has a keen eye, Lucia looks across the avenue to the small group loitering. She neither waves, nor smiles. Strangers, each and every one.

This has been enough. I have an appointment.

With who?

The General, Mora says, lifting the cigarette from Peter's lips.

Why do you bother asking? Maria says.

HOW IT WORKS

On the third day after the women saw no more the grandfather, father and husband last seen on his knees, and the son and husband and brother also, all of the women come together at a cloth-covered table under which a dish of embers has been placed. The remaining men, boys, for none of them have reached an age when their hand needs to hold a razor, are away to a cousin in Albox, who owns a farm with an almond grove.

They, the women, sit with various emotions, foremost among them for all — except one, Señora Dolores — is curiosity as to why their mother has called them to sit thus.

This first feeling, from which Señora Dolores does not suffer, she swiftly abolishes by telling them, *We must change all of our names. Everything.*

Thus, she, who had been Davila, becomes Dolores. The eldest, who had been Ruth, becomes Maria, for that is the way of their neighbors. Isadora accepts Isabella, though she cries most when the command by her mother is given. The sound of Isadora in her ear is always in the voice of her father, and she feels the loss twice over.

Moira, then the youngest, is allowed Zarzamora, the simplest change, which has always been Zarza. *Zarzamora* to every Spaniard means blackberry, and it had been the father's name for his pet since her birth, when she arrived covered with fine black hair and black olive tones to her skin.

But she will not be excluded from transformation. She claims for herself Mora.

There is no change to the youngest, for not one among them except Dolores knows of her coming. She is to be named Luna. As they feel the heat from the brazier against their shins and knees, there is more to decide, or rather to impress, for Señora Dolores — as she will be forever thereafter until her death — has already decided: to remain who they have been is to invite horror, and to remain where they are is to invite more horror.

The names of the young brothers had been given to them an hour before Señora Dolores dispatched them under the cover of a moonless night, putting them and their futures into the care of a neighbor they have to trust.

Only their mother and eldest sister saw them off, or know to where the boys had been sent.

Isadora now Isabella cries, as she has since the beginning of that lightless day of cockroaches.

Mora only stares black-eyed at her mother's explanations. She feels she may possibly miss Israel, thereafter named Ignacio, Nachito, whom she forever refuses to call anything except Izzitito.

What also stops as commanded at that table under which they warm their legs, is ever to speak again, to anyone, tomorrow, soon or forever, about what they there together all agree is the blackest of all possible nights for each, though the night of cockroaches remains not as black for Mora as it had, is and will be for her sisters, mother, her brothers, and had been for her father and a brother.

It had been the butcher who saw to her preservation, dragging her by black hair, forcing her into a closet with him and slapping her so that she would scream, loudly, holding her down with one meaty hand as he drew out a knife to cut his own belly meat so that there would be blood between her legs. And it had been the butcher who ripped her gown and tied her with it, begging her to stay quiet and in the closet but, knowing the spirit of the child as he did, had to strike her until she fell unconscious, to remain so until the other men, finished with those they wanted, and one of them wanting the youngest son instead of a woman, forgot about the child and left the house.

And no one was ever again to explain what had happened after the men left. Mora asked, *Where did Papa go? And David?* And Señora Dolores built the first lie upon which all others would become built.

This is what you will say. Your father is gone with David, gone. He had to escape the General. He had to take our money, what we had, and he will live in England.

With a new family?

Señora Dolores did not answer, but her eldest sister began to nod.

New boys and daughters?

Again, Maria responded.

Forever?

That there was no answer was enough, and that is how everything worked, thereafter.

HUNGER AND SMOKE

The street teaches, and does so with necessities, and through those who have already learned.

By noon the shade is gone, and the soured nun watching orphans takes back the care of an infant from a ratty, black-haired girl. Her words of instruction are not necessary, they never change. *Return after vespers, no sooner. Go.*

Where the the children go is to find food. Cast aways, bread. Lucia however seeks something else, something the orphanage has taught her to want, and the street has taught her to get. Pulling the next youngest girl, a child of four, along the road, she leads with determination torward a corner where buses stop, and where people who wait for buses toss the finished butt of cigarettes, sometimes still lit and smoldering. *Easy to find,* she says to the child. *You'll see.*

For those who must wait for the arrival of always tardy buses, a cigarette assists patience. For Lucia, as it had been for the older girl who had once shown her, a bit of cigarette is a balm against hunger.

Hunger. Orphans that have nothing hunger for everything, but none ever reveal that, even to each other. They hunger for water, which they sip from the glass bottle a nun has placed by the wall she leans against. They hunger for food, for all the Church can supply is bread and sometimes thin broth made from a donated carcass of a picked-over chicken, or — when the *corrida* is active with the slaughter of bulls — the boiled bits of bone, sinews and snouts. The children hunger not for a place to lie down, but a place to lie down in safety, even a cloth-covered board ranked in rows and inches from another dreaming of the thing they each hunger for most: a home, a family, kindness.

No one understands the meaning of kind more than an orphan, for each is an unkind, each is someone without anyone to whom she resembles, without anyone by whom she might be heard, held, lifted, without anyone who will wash her gently and comb her hair.

Merde, Lucia whispers, finding all of them smoked down to nubs from which she can't even prize out a stub, no matter how carefully she lifts the bits from the paper.

Come on, she says. *I know another place. But you keep up, and you run when I say run.*

It is a long walk to the *Parque de Maria Luisa,* but there are places along the way where restaurants have begun closing their doors for the siesta. Lucia knows this is a good time, because those who work inside may already be scraping shreds from the merienda into waste cans that they will set out by the back door for beggars and cripples. Old cripples and experienced beggars, that ragged flock of adults not likely to allow the likes of a seven-year old girl and her smaller ward to have a pick from their pickings.

Lucia knows tricks, and she has a partner for the crime, one good enough to snatch at least a crust once the ancient beggar's head gets turned.

You don't run, we don't eat, she says, having told the child how to move toward the man in mincing steps while she waits a dozen yards off. The child nods.

Once Lucia thinks the child close enough to the filthy man scrounging in a can, she whistles. Loud. The man looks up, to see a runt holding the hem of her skirt as high as her shoulders.

It works, and the child jams her hand into the can. *Run!*

And run the toddler does, and succeeds, because the man keeps looking at the bald bodied girl.

Who runs.

By the time they reach *Parque de Maria Luisa,* the partial bread roll the child has filched is hardly a crumb on their lip.

The part of the park that Lucia seeks is encircled by an intricate iron fence half buried in a lush hedge, all decoration with no other purpose. Inside is a paradise of shade, with fountains, flowers, palms and avenues overhung with oranges. The fragrant days of flowering citrus has passed, but some fruit still hangs.

Both children look on the brilliant globes orange among the greenery with an increased hunger, but the streets teach. One of the things the street teaches is that even the starving may not steal.

She has already spotted the walking gendarme in the funny hat, and she is sure he has already seen her. There are no tricks with them. Get caught, and never be seen again. That's what they say, and that's what the truth is.

But she has not come for fruit.

They walk, scouring the ground. Soon she has three stubs in her pocket, enough, and she tells the child they should go. But from where they have been a policeman comes, his brass and his lacquered hat and buffed shoes flashing in the streams of sunlight falling through the branches. He does not watch them, but the street teaches, and Lucia knows he has his evil eye working, and in it are her and the girl beside her. She guides her to walk the opposite way.

Neither are as tall as the hedge they pass along, and when a sharp left can be had behind one that will, for a few moments at least, confuse the policeman about where they have gone, Lucia pushes the child and says, *run*. But no sooner does the child lift her foot to flee than the older girl tightens her fingers on her loose shift to stop her. *Look*.

Whether the child knows at what she is to look is not known, because Lucia pushes her down and commands, *Quick, crawl in there,* indicating a small hole in the otherwise thick hedge. *You stay until I say run, you got that?* The child nods.

On an intricate ironwork bench rests an old woman, an *abuela* to someone, who has just fallen asleep with a full cigarette smoldering between her fingers. Lucia creeps closer, looking back to see if the policeman has come around the corner. He has not, and she reaches for the cigarette. It comes loose from the woman's fingers with more ease than an over-ripe fruit. Lucia puts it between her lips for a quick draw. The woman shuffles but doesn't waken, and the girl moves out from an arm's reach.

Run! she yells.

But the timing is poor.

The woman wakes. However, it is the policeman who causes worry. The four-year old clambors out of her rabbit hole just as he rounds the corner, moving too slow and too awkwardly not to be snatched by the long ratty hair already caught in the hedge.

The street teaches, and one lesson it stresses is that to survive, one must save oneself before any other.

Later, Lucia relearns that a thick cane striking her back again and again is preferred, greatly preferred, to what the police do, and though she suffers inside and out, she lives.

But what surprises and confuses her more is that, having been dragged back to where all will eventually sleep, the child she had lost is on her board, a thumb in her mouth and a cleaner face than she should have, asleep.

AN ACCOMPLISHMENT

Must you come back so late?

Yes. Mora does not want the conversation, but Señora Dolores owns the door key. *What do you care? And why do you stay awake?*

I am always awake.

Yes, I suppose you are. Not me. I sleep.

Of course you do, stinking of that.

What? Cigarettes?

That, and the rest.

No surprise you recognize it, Madre. Wearing some yourself?

Of course not. It's the perfume of whores.

Had Mora not drawn out a number of unwrinkled bills and creased them down the center before settling them on an aluminum tray on the table, Señora Dolores might also have struck her.

Trials teach, though, that it's not the money's fault for how it crosses the threshold.

The following morning Nora tells Luna to put on a pretty dress, teasing the young girl with an insensitive poke at her swelling bodice.

Mora then points to her own. *You'll never have any like these.*

How you know?

Because I know. It's not what they look like, it's how you use them.

You use them?

Every time, she says, turning away with a smile. *Hurry up. Get dressed.*

In Mora's opinion, their walk from Señora Dolores's barrio to the strand running along the Guadalquivir is long, too long for two girls who wish to remain pretty in their pretty dresses, so Mora does the unthinkable in the barrio. She calls for a cab.

Luna has never been in a cab. For her it is as mystical as a fairy tale coach. She dresses for her role. The first choice is stripped from her hands and tossed onto the bed. Mora then takes from the closet a simple yellow dress, one with puffed sleeves and lace that Maria has made.

Lace-making made money, and Maria makes money.

You'll look like a Princess, her sister says, tugging a vicious brush through Luna's thick blonde hair. Luna believes her, and sits straighter, and does not cry out.

The cab leaves them at the *El Tor del Oro,* for which Luna only has widened eyes, but Mora's dart south along the cloudy river, then north, then to the street behind them, searching. A man near the tower's door explains to a knot of tourists that all the conquistador gold carried to Spain had to pass through the tower's doors, that the stairwell inside is wide enough for a horseman in armor to pass, for he guarded the gold coming from the Americas after the time of Cristoforo Colombo.

Luna is fascinated, but Mora, with sharp, fast words, demands, *Let's go.*

Luna has a difficult time keeping up with her sister. *Why are you running?*

I'm not running. Just keep up.

But what Mora pursues, she does not find. Stopping to look around again, she stamps her foot and grunts.

What?

Nothing. I thought he...

He who? You know somebody here?

I know lot's of somebodies. Or I should say lots of somebodies know me.

Why?

You are an imbecile. Mora spots a bench and drags the girl. Both sit, and Mora takes out her cigarettes. The hurried rush south has tired Luna. She does not argue but swings her unstockinged legs. Mora looks down at the flash of pale. *You have a boyfriend?*

Luna shocked, spurts, *Of course not. I'm only a girl.*

There are women younger than you.

What do you mean?

Mora smokes, still watching for what she does not see. Eventually she smiles. *Come on.*

But I like it here.

You'll like it better somewhere else. Come on.

They wend through a colorful cloud of strangers, many of them chatting to others in languages Luna does not recognize, but out of each are words that Mora does. Some of them, as the two sweep past, are, if not meant for her, meant about her. They keep her smiling.

Not far from a bench Mora stops herself and her sister, and Luna is aware that it is a man in a *Guardia de Civil* uniform who has stopped them, even though he has not yet noticed either. Luna fears, having learned from myth and tale that men in those clothes ought to be feared. But, she realizes, he does look nice. When the policeman turns their way, for Mora makes her sister stand in quiet until he does, he does not look away. Nor does his expression change, which surprises Luna, for it has been her experience already, though she has not seen her sister for a long time, that men who look on Mora always change expressions, and sometimes the expressions do not make Luna feel comfortable.

Mora seeks and finds the young girl's hand, then tugs her toward the man watching them.

Been a while.

He nods, does a small bow toward Luna, who blushes. To Mora he says, *Nothing to throw at me?*

You look handsome.

All he does is tip a bow towards Mora.

If I remember correctly, you have a tongue. Luna looks up at her sister, frowning. All people have tongues. *Nothing to say?*

I remember her, he says. *Quite well.* For Luna he manages a smile, but even Luna sees that it is not a practiced expression.

I'm sure you do. And probably often.

At that he glares. And the glare is for Mora. Again he nods toward Luna, something in his eyes, which linger on her but not on her face, makes Luna uncomfortable, but not very. Then he says, *Ladies,* and walks away.

He gets no more than a pair of steps from them when Mora says, *Not to your liking? Surely not too old. Not what I remember, or hear.*

He continues on, but with a brisker step.

Who is he?

Oh, someone I knew, once upon a time.

Was he your boyfriend?

So long as I thought so.

A LITANY OF ACCOMPLISHMENTS

It is a thing she likes to do when the boredom has set in, or when the presents become a bit less costly than the prior, or when the attentions of men who give presents predicts unpleasantness on some future evening: she recounts.

Usually she begins while reclined on a divan, for clichés appeal to her, or on a mussed hotel bed, or while inspecting her lipstick in a flecked mirror at some small apartment borrowed from a friend who also likes presents, once or twice prone but usually supine, her slim ankles crossed, perhaps her Chinese slippers still on her feet, blue smoke wreathing overhead, and him urinating with too much noise, or pouring yet another glassful of liquor, or — as she most prefers to time her recounting — after he has slipped and said something about his children or, even better, his wife.

You remind me of someone.

If he responds at all, it's usually with a grunt. They never ask *Who*, unless vain and supposing she'll respond with the name of a celebrity. But she avoids the vain, for who wants a man prettier than oneself? This one says nothing.

Actually, you remind me of a lot of someones.

This, he understands, from wherever in the close quarters he has retreated, is a recognizable moment, and his first thought is about the expenses. He really does not mind what is about to come next, welcomes it, so much that he finds what he has to say next comes rather easily. *You remind me of a lot of someones too.*

Mora smiles, though she does not let him see it. No longer is it about who can win, but how swift the pieces may be cleared from the board so that another game, with another opponent, may be had.

Who was your first love?

You.

Liar.

He smiles, and does not care if Mora sees the smile. *A girl in my school.*

Naturally.

What can I say? I was learning.

You learned?

Don't be a bitch, Mora. You're not the only teacher in the school.

She draws on the cigarette, but instead of blowing the smoke into the air over her head, opens wide her mouth, and the smoke finds its way out, though with tentative shifts and liftings. But it takes too long, and with a blast it dissipates.

Who was your real first? I'm betting the wife.

Don't bet.

Why not?

My uncle took me to a whore.

Ahh.

An uncle's duty.

Ahh.

I made a mess of it.

I can well imagine.

He comes and sits with her, their first real intimacy. He almost likes her. *What about you, Mora?* He places a hand on her stomach, her tell-tale stomach.

Mora does not answer. He already knows that story. Instead, she asks what will lead into the recounting.

Before me, and since the secretary, many?

Enough. He wonders something he had not wondered before, not cared to wonder, not thought the possibility about which he wondered as a possibility. But since the thought arrives so suddenly, unexpectedly, it comes out of his mouth before he thinks to stop it. *Ever in love, Mora?*

You think me stupid?

I thought maybe human. She smiles. Perhaps the naming of men will not be necessary this time.

How about it? Love happens to us all, eventually.

Got you a wife.

He doesn't smile, he laughs. And he doesn't respond, for she already knows that story. *Come on, girl. Bad luck?*

Every time, she says. *But theirs, not mine. I don't depend on luck.*

A DANCE WITHOUT MUSIC

Lucia knows the ritual sometimes changes. Some of the girls, especially pretty ones, long for it. But she is not among the pretty ones. Her hair, they say, is too black, her legs too bowed, her teeth crooked and already yellowed by the stubbed cigarettes and damp-ended cigars she always finds. And, they sometimes say, she is too short, her long red hands already tell them something and they shake their heads.

But it is not any of those things, nor even all of those together, that tells Lucia that her heart is never to be one called to the different ritual. It's her black eyes, the ones that grow tender only when caring for the little ones. For the nuns, for the pretty girls, for the couples and women who come for the ritual of the clean shift and loaned dress, her eyes are always coal, adamantine and immovable black stones, and sometimes, after the woman shakes her head from side to side, Lucia whispers words whose meanings are always polite, but whose suggestions could slice stones.

Every time before the ritual called for a cold bath in a gray basin, the vicious hands of a sister scraping dirt away as if filth had found a way under the surface of her skin, scrubbing as though only vigorous ministrations might eradicate the original sin of her misbegotten birth. In the usual rituals, after the bath, after being made to stand naked in a square of sunlight so that the skin would dry, there would be the pains of a thorough combing.

On this day her hair has still not grown past her shoulder. It has not been a year since her last shearing because of lice. Finally comes the folded, clean, white and washed shift to be pulled over her head.

And every time before, for there had been many times before, there had been a woman — sometimes with a man, sometimes not, and sometimes, feared times, a man alone — seated cross-legged on a chair, the expression on the woman's face sometimes as terrified of the child as the child was terrified of her, sometimes, though, the woman's face, inspecting the child from head to toe, is the same as on the women who look over meat cuts in the market.

And every time before, despite the washing and the clean white shift, and the temporary dress, and the demonstration of good manners and the showing of hands, Lucia would be dismissed, the shift removed, the rags replaced, and she would run off again an unwanted orphan.

But this time there is a different dress, for she is, even small, bigger than all those usually called to the ritual. And she knows what alterations to the ritual a different dress can bring. And this time there is no woman, only a man. And Lucia knows what that alteration to the ritual means.

She has heard stories of the single man.

A man seeks a bride, or so he might call the girl whose breasts had begun growing.

All through her bath, Lucia stares at the yellow square of fabric resting on the cot. She remembers having seen one like it on Begonia, gone now six months but every day missed. The only older girl Lucia had ever missed. Babies had been missed, but not for long, and three times a girl barely past walking got snatched out of her caring embrace and settled into the arms of a cooing woman, then never seen again, and was remembered, but not missed. But only Begonia's vanishing into the love and comfort and protection of a family, which is desired by every one of the orphans without alteration — even though sometimes the new life turns harsher than that in the convent — only Begonia's absence left an unforgotten hurt. And, Lucia discovered, only the girl's sweet smile and golden hair remained — as will the scent of a blooming gardenia on the other side of a courtyard wall be all that's had. The sweet smile and yellow hair were the parts that had taken Begonia away.

Lucia stands obedient if not patient at the repeated tugs on her hair. She knows the coming changes in the ritual, for others before have explained it, whispered how — before her and after her — once she has been bathed and combed and made to stand erect and silent, the man will look her over, and maybe even touch her as no man has before. She also knows there will be others with her to be prodded and inspected, others among whom one will get selected, some other who will be taken as the bride, another who will have a wedding dance. Another, not her.

None of them have been touched?

The sister shakes her head.

I'll know.

She nods.

All right. Have them remove their clothes.

He inspects each, stopping before Lucia with a sneer. *You're serious about this one? She looks like a boy. This?* He lifts an end of her hair. *Lice?*

It happens.

I'd have to keep her cut like a sheep. He drops her lock and jabs a finger into her breastbone. *You think anyone wants a girl looks like a boy?*

She will not always look like a boy.

You've seen the mother?

I've seen the aunt.

And this is the first time Lucia has ever heard that word, aunt, or any with a like implication, used about herself. Hearing it both hurts and thrills.

Well, these are what you've got?

Cisca, step out. The girl at the far end, the tallest though not the oldest, for that is Lucia, does as she is told. *Turn.*

Again, she does as told.

You won't get better. And she has been regular for several months.

Fine, fine. I'll send a car.

That evening, well after all have been warned that swift sleep is preferable to conversation, Lucia hears someone also crying.

She remains awake through the cries, certain they come from the next prettiest girl in the line.

A CONSIDERATION

Yes, indeed, he does remember the child in the simple dress, and the day he had last seen her, and her crown of golden hair. And, as Senna walks through the crowd of fellow Spaniards and strange tourists, who separate at his approach, he sees none of them, for he has seen again, and liked, the crown of golden yellow hair.

Surprises every native passer-by when he begins to whistle. It even surprises Claudio approaching from the direction of Torre del Oro.

Whistling?

Alejandro Senna stops whistling, but only long enough to smile, and shrug, and give a little laugh, before he starts to whistle once more.

Got another address, have you?

No.

Come on. She's got a name?

Luna.

Luna? Ominous. She's got a sister?

Oh, yes, that's she's got.

Old enough for me?

Alejandro recalls the sharp features that have replaced the soft young curves his fingers had once known. *Not very much, but far too old for you.*

No woman is too old for me, Sebastiano laughs. *Unlike you, bastard. For you, if she's a woman, she's too old.*

They walk away from the river, toward the old city, both whistling.

AMERICA

Any child abandoned to her own devices will rely on her nature to do one of two things. She will either find collaborators for her entertainment, or she will find quiet and a safe place.

Lucia, when she does not have a ward in tow, with Begonia long gone, prefers the latter. Her safe place in whatever town — and she has run away from the sisters in Seville, in Valencia, in Barcelona, Madrid, Cordoba and today in the port city of Algeciras, the ferry to Morocco already having pulled away from the dock, the nun on board realizing that, again, Lucia has slipped off — is always by water, almost always on a stonework wall fronting muddy flats left by a falling tide, somewhere that she can place her branches and sticks end-up in the mud to attract and host dragonflies.

But the tide is not always low. When it is too high for her to drop down from the rough bulwark onto the unctuous silt that she likes to feel oozing between her toes, she watches the boats gliding on the Mediterranean, especially those bound for the open Atlantic. Today she studies all of the traffic on the sea, each moving in a cinematic slowness whether a cargo ship or a fisherman under sail. Some pass close to her, and she sees on the decks and in holds the nets, ropes, crates and tossed rags. She hears, when there talk is to be heard, commands shouted from one seaman to another. Some in Spanish, but sometimes not. Whether the unknown words are Portuguese or Russian, German, English or French, she does not know.

Nor does she care. They are parts of a spell, enchantments, and she believes them all to be the sound she will someday hear in America.

Across the water to the East rises the mountain of Gibraltar, where many boats still press against the shore. Between them and Lucia, churning the waters to the south and already a mere swipe of dark on the horizon, is the ferry from which she escaped. The ferry that would have borne her into a dark and pungent house of a Moor, a house already where three wives fight each other for supremacy, a house of labor and loneliness.

She has been warned by one who has told her everything.

Lucia watches the ferry shrink into a dot until it vanishes.

They ever say you going to Morocco, you run, girl. You run and run until your feet bleed and your toes are gone.

Why?

They do things to girls over there. Bad things.

What things?

Bad things. You never mind. But you mind me, girl. They ever say the word, or Algiers or even the ferry, your life is over and you won't be nothing but forever a slave. But you so dark maybe they won't take you. They want us light, like me, and really like Brigette Bardot. They start wars for a girl who looks like Bridget Bardot, them Arab savages hacking each other to bits with their knives just to get one taste of a woman like Bridget Bardot. You mind me. You run.

Where do I run?

The other way, of course. You an idiot or something?

I'll run. Until my toes bleed and my feet hurt.

She looks down at her naked feet, the water under them glittering like a field strewn with diamonds. They have not begun to bleed. *I guess I run the wrong way.*

The memory continues. She looks up at the woman talking to her, whose face is scrunched tight and her eyes fixated on something before them that could not be seen by anyone but the woman fixated and remembering.

Where's the best place to run, besides the other way?

You are an idiot. Everybody knows where that is.

Well I don't. They didn't never tell me.

They wouldn't. They don't want nobody going there, because they can't get you when you there and snatch you back and sell your bag of bones for money to the Arabs and Moors down there in Africa. They got gold, and them nuns and priests got a thing for gold.

Lucia nods, having seen it in multitudes and in every church she had been brought to, whether Seville, Valencia, Barcelona, Madrid or Cordoba. Yes, they have a thing for gold.

But where's where they can't get you?

Idiot, the woman smiles. *America, of course.*

East of where the ferry to Morocco disappears over the horizon, a white-sided ship of immense size plies a line through the Pillars of Hercules to the open Atlantic. Lucia watches it creep. As she does for every ship or boat or sailing craft moving past, she ponders its destination.

Then, surprising her, a dragonfly swoops by, returns, hovers in a jiggy-jaggy dance before dropping onto her knee, its wings out and steady as a street.

I know where they are going, Lucia whispers to the creature. The dragonfly twitches its wings once. It waits.

Don't you know? You must be an idiot. America, of course. They both begin to laugh.

An American Sailor in Seville

The American in uniform studies a sheet of paper held on a clipboard in much the same way he does the specifications for rudder alignments on a destroyer. What he reads has nothing to do with the forward direction of a U.S. naval ship, but everything to do with the forward direction of his Naval career. He does not understand much of the language except the one word, *Terminal.* It has to do with coming to a full stop.

Thought it best I tell you before I tell Diana. Give you the chance to do it. You tell her, if you want.

Who wants to say that to anyone, ever? But Ned, finally lifting his eyes from the paper, says, *No, yeah. Okay, sure. I can. If you want me… to.*

You were pretty sure, before. Weren't you? I mean, it's a shock, sure, but Lieutenant, you knew this, right?

Ned looks out the window. The air in room had grown dark, but what filters through the orange trees helps. He settles the clipboard on his lap to still his hands.

You think I should get her back to the States, have them see if it's…

Her diagnosis won't change. But get her back, sure, get her home. That's what I'd want. Here, I mean I love it, but it's not home. You know?

He shakes his head, unsure, though, to what he's acceding.

I can't, just yet. I mean, Christ, we have so much work.

I can clear channels for you. Rank has its privileges. I'm sure you want...

Let me tell her first, see what she says. We'll probably go, but... she can barely do the laundry, the stuff you gave her.

Yeah. Maybe you should get her help.

Yeah.

The doctor sits back in his chair, scans his desk for any distraction. Ned isn't rising, and he knows that he will in his own time. But until then... *You know where you can get good help, and cheap? The church.*

I don't go to church.

No, I mean the orphanage. At the big cathedral. They got kids and they're good. Taught by nuns. Polite, work hard, never complain. Might steal stuff sometimes, but Hell, they all do that. And you might get one who doesn't steal, if you treat her right and slip her a few coins on the side, maybe a smoke.

A smoke?

They all smoke. Helps keep the hunger pains down, so I've been told. I do pro bono there. Go see. In fact, the doctor leans forward, shuffles through his Rolodex and selects a card, the address upon it he writes down on a subscription pad, *go see this person. She'll fix you up.*

Ted does not take the note, his hands still in tight grip around the edges of the clipboard.

Go on. It's for Diana. You don't like the one you get, you go get another. But they're good kids, what I've seen. And work harder than a new recruit. What you got to lose?

Ned takes the paper. *What have I got to lose?*

Both know the answer, and both regret the question.

DUPLICITY OF THE WOUNDED

Mora at the unshuttered bedroom window does not sigh, does not pout from the heat within and without, nor does she think about her sister asleep on a mat. Nor is she lost in nostalgic recollections. She is thinking.

What she thinks is what she has thought before, the steps needed, all taken with sure footing. Senna has seen Luna, and he has looked at Luna, and he has thought what Mora knew he would have thought seeing the girl child in a pretty dress.

The empty courtyard below keeps no magic in its shadows. What glimmers from the moon on the tiles and sills of the surrounding apartments are watery gray. Nothing silvered.

Below her mother does what she does, feeling about in the dark to check and recheck windows and the door, muttering whatever prayers or incantations she recalls from her days as a dutiful wife. Mora's lip curls in each corner.

I am a spider. I spin a web. I will catch them all.

Then she turns toward Luna, whose pale shoulder is all that is visible.

And you, little Nazi princess, keep sleeping. A busy time ahead.

A MOMENT FOR PROVIDENCE

The American in uniform holds her thin hand, the wedding band rolling between his own thick thumb and finger. It rolls about easily.

I don't know, Di.

She's been an angel, the poor thing. Such an angel.

Ned looks at the child standing in the doorway to the bedroom. *I won't be able to send her back.*

You know your dad wouldn't let you. I know what I'm asking. We'll need someone, and I want her. I certainly don't want Edith or Stephanie coming round to do what I can't anymore. They'll kill me with kindness sooner than the cancer will.

She is right about that, he thinks. They'll fuss and insist her into an earlier grave.

She doesn't get a word we're saying.

She'll learn.

He is not so sure. *And who would teach her? You?*

You know Tata will. You leave her to him.

I hate talking like this.

We have to. We go Saturday. I'll need her.

What if the Church won't let us?

Right. One less mouth. Like they care now.

Okay.

You hear that, Lucia? We're going to turn you into a little American princess.

The girl does not show it, a rigid creature in the doorway, but she understands some things. *American,* for one.

CONQUEST

Alejandro Senna pauses before the gilded mirror in the hall, tugs his jacket square, smooths his hair, measures his reflection with his head turned left, then right, less interested in how the uniform intensifies the confidence in his countenance than whether resolve appears at all.

Asking Luna had been nothing. Asking her mother had been nothing, though he could see, when he confronted the sorry sack with a bitter face, her permission came forward despite reluctance. *Dolores,* he thinks, *is a perfect name for the woman. I'll have to suffer that, but...*

Señora Senna arrives at the staircase landing wearing no look of joyous surprise at her eldest son's arrival. Alejandro's desired expression begins to weaken. He tightens the muscles not only in his face but down his back to his heels. His message remains unaltered, the need to express undeflected.

Mama.

She begins to descend, a tight grip on the handrail. He starts forward to assist, but she raises her free hand and he ceases.

The steps down are few but interminable.

She does not descend them all, stopping on that which leaves her head above his, her eyes thus lowered, and his upturned.

What is it?

As must be natural, he redirects his attention to the room at his left. It is filled with flowers and houseplants, the sword-like leaves of a sanservera being wiped clean of the thinnest layer of dust by a woman also in uniform, though hers has limp frills and unstarched lace. He catches the servant's eye, and she his, and a silent acknowledgement passes between them, the phrases and regrets of two people who once had pressed against the other for their own distinct reasons, his reason no longer in the world, hers always. He knows she is a distraction, one that must vanish if he and his mother are to enter the room, and one who would remain as she is if they do not.

Come on, Mama. Let's talk in there. And send Sophia off.

Her frame refuses, but only for the few seconds it takes to reinforce her displeasure. Finally, the air about them beginning to thicken lest it become stirred, she shifts one black-booted foot to the lower step.

The woman in the room has time to vanish.

He allows his mother to compose on the brocaded settee, a ritual that requires a squaring of her skirt, the crossing of one ankle over the other, the removal of an antique fan from an almost invisible, undetectable pocket, the undirected gaze that continues until she settles, which announces she is ready to hear what she knows she does not want to hear, the confirmation of a rumor that his young brother Sebastiano has already brought to her.

I suppose this one is also pregnant?

About her deduction he shows indignation. This one is decidedly not pregnant. He shakes his head.

You've found yourself a virgin in that family?

He has not come for an interrogation but to state a fact. His lips whiten as they thin.

I am asking for nothing except that you will attend.

You'll get nothing except that, and that is only if it is what I will decide.

And I want Sebastiano to stand with me. It is only right. His right.

So you do ask for more than one thing.

It is as he expected, *el toro y el matador.* But which is he? Must he suffer these *banderillas?*

I am not asking, he says.

No, I see that. How is life among the Jews?

She is not a Jew.

You can think that, the pretty yellow hair. But every child of a judía has that infection.

She is a Catholic, baptized.

There's not enough water. Señora Senna turns slightly on the settee to call the woman back into the room. *Sophia, agua frío. Ahora.*

Alejandro Senna has been standing at attention as he would during inspection by his captain, wordless, white-knuckled, fully aware of the perfection of his dress as much as he is aware of the imperfection of the man in it. But at her request to the maid he cannot help the allowance of a small smile into evidence. His mother sees it, says, *I wonder how her sister has taken the news.*

Finally, it is the moment to sink the blade, the *tercio del muerte.* Alejandro almost feels the need to sweep his arm in a wide pass, which he doesn't. But it is with joy he says, *I have spoken to her.*

Señora Senna raises an eyebrow.

Alejandro's smile broadens. *She is as happy for us as we are for ourselves. She has encouraged it from the first.*

A Shadow in the Doorway

Lucia gathers clothing in her arms and sets them into a cloth spread on the stone floor. Some have blood stains, some smell. She pays both little attention, for it is always the same.

The prospect of a walk to the river overrides what she knows will be pains in her back, weariness in her arms. The sun is warm and yellow, and there is nothing more worthy of her worship.

A noise and commotion comes from the office of the Mother Superior. Lucia knows why the sounds are made. A couple has arrived to claim an older girl. They have not come for her.

She crosses the room where the nuns sleep, to draw out from beneath one of the beds a last remaining receptacle. It has been pushed far under, back against the wall which the bed itself has been pressed, so Lucia drops onto her stomach to crawl. Because of her size and thinness, when she is close enough to snatch at what she seeks, almost all of her lies hidden, though, she knows, there's no one to wonder where she may have gone.

Her fingers fix on the woven basket when she hears a heavy footstep more close than expected, and more differently made than are those of any nun she's heard. It has a decided snap.

Under the bed she arcs her body, an effort to crane her neck for a look at who may have come in. All she can see at the doorway are the rich folds of a man's cuffs atop shining black leather shoes. As she moves for a better look, her shorn head scrapes against a naked bedspring, and she cries out.

Hello?

She does not understand the word, nor when the man says, *You hurt yourself?*

She stays silent as the stones upon which she lies.

You under the bed?

Lucia has no reason to hide, and considers that it is better to reveal her presence and suffer a chastising than to be thought remiss at her chore, so she crawls out and stands.

But by then the man has abandoned his curiosity and left. Or so she believes.

She returns to dragging out the basket, lifts the clothing and carries it to the white puddle she's already formed. With practiced fingers she ties up the bundle, making a loop through which she pushes her head, to use her neck against the weight. Then she struggles to stand, wobbling on her bowed legs until she manages the sack into a bearable position. The weight nearly equals her own, and she leans far backward to counterbalance.

It is then she notices a shadow in the doorway. The man who had called out to her stands and watches. But Lucia stops to keep an eye on him, well aware what it means to be caught alone with a man in a close space, even if it's the dormitory of nuns. She has heard stories, and she has a few of her own.

Although she cannot see his face where he stands in the lightless hallway, she knows he is studying her. The weight of the bundle places an uncomfortable stress on her shoulder and she shifts the load. The man walks off.

With a roll of her eyes, Lucia takes up again her chore.

LETTERS FROM THE DEVIL HERSELF

Señora Dolores spreads open another letter written on scented blue paper so that the light of the candle beside them can spill an unshadowed light. This is the fourth she's flattened, and as out of order as had been the prior three. The letter is not meant for her, though she has been aware from the first that Mora has been writing often to her youngest.

The child sleeps in a different room, and Mora — in a different house in a different town in a different district of her Spain — may or not be sleeping. Señora Dolores suspects not, for the clock has not struck off its twelve notes. Mora is not one, she believes, for sleep at such an hour. Bed, certainly, but not sleep.

Of course you love him. He is very handsome, and he is rich, though I suspect not as rich as he might have been, or may yet be. They have a very large vineyard. I had once hoped for such a place for myself, before I saw the world. And that is far larger than any vineyard. But you shall not see the world I have seen, nor would I want you to. No, dear Luna, it's not a place for you. Do what you must, but do not let our policeman get away. You are a perfect treat for him, a match decided by the stars well before you were born.

But not much more, Mora had thought, pausing over the paper to consider the implication of what she had just then written. *Oh yes,* she had thought, *decided the moment your cockroach father spent his Nazi seed.*

Señora Dolores does not know this is what Mora had thought, but it is what she believes her dark daughter keeps in her heart. Mora had the memories too, and though the darkest night among many dark nights had never been mentioned since, not once, for she forbid it and kept it away with all of the sternness she could exercise, a mother knows who shares her memories.

Under the unwavering yellow of her upright flame, the words from the fourth letter reveal, *And by all means, no, very much no. You should not allow him that prize. Do not allow it. Keep yourself safe and away from him. From now on, insist on a chaperone. Maria, not Madre. Maria will fight you. Maria will do this. I will insist. Let him into your prize, and you will lose him. Everything. And you do not need that. I know his heart, men's hearts, much better than I should, so trust when I say his heart loves you with the same aches and pains your little one feels right now. I insist, Luna, do not let him touch you any more than he already has.*

Señora Dolores sets loose a sigh, and the candlelight quavers. The folded papers curl back into a tight shape. She pushes the pile away. The clock has yet to strike twelve, but she feels more weight than ever suffered from wearying, implacable worries. An uncomfortable surprise, this pain to the heart.

Unlike as on every other evening, on this she does not walk with the candle to check a third time, or possibly fourth, whether the locks on the door or on shutters remain in place. Instead she sets the holder on a small trunk against the wall, then takes herself to bed, to fold her hands atop her breasts, ready for a grave.

WHY COMES THAT?

Candies, candles, cakes, even in her two hands someone has placed a glass, a real glass, of wine. Of real wine. Not that Lucia takes a second sip. The first to pass her lips convinces her that strangers have brought her to a party with no less an intent than to poison her. She eyes the candy and cake with suspicion.

She knows no one, and no one speaks to her. Several of the adults keep watching, their glances sour, their heads together. There are other children, though they run about laughing and screaming, they do not run to her. What they do is a thing Lucia knows is not to be done. Have they no sense? Once, three running past stopped to stand before her. A boy reached for her hair, but she knocked the hand away with a growl. *Un salvaje*, shouted the smallest, and they began laughing. *Gitana sucio.* And the bigger girl stuck her face in Lucia's to shout, *¡Claro!* Then they ran off.

Why and how an orphan-child continually starved has learned to stand silently with her hands clapped behind, a table larded with sweets an arm's length off, well, that would astonish any fat man, a fat man says, loud enough for Lucia to overhear. *The Church, yes, the Church does a good job with them.* The disconcerted man has been watching Lucia stand flatfooted and alone toward the end of the table, and now he has beckoned the bride, a pale, golden-haired child herself, to come hear what he has to say. Luna looks to where he points. *Pobrecita*, she says, shaking her head, a gleaming lock falling free of a flower circlet.

She then walks toward the child, tucking the errant hair back under the band, and asks her, *Aren't you hungry?*

Lucia shrugs.

Well that's foolish. I'm always hungry. Luna snatches up a bit of cake and pops it into her mouth. *Delicioso.*

She takes up a second and offers it to Lucia. *Eat it, silly. You don't I'll have to, and I'll get so fat!* She laughs, a tint of pink flushing under her otherwise clear white skin. No *Gitano* here. To Lucia, nothing and no one has ever been more beautiful, not even the unforgotten Begonia. The presence of such beauty alone is enough to stay her hand from the offered cake, but it is the prospect of accepting a stranger's gift without having to deliver it to the Church that puzzles her.

So, who are you?

Lucia consider it a strange question, for after all, it was the child bride's party to which she'd been brought, not the other way around. But she answers.

Lucia what?

Just Lucia. That's all.

That's impossible. Nobody has only one name.

To the child's thinking, few have more. And she says so.

Well I have more, now. I am Señora Luna Maria Senna y Soledad, and that... she points to a laughing policeman bent backward in an exuberant laugh, *is why.* She giggles, blushing, covering her face with her hand. *Gah! I can't believe it yet! How old are you?*

Again, Lucia shrugs. She has no way of knowing.

Well, you look six, but you seem ten, so maybe you are eight.

I guess. I don't know.

Who doesn't know how old they are? You are some kind of dummy, aren't you. One name and no, when was your last birthday?

A third time with a shrug.

Uh, you are not fun to talk to. But I like you. I am glad you have come to my wedding. Who are you with?

Lucia looks around but does not see the nun who had brought her. She has been in the midst of strangers before, and being left does not upset her.

Are you sneaking into my party? I think you're only here for the cake.

I don't know why I am here. The Sister brought me, but she is gone I think.

Luna looks at her wide-eyed. *You're one of them? You're an orphan! Oh what great luck! It is lucky to have an orphan at your wedding. Everybody knows that. My sister said so, and she knows everything and everybody and everything about everybody, and I bet she even knows who you are, and even your last name.*

I bet not.

We should see. Luna grabs the girl by the hand and begins to pull. They cross the flat courtyard, skipping between white and frothy tables already filled with dirty plates and abandoned glasses. *That's her.*

Lucia sees a dramatic woman holding a glass before her lips, the other hand tucked under her elbow gripping a closed fan. She wears a shimmering gold dress that has red ruffles pouring out of a rupture along her near leg. Her hair is done up with a high comb and a glittering mantilla embroidered with poppies and carnations of the same violent red as the dress. She is speaking to a rotund woman in dull purple, a color gained more by innumerable wash days than by regal dye. Her head tilts down as she addresses the older woman.

Mora! I have made a bet. And you have got to help me win it.

Mora turns to her sister and, seeing Lucia, smiles, though coldly.

What?

I've made a bet you know who this poor orphan is. Maria, what's the matter?

The woman in purple, Maria, has grown purple herself. She glares at Lucia. *How?* she says more than asks Mora. Then, *You incredible whore.*

Mora flips open the fan. To Lucia she says, *Don't believe a word she says. I am a very credible whore.*

Another day among cockroaches

Lucia makes a mistake. The alley is blind, and long, and though she sees it is empty she does not see that it is blind, and from it no one may escape once that need arises. But there are cans, and in the cans may be food, and this time she is determined she will not return to the Church from which she has fled. But it has been days, and she is hungry, and the cans in the alley may contain food.

But hunger misleads, and it has misled her into an alley from which there is no escape, for it is blind. And blind to what follows her in.

Later, washing away the blood with a rag shoved under the river water, parts to her stinging as they never had stung before, and while wiping off the filth and slime the man left on her skin, Lucia will wonder, *How'd he know I'd go in there?*

A decision with implications

Ned detests the process, and rises from his chair in the antique office of the Mother Superior. The eyes of four pretty girls in clean dresses and shoes that pinch follow him as he leaves, each face of the four twitching with disappointments and fears. That of the Mother Superior herself is concerned, but not surprised. The reactions toward claiming one of the orphans vary, as do the intentions of those who claim them.

He wanders along a corridor that he believes will lead to an outside courtyard, to smoke. However, it does not, and returning he hears a child's voice come from a room whose door is open. Looking in, he sees no one, nothing except a pile of clothing centered in a bed sheet in the middle of what appears to be a dormitory, a number of flat, spare cots aligned with their heads against a wall.

He hears scuffling and discovers a child's feet bobbling under one of the far beds, the soles black with dirt. Then he hears the rapid, throaty Spanish that sounds a lot like the cursing he's heard on the street. He watches as she backs out, the rag of her shift climbing up her skinny but muscular legs. Finally the child, clear enough of the bed, the prize of soiled clothing in each of her hands, stands up. Ned steps back, not wanting to be seen watching her.

The child does not see him. Her hair rises no more than an inch from her scalp, and he feels a momentary sadness, remembering his own getting shorn at her age for the same probable reason. The child fiddles with the bundle, which she then struggles to raise into place. A bundle, Ned feels certain, half the weight of her scrawny self.

When she reacts as though she has spotted him, he walks away, back to the Mother Superior.

A child with laundry? The Mother Superior turns to one of the three nuns standing in the office with the girls, the one who translates Ned's words into something understandable. A second nun whispers, *Lucia.*

The Mother Superior turns thoughtful, as though considering a misplacement of her bible always at the corner of her desk. Then, in Spanish quickly converted into English, she says, *If that's who you want.*

Ned looks at his wife, who keeps her wearied blue eyes on his face. *I liked her immediately. She has spunk. You want to see her?*

If you think she'll do, I am fine with what you decide.

Word passes quickly among all living inside the orphanage, and the word is, *finally.*

MOTHER INFERIOR

Such calls to the office of the Mother Superior are never good, but all too common. *What did I do?* she wonders, padding barefoot from kitchen with her hands and the front of her sack wet and red from the hot water used to scrub the tables. On another day the call might been from getting caught with a stolen crust, but not that day. There had been none to steal. *Forgetting the ashes?*

Turning onto the corridor leading to the office, Lucia sees an old nun holding a blue package, the woman's head bent forward, her wimple shadowing her face. As the child approached, she raises her head. Sister Concordia is smiling, her coal eyes bright.

Contrite, Lucia lowers her expression, doubly worried that her transgression — whatever it may have been — has delighted the nun with an opportunity to punish even more severely than a beating with a rod. She curls her hands into a fist, not in opposition, but to protect the small bones. Though she knows to do so is discouraged, she approaches the nun in smaller steps, more slowly. It is the consequence of fear and awareness of it.

But the blue box entrances, and Lucia cannot ignore it. Once she has come close enough to hear her crime, she raises her eyes, but no higher than enough to see its shape and size.

Por favor, she whispers, again dropping her head, though only a little. *I come to be improved. I accept that I have not served God as He expects.*

Dios mio, the sister says. *It's not that. Come with me.*

Instead of opening the door into the chamber of the Mother Superior, the sister walks on, knocking the child in the shoulder with the box, not by accident but as a further command to follow.

She leads to a closet in which are rags and a tin basin used on wash day, when there is a wash day. *Get the basin and a towel.* The sister herself, tucking the box under one arm, takes a scrub brush and a shard of lye soap from a higher shelf, one that none of the orphans can reach without help. Without a word after closing the closet door, she spins about and walks off toward the children's dormitory, her movements only commanding Lucia to follow.

You know what to do, so do it.

There are two other children in the room, both more than a half dozen years younger but old enough to understand and become curious. They have been smoothing bed covers, rags that they are, but all of the beds are done. The nun scowls at them. *What next?*

The children flee. Lucia is alone with the nun, the wash basin heavy in her hands, the towel carried on her head drooping down over one eye. She has to tilt her head back to see the woman's face.

I said, what next? Why anyone would want an ugly imbecile like you is beyond knowing, but God does work his mysteries. Come on, put them down and fetch the water.

It is a chore she likes least, dipping hot water from a cauldron in the fireplace into a bucket and then having to carry it back to the dormitory. The wooden bucket is already heavy and, once filled, she must not allow any to slop over, which always happens and scalds her feet.

As the oldest, and oldest by years rather than inches, she has earned the last bath, but no one else has arrived in the dormitory. The need for a solitary and unexpected bath in clean, hot water and the presence of that blue box terrifies her to the core. She sets the bucket beside the tub, the nun demanding *strip*, and one thought possesses her.

She has been sold.

And there will be nowhere to run, because there will be nowhere to let her return. The Church will close its doors to her, in the way it has never been before closed after she has run away.

She has heard stories about those who grew too old and got sold. These whispered fantastics told from one sleeper to next, tales told since the Moors overran Seville, make her knees — she lowers her foot into the cold zinc tub — worthless. She squats, and the first ladle of boiled water pours over her.

Lucia suffers the brush and the *picanté* bite of the fresh hot water, the stinging torture of lye soap eating the filth and sin off of her body, all of her strength centered on keeping the tears from mixing with the rinse water. She hates the blood and hairs, and the pains visiting her more often than ever. It seems continual that blood seeps out of her, and she knows the consequence of the blood.

Her time has come, she has been sold.

She wants to ask Sister Concordia whether she knows what kind of man at whose side she must go to lie. She is certain it is a Moor, her ugly self worthy only to one of those Moroccan devils. The tales say that once he is done what he will do, she will become a mother to a bastard like herself, and if it is a girl, it will die, for they only want boys, and that she'll have to lie with him again, and if another girl, you know, it too will die, until there is a boy. And she will have to kill it herself, either by holding the infant under water, or twisting its head around on its neck until it comes off, or even boiling it in a big iron pot like the one in the kitchen. Or stabbing it with one of their enormous curved knives, or using the blade to chop off its screaming head.

Lucia hates her blood and the hair growing between her legs, and the swells that will change her from looking any more like a boy. She cannot help prevent the burst of a sob.

Sister Concordia slaps her head. *Hold still,* she says, *and let me clean your ears. It's going to be fine. You'll see.*

AN UNEXPECTED KINDNESS

It happens quickly, unavoidably, and on the fast streets of Seville, too often. This time it happens to Lucia, who is returning on the orphanage's one bicycle with a heavy basketful of vegetables begged at the market, each specimen handed over to her with a prayer to the Virgin at the giver's lips.

Whose fault it is cannot be determined. Children are easily distracted during their perambulations, and men in cars are too often focused on what will happen rather than what is happening. Because of the cobbles, she lurches more into the street than she should. All Lucia then sees is the toothy chromed grill of a huge vehicle, and then the sky, and then several of her fruits bouncing and rolling away, until she closes her eyes to see nothing but stars and the swirling color of blood.

The man driving stops, *Dios mio, Dios mio!* He crouches over the child, whose eyes open and she looks up at him like a landed fish, her mouth gawping. *Dios mio.* He checks her twisted legs and arms, asks her if she's hurt. Lucia feels herself bruised but not broken. She has felt broken before. Then she spies the bicycle's rear wheel, and she closes her eyes knowing how many times the cane will strike her for this. They trusted her with the bicycle, and she has failed God.

But she refuses to cry.

Then the man helps her sit. In an incoherent stream not meant expressly for the man with his arm under her back, Lucia begins talking about the bicycle, the vegetables, the nuns, the orphanage, and she feels herself rising into the arms. Twice her head falls back and the world she knows distorts, the people upside down, the buildings tilting this way and that. Then she is slid onto the back seat of the car. She hears the man ask again, *Which church?* And someone telling him the street on which it sits.

Then they are driving.

Lucia at last sits up. *My bicycle,* she says over the seat.

Not to worry, little one. I have it.

One of the nuns gives her a stern look, the fault always hers. Then she is led away, to be inspected and washed. The man watches her go, his hands twisting the brim of his hat, contrite, apologizing often.

She never sees him again, but in three days she is shown a shining new bicycle, and told by one of the other orphans about several large cardboard boxes filled with fresh food, oranges, dates, meat. And bread.

She is given bread.

AN UNEXPECTED KINDNESS THAT UPSETS MORA

Though it has been many years for Señora Dolores, nothing about where she sits has changed. Indeed, notions of change violate everything for which everything in the room stands. She keeps her veiled head down, less aware of the chants and songs rising from where the men gather on the far side of the mehitzah than she is on what she carries in her pocket, a letter upon whose folds her dry and tired fingers rest.

They touch a letter she has written, one composed with unkind joy. It bears news that has drawn her into the room after so many years of keeping away. The Señora feels herself compelled.

Dear daughter,

I hope this finds you well. Maria has another child, and we have not heard from Isabella in four months, but I suspect her new family treats her well. Luna is swelling daily. We are all convinced she carries a boy.

I am certain you will celebrate with us, for we have been given news. Your daughter is now with a new family, at last, prayers answered. And do not worry, she has not been sold. She goes with an American naval man to help care for his ailing wife, who is dying.

And I have been assured, or rather Maria has, by the head woman in that place, that she will never be returned, even should the woman die. It would be too difficult, too costly, too unwanted. And too far.

Our lost child is gone to America.

It is that line which had been written in unkind joy, and the line that has Mora — alone in a dismal hot room in a dismal hot town awaiting the arrival of a dismal dry man — casting the letter onto the floor.

AMERICA

A SHIP TO

All of her terrors pass. In a conveyance up on which she has never before ridden but daily seen, Lucia feels herself, because of the thick leather seat and great height, if not a Queen in her lacquered carriage, at least a princess, though a princess whose feet hurt.

She raises her shining patent leather shoes to admire the straight black line of the straps across her white socks, each strap held with a gleaming gold buckle, things of fancy, and things not one of the nuns would have given approval, but within the hidden heart of each would have lived some envy. Shoes. The straps bite, and Lucia is certain that any minute blood will begin staining her white socks, but she refuses to say a word, offer any complaint. And what good would that do? The couple speaks little Spanish, and she no English other than *cigarette.*

Even though she has been sternly admonished against complaining by more than one red-faced nun as she was paraded out of the church, Lucia recognizes how great her fortune, and knows she will do nothing to imperil it, now that it is hers.

Fortune is hers. In so many, in various ways, and people have told her so. And, by some, said so with spit.

But that lies behind.

Lucia keeps her gloved hands together as in and out of sunshine the carriage bears them all, the clop of matched black horses ringing. On her shoulders the woman rests her arm, every now and then tugging Lucia more tightly against a thin body. Lucia accepts the discomforts, does not mind. She is going to America.

Cruise liners require too much depth to dock alongside the Gibraltor quay. Ned lifts Lucia from carriage and carries her all the way to a rocking launch in which a dozen other well-dressed people already sit. He sets her down at the gangplank.

A chubby youth in white holds out his hand to assist her onto the craft, but it is not a gesture with which the girl has any familiarity, so she ignores him and stumbles her way to a seat.

With some difficulty, Ned helps the frail Diana. Lucia watches the fat boy fawn before the couple. *Dios mio,* she thinks, *Royalty.*

For anyone isolated by language, there remains only observation. She switches attention from the vanishing wharf already the foam from waves crashing that bulkhead is a thin line to the growing white-sided *Michaelangelo,* at which other launches unload. Those passengers scramble up the gangplanks like ants onto a dinner roll, disappearing into holes in the side.

She also looks at the waves, fearful that Noah's Leviathan may still be hungry. Her knuckles whiten inside the gloves, and her bitten fingernails sting.

Diana kisses her on the head, whispering something that soothes.

For Lucia, all amazes, all bewilders. She is guided by a firm hand on her shoulder to the belly of the ship, then along many corridors. Several times they stop, someone speaking to Ned, one of them also in uniform snapping a salute, but then they walk and walk until reaching a metal door painted to resemble wood, with a number on it.

Lucia says out loud, *Catorce.*

Fourteen.

The girl looks up at Diana, confused. She will not be confused. *Catorce.*

Right, right. Both Ned and Diana smile, the porter unlocking and opening the door before attempting to hand over the key. Ned puts up both hands, refusing the offer, then points at Lucia. With a stiff bow and a click of his heels, the porter lowers his offer of the the key, presenting it to the girl as though she is, indeed, a princess, and his gloved hand a silk pillow.

She takes it, but with no pocket on her dress, she slides it into the palm of her own gloved hand.

Against the wall are two bunks, Ned asking by gestures for her to choose one of them. She eyes the higher, again confused at what he indicates, but when he pats the upper, raising his eyebrows, she begins to understand. He lifts her up and plops her down, perching her there as one would a doll put way after play. She swings her feet and looks around.

Already there is a suitcase tucked beside a small dresser, and Diana is at it, lifting it to the lower bunk, opening it and removing new clothes. When she removes a powder blue dress with a chiffon skirt and shakes it, Lucia feels she must clap, and as she does the key slips from her glove and tumbles to the floor.

Ned, retrieving it, says something to Diana, who nods. She takes the key and puts it into her purse.

The porter, who has remained in the corridor, says something in Italian, and Lucia knows enough of the words to understand he wants them to go with him. Ned says something to the man, and then to her. She accepts his hands about her waist and the lift down from the upper bunk.

They are led to the next cabin, again a key which Ned, this time, accepts. Theirs is a larger room with a full bed rather than bunks. On it are several suitcases that Ned shuffles down to the floor, clearing a space for his wife to lie upon.

Diana pats an empty space at her side, calling Lucia by name. The girl understands, but hesitates until Diana pats again, then she climbs onto the bed to sit.

Diana asks Lucia to hold her raised hand, then closes her eyes, and soon she is asleep.

Ned sets a finger to his smiling lips, a jerky nod calling her to follow. She slides from the bed, careful not to disturb. Diana is not disturbed.

The boat goes nowhere for much of the morning. Ned leads the child along the deck. Already people sprawl in chairs, some reading, some talking. As they pass two women, Ned bows and says, *Hello*. The women smile up at Ned, but give Lucia an up and down. After Ned moves on, Lucia hears one of them say something aloud in French. The nuns taught her to understand and speak it, to prepare her for an eventual marriage to a Moor, from whom she repeatedly ran. The women say something kind about Ned, but not about her. Lucia, who had begun to follow

Ned, stops and spits on the deck at their feet, then she tells them that she believes she can guess their primary occupation.

Ned, who does not understand French, who understands tone and rhythm, turns on his heel and scowls at the child, but her back is to him. He calls her name in the way that means, *Forget them, come on*, but Lucia does not break from her accusations. He calls again, Lucia spits again when she also hears the woman who had said the unkind thing repeating it. Then she kicks the edge of the woman's chair. Her companion laughs, then calls Lucia a whore's daughter.

Lucia, feeling Ned's hand come down on her shoulder, tells the nearer woman that she is aboard with royalty, and they had better watch their necks or their heads may be taken off.

Ned is not pleased, but he does not say much, though he smiles, a small smile, which stays on his lips a while.

AN ISLAND OF FOOD

More than the sea can hold, more than a bevy of nuns can swallow, almost as much as a hungry orphan might want, the ship's buffet seems endless. Cherries, oranges, pineapple, mangoes, heaps of purple grapes, barrels of soups with steam quivering from under and around the rims, a man in white behind an island of fish — some as large as she. Another in white draws a blunt-tipped sword along the blood-dripping side of a roast beef twice her size. And mountains of potatoes, platters the size of shields upon which are hills of boiled and roasted greens.

Lucia feels herself growing dizzy and she grabs for the tail of Ned's jacket. He has been pointing, gesturing, eyebrows scrunched upward on his forehead. She can only stare and gape open mouthed.

There are small, smelly balls of green that roll when she tries to stab one. Ned laughs. Finally she holds it between two fingers, to jab, *picador*, with her fork. The ball is not too hot, but it smells and she makes a face.

Ned laughs.

She does not laugh. She looks at him with a dark frown, then puts the entire ball into her mouth. A taste never had before.

Ned says to her, *Brussel sprout.*

She tries to repeat it, but her mouth is still full. One of the mashed leaves comes out of her mouth and lands on her chin. She shoves it back in, grimacing at the queer texture of the green ball.

You don't have to eat it, he says, slicing into quarters one of his own. Lucia chews and chews, and eventually the mash is swallowed. She does not take another.

The fish disappears in rapid bites, but the wedge of brown meat goes untouched. She has heard stories about beef, told to her by the sisters, sometimes by the girls who had been older, that *if you eat it before you are married, you will grow hair on your parts and no one will want you ever and ever.* Already she has hair on her parts, a few thin strands, and she fears the beef. She will not touch it, or the man beside her will take her back to the convent.

Ned does not understand, but finally quits pointing at the slab, lifting it with a fork from her plate onto his own. She is glad. She studies the nubs on his chin as he chews, and she feels very glad, and wise.

A MOVE OUT TO SEA

The blast startles her beyond frightened, and when the second begins she claps her hands over her ears, looking for a place into which she might crawl. Ned is laughing. He points up toward the top of the ship, which she cannot see, and then holds up three fingers. At the third blast he drops one, leaving two. She understands, but she does not drop her hands covering her ears.

Many people move toward the rails, and Ned waves for her to join him there. There is a shudder, then rattling of the great chains.

Once, having been told to leave the convent and to not come back until dark approached, she found in an alley a man stinking of urine. He had been discovered because he groaned loud enough for her to hear. His head was askew, his mouth and eyes open, though they had rolled up and all she could see, almost, was the dry, yellowish whites. When she came closer, he groaned again, one hand fluttering above his chest. Then his body shook, she could hear it rattle. He trembled for a long time, then collapsed, crumbled into a heap. The man no longer groaned but lay still, the odors of a chamber pot arose and mixed with the urine.

She backed away. When far enough from him, Lucia turned and ran.

She understood.

The ship trembles once the shudder has run through. She feels a growing rumble through the soles of her shoes, in her hand on the rail, inside her chest, and she wonders if the ship dies, will she not reach America?

She looks to Ned for something, anything reassuring, but he looks only landward. Following his line of sight she sees what she needs to see, that the relationship of the giant rock of Gibralter to that of the ship is changing. They are moving out to sea.

Not the apparent breeze, nor Ned calling her away from the rail, nor any of the passengers vanishing one by one, draws her from the unending vigil she has determined must be kept. It is not until Gibraltar vanishes, not until the thin line of yellow sand eternally suspended in the air over the Spanish coast ceases to color the sky, does she come away. But then, she only comes away to take Ned's hand, not to accompany him back to the cabin in which Diana sleeps, but forward toward the bow. For there, Lucia knows, America will soon be seen.

DUTY

Forgoing the shoes, the socks, certainly the gloves and the yellow dress, Lucia wears only the slip that hangs straight down over her body. She keeps the key in her hand when she closes the cabin door behind her, and it bites her palm when she knocks lightly but firmly on the couple's cabin door.

She knocks again, and finally the door opens. Ned, wearing only trousers, sockless, shirtless, blinks at her. Lucia says, *If I am late, it is because the bells have not rung.*

Bells she has risen to since she could walk.

And then she asks, *Do you want your pot removed?*

But Ned does not understand a word. Nor does Diana, who sits upright in the bed, her thin hair down to her shoulders and against her cheek.

Lucia sees that his shoes sit far from the wall, his socks balled and stuffed into the heels, a shirt drapes the arm of the cabin's chair, Diana's dress across the back. She darts for the shoes, drawing each sock out until the pair hangs together, which she then folds. The shoes she sets in rigid parallel. She is lifting the shirt and glancing around for a place to hang it when Ned barks something at her.

Diana says something to her husband, and then she smiles at the girl. All Lucia understands is the woman saying, *No, no no no.* This is followed by something else, and the girl stops folding the shirt. Ned takes it from her, tosses it onto the foot of the bed, then with a hand against her shoulder directs her to the door, which he opens. Then he pushes her out, saying something, indicating the direction of her room.

The door shuts and Lucia remains in the hall, confused, until she hears someone farther along the passage coming nearer.

A THING NEVER DONE BEFORE THAT SHE LIKES

At the far end of the table sits *El Capitan,* two words that Ned has whispered in Lucia's ear, two words she understands but only partly. *¿Policia?* Ned smiles, *No, the captain. El Capitan,* then with a sweep of his hand, *de la barca.*

¿Sí?

Sí.

Ooo, she says. *Claro.*

At that moment, from the far side of the seating area in which many well dressed men and jeweled women sit with food still on their plates, a band strikes the first flourish of a tune she had once or twice heard coming from a radio of some car passing near where she begs. But it sounds differently than that. Better. Brighter, bigger. And there is no singing.

Diana settles her hand on her husband's forearm. Lucia sees the captain looking their way and hears him ask something of Ned. By the rhythm of what he has said, Lucia knows he has put forward a question. Instead of answering the captain, Ned turns to his wife and repeats the question. Diana laughs, a thin, glittery laugh, shaking her head from side to side, a silly wave toward their host. The captain, however, goes on, but this time to Lucia. All she understands of his words, though, is the single use of *señorita.*

For her, Ned answers, and they all laugh. But then he puts out a hand before the girl. She looks at it, unsure of what she has that he may want. But then he slips his hand beneath hers, stands, bows, and in a very solemn manner, asks his question. A gentle tug on her hand tells her she has been asked to rise. For what, she does not know.

Ned leads her to a knot of dancers, the men erect and elegant in their postures, the women swirling the chiffon skirts out from their knees. Ned holds her hand aloft, and places another behind her back. Then he shuffles, Lucia standing in place. Pressure against her back makes her move, but she crashes against his legs. He stops, looks down and says, to the beats of the music, *ewno, doze, trace* and then he repeats the triplet, *ewno, doze, trace*, moving a foot with each word. It is something at first Lucia does not feel, but soon something happens to her legs and feet, and she no long bangs against the tall man's legs.

They are dancing.

Later, forward at the bow, Ned shows her the stars, and there are many, many stars. She looks up at them as he points and speaks, looks elsewhere in the night's brocade at where he points again and speaks again, and she forgets the unseeable horizon, forgets to look for America.

In a part of the sky into which she does not look but of which she can see, a brilliants streak flashes and is gone.

A LADY WITH A LAMP IN HER HAND

Once before, when the Pope deigned to come to Seville, and many times on Easters when the Macarena, prepared for her parade through the streets, had yet to emerge through the cathedral doors, Lucia had experienced the collective electricity of a community waiting. So it is, there on the foredeck, again. Ned above her smokes a cigarette while Diana holds down her wide brimmed hat. Lucia and a number of women lean forward over the rail. It is cold, and she shivers, but it does not stop her from jabbering her many and oft-repeated questions, for which there is no one to answer, for there is no one near who understand what she asks.

She asks, *What is the fuss?*

Already America had appeared, a strip of darker gray on a gray horizon, buildings and shapes only making thin scribbles in the gray fog. Ned had pointed out the coastline to her, said the one word she understood as meaning salvation from every plague and ill behind her. He had not been the first to see it, and whoever had caught sight had passed the word, and already an eruption of excitement had animated the company. But this electricity feels different to Lucia, for it is one affecting all of the adults.

She is not the youngest against a rail, but she is one of the few children straining to see. Those near her have puffy eyes and deep, childish scowls at having been awakened too early and dragged from comfortable beds.

Within his glass-fronted helm the captain nods to a second man, who depresses a button, and the chest-thundering blast fills the air. And there, Lucia sees, her hands clapped over her ears, is what everyone on the port side sees. A giant woman holding aloft a lamp.

She has heard there are giants in America. She thinks, it must be true.

None leave their posts against the rail until the green unsmiling lady slides into the past.

NOT *ABUELO,* NOR *SEÑOR.* GRANDDADDY

Huge, even more giant than Ned, red-faced and jowly, with eyes bluer than even the Madonna's robe, a laugh more loud than the ship's blast, each of his soft and meaty hands holding Lucia's by the wrist, he swings her about, her legs no more than extended ropes, her hair crisscrossing her face, covering her bewildered eyes.

Ned smiles, Diana laughs, and finally her feet again touch ground. But not for long. The thick hands slip under her armpits and she is hoisted aloft until she is settled, like an orphaned toddler, against the giant's hip. She stays there until they are no longer in the midst of fellow passengers. The giant swings her from his hip and into a horse-drawn carriage.

Ned and Diana face the small dark child and a blonde, blue-eyed giant, constant smiles frozen on their unspeaking lips. No need to speak, because the man beside Lucia has not ceased since first finding them in the disembarking crowd.

It is the land of giants, at least of giant things. They enter Central Park, where giant statues of men on horseback, soldiers with swords aloft, are frozen into indifference to their passing. The party drifts under giant trees and huge striped flags, and everywhere there are people lounging, smoking, laughing, some even dancing to music that comes from nowhere.

Emerging from under shade into a cool but bright light, Diana calls Lucia by name, and, pointing at the newest of their company, say, *Abuelo.*

She looks at the man. *Imposible. ¡Sus ojos son azul!*

The man returns a confused look. Diana says something, to which he replies, *Abuelo my ass.* He jabs Lucia below her collarbone, then thumps himself on the chest. *Granddaddy.*

He says it again, thumps again, says it a third time. Lucia tries, but it comes out with a different sound, and the three adults all laugh. Lucia purses her lips and her eyes turn blacker than the black they always are.

¡No es mi abuelo!

The three laugh louder, and Lucia's eyes turn even blacker.

After a long drive at the curbstone before the towering Essex Hotel they stop. Ned climbs down, and then the giant and Ned assist Diana, who exclaims and frets until she reaches ground. Ned calls Lucia, who rises.

The giant reaches to lift the girl down, but Ned sets a hand on his father's arm. He says something, the man nods, and holds forward one hand. Ned, too, holds out a hand, and Lucia, taking each, steps carefully onto the America sidewalk in royal fashion.

AN ISLAND OF BEEF, A CONTINENT OF AUTOMOBILE

The plate cannot contain the sizzling edges of the Porterhouse set down before her, and melting fat drips onto the white linen tablecloth. Lucia does not move her hands from where they have been folded in her lap, despite what she knows is insistent urging from the giant that she take up the knife and fork in the manner he holds his, and shows her how they must be held.

She will have the hide of a gorilla. Of this she is fully aware, and it stays her hands. Ned, understanding her reluctance toward beef, takes her plate and sets it beside his own. He then slices the meat into small, precise squares, one of which he stabs with his fork and, saying *Lucia,* puts one chunk into his mouth. He bites, chews, and then swallows before returning the plate to where she sits.

She feels as though she moves her hand through the silt and low-tide mud of the Guadalquivir, but finally she takes a fork, presses it into one of the bleeding cubes. With a shaking hand she lifts it into her mouth.

Within minutes, Ned, Diana and the giant are all stares, astonished at how much meat has vanished into such a little girl. After every morsel gone, Ned understands that the child's imploring eyes are asking that he cut up even more. He shreds the meat, even from the bone.

Lucia chews in silence, when she chews. The three speak among themselves, the conversation hovering over the table like the shifting smoke of Ned's cigarettes. Questions asked and answered, questions from the giant, questions to Diana, some of which are answered in whispers and with lowered eyes. But on and on, Lucia chews.

At one pause between bites, the giant shows Lucia how to load her fork with the white mash and then how to lower it into the green peas. He chews with exaggerated expression, which makes Lucia laugh.

All she remembers is floating, her head on the giant's broad shoulder, the giant rattling the air in a bed beside her. The room is dark, and for several moments she fears being eaten. Giants eat children, and as she still does not understand what she has been brought for, it is all in the dark she can picture.

But the giant snores on, and soon there is light in the room.

She has seen automobiles, even ridden in some, and she has seen ships, and now been at sea in one, but she has never seen anything so long, so sleek, so beautiful, so blue.

With a light touch on every letter, she spells out the raised chrome letters at the rear, while Ned and the Giant load suitcases. *B-o-n-n-e-v-i-l-l-e*. She knows from the French the nuns taught her that it means a good city, a beautiful, wonderful city, and she is certain this impossibly long automobile will take to the skies and sweep her off to a land where there are golden streets, the houses with doorknobs cut from fist-sized pearls, and the streetlights hanging with diamonds. This, too, she has heard from the nuns and the many orphans now so far behind.

Ned assists Diana into the back seat, handing his wife a scarf additional to the one she has already tied under her chin. There is no roof to the car, and Lucia accepts having the cloth tied under her chin. Ned slides behind the wheel, the giant already in his seat turns, points at her head and calls her *babcia*. Ned laughs, but Diana doesn't know the word. The giant says, *Abuel*, at which Diana, shakes her head. With a gentle caress on Lucia's scarved crown, she correct the old man.

No, she says, fingering the fold near her cheek. *Abuelita*.

The car pulls from the curb, and they drive past so many huge and wonderful things before entering a long, dark and smelly tunnel.

Perhaps, Lucia considers as she watches lights flash over their heads, herself holding her nose, *the golden streets still have dogs and pigs*.

Eventually, though, the stinks give way to shaggy, placid creeks, still estuaries and tree-shaded coves, and she wishes they would stop so that she might attract and speak to a dragonfly. She wants to ask, but knowing they will not understand either a word or the sentiment, settles for the satisfactions of strangeness.

At some point in the monotony of traffic, she slides down onto the seat and does not again awaken until the sounds of the slowing car have changed.

When she sits up, Diana says, *Philadelphia. Home.*

HEY, SAILOR, LOVE YOU LONG TIME

Come on, sing it. I realize... the way your eyes... deceived me... With tender looks... that I mistook... for love. The giant old man raises a foot, hers atop it, stepping forward, her backward, to the rhythm of the song. *Paper roses... Paper roses... Come on. Sing it. Oh how real...*

O, ha weel...

Those roses...

Dess rosses...

That's it...seem to be...

Seem be...

But...

Boot...

They're only imitation...

Lucia leans away, all her weight on his insteps, all her safety in the clasp of his hands. *¿Que?*

He laughs. *They're only imitation...* He leans back, swooping her up into a bear hug. She laughs. *Like your imitation love for me.* He swings her dangling legs and body in a wide arc, nuzzling kisses into her neck. *Mwah, mwah, mwah, mwah.* She cannot stop laughing. *Mmmmwah.* He kisses her more. *Paper roses... You'll get it, honey. Keep singing. Oh, damn, the soup. Hop down. No, stay on my feet.*

The old man walks her backward from the living room, past the never-used dining table of dark, thick, red-veined wood, into the bright yellow kitchen and across to his stove. He pulls her close, one arm holding her away from the stove as he turns down its flame. The soup pot steams and the kettle lid dances, a hiss of broth running down the side explodes on the hot cast iron. Lifts the lid, checks, resettles the lid with a *yumm,* then he walks backward, humming.

Lucia presses her cheek against the broad stone belly. *It is a place I could live,* she thinks, *forever.*

The back door opens and Ned in his working khakis comes in. They can see him from the kitchen, bent, dirty, a long streak of oil along the thigh of his left leg. By the back door hangs a laundry basin. He turns on the cold-water tap, picks up Lava soap and begins to spin it between his hands under a gush of water. Ritual. Lucia, stepping down from the old man's shoe tops, waits until Ned, shaking the excess from his hands, splattering the wall with soapy drops, reaches for a hand towel hanging from a nail. Then she goes for his kiss on the top of her head.

Granddaddy continues the song. *I thought that you would be a perfect lover. You seemed so full of sweetness at the start. But like a big red rose that's made of paper, there isn't any sweetness in your...* he swallows deeply, then bellows ...*heart! Paper roses, paper roses... hmm hmm hm hmmm...*

She smiles at him.

Hey, Lucy, you go on in and learn some more English from Popeye. I want to talk to your dad.

How is she today? Ned asks, his glance upwards toward the ceiling.

THE SOUND OF NOTHING TO SAY

Lucia studies the television, and she hears something she has heard before, the sound that ends a word, *sss. That's all, folks.* It reminds her of *What's up, Doc.* It reminds her of the gray-faced man with the small mustache. *And that's the way it is.*

On her stomach, she must twist to look over her shoulder at the old man in his armchair. He is staring, though at nothing, while continually flipping an edge of a lace doily with his fingertip. His cigarette showers ash onto the arm of the chair.

The chair facing the television has a pole lamp beside it, the pole running up through the center of a glass topped table and ending at fringed shade. On that table is a bible, in the bible's gutter is a rosary, Diana's. Behind that chair rises the stairs to the second floor, up which Ned and a doctor have gone. Below the treads but above his head, almost level with the lampshade, a cuckoo clock ticks. She sees that the bird will not appear for several minutes, a thing she always enjoys, so she returns to watching the television.

Before the bird appears, Ned and the doctor come to the top of the stairs and they speak in low, unhearable tones. Lucia turns again, but all she can see of the two is their pants legs, and of them only the doctor's. Their combined voices have the old man in the chair turning as well, both he and Lucia craning to hear what they can't.

Ned?

Not yet, Dad. Soon. Lucia, he calls.

The old man says to her, *Lucy, go on up. Your father wants you.*

She rises and climbs the stairs, her eyes on the kind, charitable face of the always smiling but not then smiling doctor. There is a book and a pair of work shoes on the third step, which she gathers to carry.

Forget them, Ned says. *Put them down.*

Hello, Lucy, Lucia, the doctor reaches her. Now he smiles. *Which is it, Ned? Lucy in the house, Lucia in the waiting room? You're filling out nicely, at any rate. Good food, good people, eh?* He chucks her under the chin as he always does, and as always, Lucia tolerates what she does not like. *Well, anyway. I'm sorry, Ned. Gonna be tough. But you're tough, and you* again chucking Lucia under the chin *are tougher than any of 'em. Y'all take care now. Call me when it happens.*

Ned nods, finishing with his eyes down, then shakes the doctor's hand before the man descends to the lower floor. Ned puts a hand on Lucia's shoulder, to lead her down the hallway to the room in which Diana lies. It is a bright room, full of summer sunlight, though too warm and too close. It has the smell of rust about it.

Diana lies with her eyes wide, as though to swallow into them all the world, but she only looks up at the ceiling, not even moving when Lucia enters, Ned waiting at the door. Lucia goes to the wooden chair at the bed's side, sits, folds her hands in her lap. Her feet do not reach the floor, her legs dangle, and she crosses her ankles to keep herself from swinging them, something she finds herself doing whenever in a wooden chair where her feet do not reach the floor.

Diana looks at Lucia, who is looking out of the window on the opposite side of the sick bed. There had been a sycamore tree whose leaves cast shadows made from the streetlamp at the corner, but Ned had it taken down when Diana asked to see nothing but the sky over the rooftops opposite. Lucia watches the sky.

Diana whispers, drawing the girl's attention back into the room. ¿Que?

English, use your English. Please, lean down. She does. *Take good care of my husband. And be a good girl.* Diana coughs, and Lucia leans away, retaking her erect posture on the chair. When Diana stops, she then says, *Buena chica, you understand?*

She does.

It is a not so distant an evening from that afternoon when Granddaddy at the stove says to Ned seated at the enamel-topped kitchen table, Lucia holding dinner plates behind the old man, *Ain't good a little girl in a house with two grown men, you not the father. Not really. And what about school? You take care of that? No. You're down at the Yard more than you got to be, you know that. I took care of that. I don't mind taking care of things. It's what I do. I don't mind. But you know what you gotta do, and I'm telling you you gotta do it, and sooner rather than later.*

Ned does not respond. Lucia watches them.

I can take care of her until you get back. You got the chance to go, go. Do the right thing.

Ned shakes his head, then shrugs, then, *Okay. If I find her. If she will come. If I can ship over. If they let me do such a crazy thing. If, if if if.*

That's all stuff. The letter says she'd come, and they'll find her for you. If I know women like you say she is, this woman'll jump at it, and probably'll beat you to the boat. Trust me on that. Don't you forget I know what it's like to dream about coming to America. You trust me, that kid's mother been looking for a ticket to here since she first heard the word. And don't you get on about what Diana would have thought. She wanted something for the kid, and it wasn't two bachelors raising a girl. Not alone.

Ned looks over his shoulder at Lucia. Back to his father he says, I doubt she ever wanted me to bring another woman here.

I know she wanted that. She was a generous woman.

Not a mother.

She was for a few months. You get the mother, Diana'll be clapping in Heaven.

I wish I could believe that, but I just don't know.

In the ensuing pause, Lucia sets down the plates.

SO FAR, YET NOT SO FAR

No, Lucia stamps her foot. She pulls her hand from the old man's. No.

It's a good school. Come on, you'll like it.

Across from where they have stopped to wait for a light are women in black from head to toe. One of them — who has been shouting to a number of girls in plaid skirts, skirts of heavy wool, skirts exact copies of the one causing Lucia to perspire — looks across the broad space of concrete to where they stand. Then the nun returns her attentions back to the flock of children, her black skirts and mantle billowing in the September breeze.

He reaches for her hand, but Lucia refuses. No.

You will go, and you will like it. Besides, it's the law.

She steps backward.

Come on, Lucy. You gotta, and they've already seen you. You're going, and don't make me mad.

The halls smell of soap, perfumes, damp wool, perspiration and the eternity of dust, and now that all the doors have closed, the sound of their shoes on the floors echo in much the same way as had the Mother Superior's cane tapping the stones of the old Cathedral. Lucia fights the urge to bring up her breakfast.

She fights well, even after her grandfather pulls open the heavy wooden door and, with a hand on her back, directs her to enter.

She will never learn their names, but she also will never call them by the name she has carried with her for so long, so ever long. This, Lucia swears.

Third grade, half a year to learn English, then we'll move her up. She'll be fine, being she's just a little thing.

Lucia hates the desk, her knees high enough that the desk rocks on them when she draws them together. It is something to do. All around her are younger girls who sometimes turn to stare. She curses them in Spanish, two of the raven-haired giggling. The sister stops what she has been writing, and when she picks up the rubber-tipped pointer, everyone goes quiet as the empty halls beyond the door. Lucia does not fear what is coming. It has come before.

But the sister only brings the rod down on Lucia's desk, which makes it crash back to the floor. Then she swings it against the legs. *Enough of that.*

The two who had giggled stare at each other with wide eyes, then at her, then at the sister when she resumes writing on the board.

THE CONSEQUENCES OF ANOTHER'S DOING

Bouncey bounce, bouncey bounce. One, two, the bad things you do. Three, four, your mother's a whore. Five, six, beat her with sticks. Seven, eight, it's never too late...

Lucia stopped tossing the bright plastic ball against the stoop for a moment, trying to recall what they had said came with *nine, ten*. She held the ball against her nose. It felt cool in her hands and smooth against her lips, and it had a smell like nothing ever smelled except maybe Granddaddy's records in the cabinet under the player. *Nine, ten... was there a nine, ten?*

With both hands she flips the ball toward the bottom step, hoping it will come back high rather than low so she could jump to catch it. It goes high, all right, higher than her head, higher than she can reach, higher than she can get her hands up to stop its flight into the street behind her.

You go no farther than this, Granddaddy had said, dragging a toe along the line of curb stone. *You stay out of the street.*

He should have told the ball.

It strikes first the high ridge fin of an Impala that Ned bought a month before he had come into her room to say *I gotta leave a while. Gonna be a long while. But I'll come back an'll have a surprise when I get home.* The ball bounces from the fin nearly straight up, but not quite, coming down onto the rear windshield, then flying up into the street where it bumps a few times before striking against the opposite side curb. Its journey slows to a roll back towards her, but with not enough oomph to get it out of the street and to her.

Lucia watches, her lower lip between her teeth.

You ain't to get no farther than this here curb. You stay outta the street.

She looks back at the closed door above the stoop, then at the ball. She takes a step forward, then another, which brings her to the line of forbidden passage at the gap between the rear bumper of Ned's Impala and the grill of her neighbor's old Ford pickup. The ball, still energized enough to rock side to side, begins to settle into a small hole in the tar where two underlying cobblestones are visible. A distance not far, *two, three, four giant steps. That is all.*

Between the Ford and the Impala she crouches, eyes fixed on the bright colors. *Ready, set, go.* That's what they taught her with all their hollering. *Ready, set, go.* Then *Run! Run, Lucy the Spic. Run!*

102

She touches the ball, has the ball in her hands, raises the ball inches from the hole in the tar when she hears the scream of tires. She looks up in the direction cars could only come. A chromium grill like the teeth of a lion, brilliant in the sunlight, and the tires screaming like a tiger diving for the kill. She looks up and sees a man driving, his two hands atop the giant wheel, his eyes wide with terror, his lips drawn back from his teeth. The car comes closer, closer, the grill enlarging, the car slowing, plenty slow, plenty, plenty slow.

But it is not his error, nor her error, but the driver of the other car coming down the street the way cars are not to come. She hears the roar behind her, turns enough to see over her shoulder the blue curl of a Pontiac hood, its twin eyes and oblivious grin hurtling at her from the wrong direction.

That is all.

He does not let go, no matter how strongly the firemen insists. He has torn off his shirt and holds her head together, even when the fireman leaning over him spots the shards of skull stuck in the grill. Two pieces. The fireman dug under the bib to his overalls for a plaid handkerchief, into which he places the two bits of bone.

He does not let go, even though the woman in white works to pull his butcher's fingers apart so that the little fingers and hand within the giant paw can be released. She calls, *Doctor, I need help here,* and the doctor strikes him on the shoulder, saying, *Dammit, man, we got to get her into the O R.*

He does not let go, though he does look at where the doctor had struck him, then up at the stern face. Then he lets go, and the wheels scream as she is rushed away.

But once she comes back to him, he does not let go. He takes her hand, limp as veal chopped from a quarter, and presses the small brown thing between his palms, and for hours thereafter, then days, then weeks, stretching almost into a month, he does not let go.

And during all that time, not once, not even one time, does he blame her for defying him. *She was just a kid trying to get her ball*, he says, his big eyes wet, his big head rocking. *Just a kid.*

And, once, he says to a nurse, *I wish I never bought her that God-damned ball.*

When she opens her one unbandaged eye it is to behold the giant bulk of a crumpled man holding her hand. She twitches her thumb and he looks up. She smiles, and then he smiles. And then he cries, a thing never before seen in her world, someone crying for her.

CINDERELLY! CINDERELLY!

She eats popcorn one kernel at a time, no butter, lots of salt, pinched between a thumb and forefinger, face upward and an eye glued to the flickering drawings in magical color. She likes the fat mouse most of all. One piece drops and tumbles down her blouse toward the dark space between her hip and the arm of the theater seat. Like a mongoose, she's after it. But her hand holding the box shakes, and a flurry of popcorn showers down her front.

Oh, damn.

Mrs. Wisniewski drops a sharp look on her. Doris, sitting between Lucia and her mother, giggles and reaches for an errant bit that has landed in her lap. *You want it?*

Doris. Mrs. Wisniewski says. *Shhhsh.*

Doris rolls her eyes. Lucia rolls her eyes too, though only the good eye. She's not sure the eye under the patch rolls.

The mouse calls after Cinderella again. He has a voice like Lucia's, and she mouths *Cinderelly* after him.

Why, she asks Doris later, *do they put a cartoon show after a cartoon movie?* Doris shrugs. Lucia doesn't think long about it, once the curtain widens and *Cleopatra* spreads in majestic colors. She sits open mouthed, popcorn ignored, through the credits, to the first appearance of the dark Queen with black hair. *She is,* the young girl whispers, *beautiful.*

She lies that night in Doris's bed — the big girl beside her sweaty and breathing badly — drawing with a finger the dark lines of the Egyptian around her own eyes, spreading out her hair in a fan across her pillow, repeating in whispers, *Cleopatra, Cleopatra...*

Lucy, you awake?

Sí.

Did you say something?

Yes.

What?

Nothing.

Oh. I been thinking, Jeez, Lucy, you excited?

¿Porque?

What?

I say, What?

I said, Are you excited? About your Dad? When's he coming home?

She is not sure. All they have been saying is that he would be coming, and that he would bring a surprise, and the surprise is something she must want, but what did she want that she had not already been given? So she says, *I am guessing.*

Jeez, I would be excited. My Dad goes away all the way to Spain and was bringing back for me a surprise? I mean, all the way from Spain? I mean, can you imagine?

The silence that falls after a stupid question, or a question which wants no answer, descends over their conversation like a blanket flung across the bed.

The next morning Doris, struggling a slip over her head while Lucia smooths the coverlet, says, *You look like Cinderella. And Captain Hook.*

Later: *I go home now.*

I guess. You be sure to call me, you know, when you get your surprise. Okay?

Sí. Okay.

MAGNIFICENT APPEARANCES

Later, when her grandfather collects her at the front door of the brown-faced school, he says, *Dad's coming home.*

And he's bringing a surprise?

Lucia thinks about what he might bring, thinks about what she might want him to bring, and thinks of what the Sevillana nuns and those of Philadelphia would say about wanting and getting.

She decides she misses roasted sardines. That would be nice. But that would be silly, bringing stinky fish from Spain. *Silly. Maybe oranges?*

I'm picking him up at the train. You want to go too, you want to stay here?

She remembers the trains of Seville, and what they meant. She thinks, which he thinks means she hesitates.

You don't have to go.

I go on a train?

Why would you go on a train?

She purses her lips. He does not know she fears getting on trains. She likes trains, their noise, their massive promises of escape to other places, like the ships in the Mediterranean or the planes in the sky. But to get inside of one? No.

Well, anyway, you want to go, you change. I don't want her first looks to be that damn uniform.

¿Que?

Que what?

Who her?

Oh, damn. Well, you never mind that. Just you want to go, you change. A pretty dress. Your dad hasn't seen you in months, and you've grown a bit, girl. Gonna be a shock just that. So you get yourself all pretty.

Lucia touches the black patch over her eye, and then the scars still red against her hairline.

And don't you worry none about them. It don't make a bit of difference.

They enter the station at the western end opposite the statue of an angel bearing a dead soldier into heaven. The echo is as magnified as a Cathedral's, but the people are not still, not quiet, and the voices bounce and echo off the plentitude of marble, along with the sound of dragged luggage and shuffled feet. In the center, above an island, a board with rapidly changing letters spelling out destinations and times rattles on occasion. It is toward that the old man leads her.

They stop and study the board.

Any minute. We go over there. He indicates a number of pew-like benches outside of a framework surrounding a staircase leading down. Then he holds out his hand, which she takes. They approach a small knot of sailors in blue and white, and two of them study her. She thinks it is the eye patch, and she turns her head to the side. After she and her grandfather pass, she looks back at them over her shoulder. They are still looking, but smiling. She scowls.

They stand and wait.

A buzzer sounds. At the far-end stairwell a commotion rises, and, like a beehive knocked with a stick, it empties of people in a swarm. *Not us, honey. He'll be coming up here.*

Not long do they wait when the buzzer sounds again, and the number lights up. A second swarm rushes up towards them, and her grandfather, a hand against her shoulder, has her step back from the flow.

She eyes with her good eye each face, growing more unsettled when passing on to the next. The crowd thins, a few pull open the door below and struggle up with an old hand fast on the rail. *Nada.* Then, after a brief spell of no one coming from the underground platform, the door opens and a woman swathed in a fur coat steps through. She looks at the many steps rising before her with disdain. Lucia and the old man watch her await Ned's elbow.

Cleopatra, Lucia thinks.

What arrives first are the scents of nutmeg, flowers, citruses and lavender. Lucia knows the scent, remembers that perhaps a stolen bottle still rests hidden behind a rock near the orphanage, a bottle she had secreted off of a counter and out of a store, a bottle whose nozzle she had spent many an afternoon with it held under her nose, herself terrified to depress it even once to allow the cool atomized odors to fall on her, lest the nuns discover and beat her for the theft.

Maja. Cleopatra wears Maja. She feels almost like clapping.

Mora, Ned says, undoing himself from the woman's hold on his arm, *This is your daughter.*

Lucia sees the woman smile, but it is not a kind of smile she wants to see the woman smile. Hers is the kind of smile that perfectly fits with what the woman then says. *Puestaté pera pequeña, la loba esta aquí.*

The old man asks his son, *What she say, Ned?*

I don't know.

I said, the woman says in textured English, *Hello, my lovely daughter.*

Lucia, however, knows differently, but keeps the translation to herself.

Yet she will not forget what was meant by *Stay put, little dog, a wolf is here.* She will not forget, because the wolf will not permit it.

A HOUSE DIVIDED

Shouts and bellows, and pans striking the kitchen table. Mora, on the sofa with her legs crossed, a nail file against her fingertip, shows no affect from what the two men say.

What's wrong with this house?

It's your house. She wants her own house.

She's goddam lucky she's even got this house. I told you five minutes after I met her you have bought yourself a world of ruin. Now this?

She was your idea. You said Go to Spain. You said The girl needs a mother. You said, you said...

I know what I said, but you know what I meant. I said bring back a mother, not a money-grubbing bitch hound like her. You get her that house, minute you head for work the door's gonna open and she'll be flat on her back beating her heels against somebody's damn ass.

That ain't fair, Dad. You don't know that.

I do know that. I know them, and they are all a breed. And they are bred to make men like you bleed, or at least bleed the life and wealth out of every man they can wrap their legs around. Which right now is you, and you can't see it.

What do you want me to do? I can't kick her out. And she's got full legal right to Lucy, she wants it.

You can fight that.

Can I?

They stopped and stared at the other.

Buy her a goddam house. But don't you buy her a goddam palace, 'cause in a month or three you'll be right back here sleeping in your old room paying for that whore to be...

That's enough, Dad. She hears you, and you're better than that.

If she can bring me down far enough to yell she's a whore, she'll be bringing you down enough to call you a, a...

A what?

You know what a what.

WHEN A BELL RINGS, AN ANGEL GETS ITS WINGS

Lucia buries her head into her pillow, but she knows it is no use. The more that Mora rings her bell, the worse will be what she demands. The daughter rises from her bed and pads down the hallway toward the bathroom.

Mora, with her hair wrapped in a silk scarf of violent colors, rests in her bath, her head back on a small pillow affixed to a specially made, Ned-made, board. Her eyes are closed, and do not open when Lucia taps on and then opens the bathroom door. All she says to the girl is, *This water is cold*, and *I want more bath salts*. She waves her hand towards a small vanity pressed between the sink and the window.

Lucia turns on the taps, sliding her fingers under the stream to set the temperature. Satisfied, she gets the salts and pours a measure into her palm, a teaspoon mound. Mora in the tub throws water on the girl, wetting her nightgown down the front. *Not so much! Pay attention. Your extravagances are going to bankrupt this family.* She splashes again, Lucia spinning away from getting hit, though the water strikes her flank, wetting down one thigh.

Lucia swirls the water, to stir into a tepid mix that which is added to that which has cooled. Mora lifts her submerged foot and prods her daughter at the elbow. *This is my house, now. You remember that. I put you out of one, I can put you out of another.*

In the orphanage Lucia made an attempt to console another child who had discovered a litter of puppies, the mother gone. She had brought them, with Lucia's help, in a box into the courtyard. Orders were given to them by one of the sisters, the large galvanized wash basin fetched, water carried to fill it, and one by one the sister held each wriggling puppy under water until it moved no more.

It is better to let them die now than to let them starve to death later. This, however, was no consolation, and the girls cried throughout the ordeal that Lucia watched.

She recalls, as the damp toes leave her skin, how the paws and small legs had flailed, the yelping maws of unheard barks, the pink swollen bellies quivering as the beasts sucked in water, *Would it be like that?* she wonders.

Back in her own room, wet, she strips herself of the nightgown, dabbing where she still feels damp with the driest parts of the garment. She brings out another, dresses, lays herself down again on her bed, the script of a watery end playing over and over in the same overwrought Cinemascope of Cleopatra.

THE AGE OF OLD

She just forgot. Or it's that bitch, the old man says, a stub of ash-laden cigarette between the fingers of his unmoving hand. *That bitch, most likely.*

The equinox had been more than a month before, the dusk in damp November coming earlier each day, and by the time he would have decided it was no longer the time to continue waiting, he has fallen asleep on the glassed-in porch. So it is dark, and well past a time when Lucia would have bounded up his steps and pushed open the door, her plaid Catholic girl's skirt flipping above her knees. Well past even when she would have wrapped her arms tightly around his neck and squeezed like there would never again be a hug from him in her future.

His mouth has fallen open and he licks his tongue about his mouth to combat the sour dryness. Pains spider along his neck and shoulders when he leans forward to rise, and a different flurry rips through his knees and down his shins.

It is not like him, and he pounds his fat butcher's palms onto his thighs.

It's that bitch won't let a kid visit an old man even on my birthday.

Each room is dark, and his hands know where to move to find light, but he does not want light. In the dark he reaches the first step up, then the second, until he enters the silent gloom of the top landing. His footfalls sound like sandy rags dragged down the hall.

It is a relic, his wife's telephone table, wedged into the corner of the bedroom. How many birthdays ago? She had sat at that table jawboning with this daughter or that cousin or some neighbor, never happier than when talking. He pauses there, rests two fingers of his left hand on the hand piece, thinks to dial, then thinks of what will be said.

I want to speak to my granddaughter.

Zen call somebody elze. No granddaughter aqui.

Just put her on.

No. Click.

He lifts the two fingers away, goes into his bedroom and lowers himself onto his edge of his bed. With a toe to each heel he pries off his shoes, lays himself back, and hates.

OTHER VOICES, OTHER ROOMS

Sometimes it happens, caused by a test that terrifies a teenager, an idleness that sets in and drives someone to shake the monotony, a whim that has grown into an obsession when the final days of school grow closer, or when someone simply must disrupt the day. A fire alarm is pulled, the glass breaking and falling onto the aggregate flooring. Or someone has made it to the local store and closed the folding door to a phone booth, to drop in a dime and dial the main office, then to say in a terribly badly falsely gravelled voice, *There's a bomb in the boiler room* before hanging up.

Or, as is this case, a shot has rung out in a distant place, killing someone barely thought of by a teenager, let alone a child orphaned in Spain and brought to a new country.

Whatever the cause, and an assassination is the cause, the students are on the streets, told to go straight home, despite that not even the lunch hour has arrived. This Lucia does without question or hesitation.

And she does it with her usual quietness, her hands folded, her eyes on the silent streets, herself silent in a silent bus. It seems the world has decided nothing needs be said.

She steps down onto the curb and walks her way along Alleghény Avenue to her street, occasionally hearing the muffled broadcasts from televisions and radios inside unlit living rooms. Half a block from where she turns, three men and a woman shake their heads continually as if in collective reply, *No,* to some unheard question.

Lucia has her own key. *Sometimes your mother has to get out, go shopping, whatever. She might not be here, and I don't want you getting hemorrhoids from sitting on cold concrete too long.* Ned had smiled, placing the bright brass key into her palm. *Besides, it's your house too.*

The house is quiet, the rooms without voices. She had thought to go to her grandfather's house, to put records on his player, to dance, until she had to be home. *But, she thought, if she found out...* The days are growing warmer, and she is thirsty. She sets her book bag at the foot of the steps to the second floor, goes into the kitchen for a glass of water.

Done with the drink, she washes and dries the glass, returns it to the cabinet, looks out of the window into a neighbor's yard where a cat swishes its tail, eyes locked on something to kill. It does not kill, and she leaves the kitchen.

Once in her room there is little to do except extend herself fully out on her bed and study the ceiling, the patterns of the wallpaper and the shifts of light. And as happens to anyone who rests in the middle of a day, nothing to think about except the mundane and worthless, she begins to drowse.

It is a voice she does not know that wakes her, and then sounds she does know. She goes rigid and cold all the while the noises continue, stays still as iron and silent as granite when the noises turn to human, the noises to words, the words to bare feet padding behind the shod.

Her door is open, not much but enough, and with every muscle straining to keep her own bedsprings from sounding an alarm, Lucia tries to rise to close it. She makes it to the door, a hand against the door stile, another on the knob, and she slowly tries to close it.

There is only one sound, a weak sound, the hinge, but to her a cannon shot has been sent booming into the air and about the house. And it is enough.

Mora glares into the space between the stile and jam before throwing her whole weight against the door. Lucia falls back, knowing what is to come. It comes, and the flurry of Spanish, the curses in English, are all threats, all establishments of how she's a bastard, a child without rights, a girl soon homeless, a piece of meat not even worth the cocks of perverts sleeping under the bridges.

Her mother seeks but does not find something to fill her hand, so she fills her hand with her fingers and slams a fist against Lucia's temple, a thing she has been warned never to do.

The child holds up her hands to protect herself, but Mora keeps beating until her own hands are sore. More words, more curses, and finally she leaves her daughter's room.

Lucia hears her mother going down the hall and down the steps, and she pulls herself to the farthest wall, curls herself into the tightest ball. She knows that what just ended has not ended. She hides her head.

But it is no use. Mora has found the fireplace poker.

It is Ned who takes her to the hospital, and Lucia who will wear the scar on her forehead, who will suffer again an eye patch.

What she does not suffer, because she is carried into the old man's house, slipped into the old man's arms and carried by the old man to her old room, are the words that Ned will say to Mora, and the words that Mora will say to Ned, and the lines crossed and the decisions made, and the plans begun, that will change her tomorrows.

She will, however, feel the tears and chokings in her throat as she and Mora climb the ramp onto a familiar boat.

They are returning to Spain.

Two of them, and one of them is not Ned.

AT SEA

STRANGERS IN THE NIGHT

At sea in a dark hour, when one moves to a ship's bow, one goes to be alone. Everyone pressing the rail to watch silver dance on the black waves, or to count the crystal stars in a velvet night, feels himself or herself someone as unknown and unknowable as the heart of the moon. Unless one is a child. They go for the wonder.

I don't care what you do. Mora says, fitting a cigarette into a long-stemmed holder. *Whatever you get up to, just don't embarrass me.*

Lucia has marveled at the freedom all the day, as she had all the day before, and the day before that when they had been among the first aboard. She delights at the expanse of the breakfast buffet, at the lights, before the dials and brass of the ship's bridge on to which her expressions of delight and joy had won for her an invitation. She splashes in a pool in an ocean, gleeful to teach another child how to float on one's back. On one's back in water on water!

And, finally, forward to the bow to watch the arrival in a clear cold sky of more stars than trees have leaves, than the world has people, than the beaches have grains of sand.

There are a few more at the prow than just her: a young couple with heads together, two ladies jabbering out of earshot, another woman older than maybe the stars, *She might know*, but something in the old woman's fixed gaze on the plashing waves where the bow cuts the water says, *No, don't bother her.* And there is a man in a soft brown suit, a man also looking at each of the others, even at Lucia.

She climbs onto a steel box welded to the deck, to sit crossed-legged and be contemplative, a pose seen in a National Geographic of someone who looked like he knew even the middle name of God. It is a pose she often assumes to improve her chances of understanding whatever puzzles her, and though nothing except the relative number of the stars then causes her to ruminate, it is a pose she feels befits the wonder of numerous stars.

But the breeze from apparent wind occasionally flips her skirt above her knees, showing in the dark night the white of her slip's hem, and Mora has said, *Don't embarrass me,* so Lucia unfolds her legs, runs them straight before her, and frowns at the man in the soft brown suit. Then he comes near.

You're the girl taught my daughter how to swim. In Spanish, and she wonders, *How's he know?*

She continues to stare out at sea.

Thought you were. Just wanted to say, gracias. She's happy, because of it.

Not a word.

Well, I'm glad you made her happy. It's been hard, lately. She could use a friend. Feel free to play some more. With her.

Do you think, she begins, *there's more sand or more stars?*

He looks puzzled. Perhaps he should sit and think.

She points skyward *Up there. More stars, or more sand on the beach?*

He looks to where she points. The Milky Way is a wash of white. *Oh, stars, surely.*

That's what I think. But there's a lot of sand. Amazing and amazing, don't you think?

I do.

Now they both look to the heavens.

You here with your parents? he asks her.

Now she is puzzled. How to answer? *Yes* is not true, for Doris is dead and Ned is not with her. *No* is not true, for although she is not a parent, Mora is the mother. Or so they have said. *I guess.* It always feels to her a safe way to answer. Guessing wrong is not wrong like saying wrong is. This has been discussed before, when she and two others were returned the orphanage, and they all agreed it was better to say *supongo* than *yo sé.*

Is your mother the woman in all the bracelets, with her hair done up in a scarf? Señora Mora?

Sí. But she always says señorita. Even after she married my Dad.

Ah. That is all he says.

BLACK AS HELL AND TWICE AS BAD

Lucia passes the cigarette back to the boy facing her, who says, *You can have it, but let me feel you.* He looks at her splayed legs. They are filthy with summer dust.

Why?

I want to.

Lucia shrugs. *But I want a whole cigarette.* The boy digs into his shirt pocket. Then she says, *Sure.*

The boy leans forward and settles a hand on her knee. He takes his time sliding it upward. By the time he reaches the hem of her ragged t-shirt, which that day is all she wears, a shadow drops on them.

A woman bellows, *¿Qué? ¿Qué estás haciendo?* Then she slaps the boy on the back of his head. To Lucia she spits, *¡Puta gitana!* and with her free hand she grabs what hair she can grip. The boy runs off, and Lucia scrapes at the woman's hand with her broken nails. The woman, gripping harder, shakes the girl's head and knocks her against the wall against which she sits.

It hurts and Lucia cries out. The lit cigarette falls against her bare thigh. She scrambles to get free of both the burn and the pain of being held, but the woman does not let go, she does not stop slamming her head against the bricks, and by holding her as she does, the cigarette burns more, for it has rolled under her leg. She fights against both, and finally the woman pulls her to her feet. The burning does not stop.

It is three blocks, but the woman does not let go. They reach the gateway into the orphanage and the woman cries out, *Su puta católica está aquí. Yo la tengo.*

A nun appears, and the woman throws both Lucia and the now out cigarette at her feet.

What did you do?

It does not matter, and no answer is wanted. It is bad to lie and worse to tell the truth, for whatever she says will be, in the sister's ear, a lie. But it is not the worst. The punishment is.

There is the trunk, and to that they go. Nothing is said. Lucia knows, and it makes her shake.

The trunk smells with the vapors of Hell and the defecation by others needing a punishment, but there is no choice and Lucia opens the lid. In she climbs, down she lies, and within seconds all is dark. The last thing she hears is, *Para estó, tres días.*

It is not the shit, it is not the vomit, it is not the ancient dry of cedarwood returning memories; it is the dark, the black of Hell.

WHEN THE FISH BITES

Joys are many to those who seek few, and Lucia revels when they come to her. She leans out over the ocean as far as weight and the rail allows. The man beside her — a Parisian Moor with a large pail in each hand, who with a slight toss of his head had called for Lucia to follow — sets one down before hoisting the second onto the rail.

He is downwind, but she knows the smells. Fish heads, fish guts, potato parings, the spoilage of leafy greens, the top ends of carrots lopped off, parts a guest would disdain had they made it to the plate but which had been eagerly scavenged from alley cans not so long ago. She watches him as though studying for the position, to learn every trick, to understand every move. But all he does is set his feet, grips well the wire handle, slides one hand under the bottom, and then upends the pail.

The waste tumbles down to the water. As though the infinite creatures of the sea have foreknowledge of mealtime, already the water begins to churn, roil, froth with snapping, unmannerly maws fighting for a morsel. She knows the drive for bits, knows hunger all too well, even though want is a thing in her past, at least the want of something to eat.

In French, the Moor, pointing, calls out the names for the hunger-crazed fish. Some she knows. The one she finds most fascinating, *requin*, shark, in her Spanish *tiburón*, do not waste their time on scraps and offal. They dine on the hungry. *Tenga cuidado con los tiburones*, the older orphans warned. *Be wary of the sharks.*

ALL'S WELL THAT ENDS

Lucia splashes and her friend splashes back. They shriek, and the younger flees from the fury of Lucia's slapping hands, their laughter heard even at the life guard's bench. She splashes more and gives chase, churning at the pool's bottom with her toes barely scraping the rough and painted cement. But determined she pursues, until the whistle and she stops.

He points at her. The water, like a sprite told to go to bed, settles. At the man's side, arms folded under her bikinied breasts, Mora scowls at her daughter. He blows the whistle one more short burst, waves to her, her, that she is to come to the poolside below his feet.

Mora says, *Get out.*

Lucia does not know why the tone, but it is a tone she has heard before. Something done somewhere has displeased, and at the center of it must be Lucia. She turns for the ladder at the shallow end.

I said, get out.

I am.

Ahora, aqui.

The girl sets her hands in place to press herself upward. All she can see as she pushes herself from the water are the dark bare feet of her mother and the lighter of the lifeguard. It is not until she stands dripping, arms about herself against the cool air streaming along the ship, that she looks up again. Mora appears calm, but the demeanor is for the lifeguard, and for whatever other man who may look on. Below decks, she knows, will be a face meant for her.

We're going.

Where is there to go? But Mora shoves her finger into the girl's shoulder, and she knows it is back to the room. What storms may come must have a private place to rage.

And it rises up when her back is turned, no more than a moment after the door clicks closed. And it wears a ring with many stones, and it hurts where it strikes and rips her skin.

What did I say? What did I say? I said, anything you want, just don't embarrass me. So you embarrass me, and you did it, what? To humiliate me? To embarrass me? Well, it worked. She snaps her fingers, *Gone.*

Lucia stands mute. Another strike with the heavy ring, this time her lip bleeds. Then a kick, and then more, for hanging on a hook behind the door is a buckled-belt.

You told him you were my daughter? You told him? I said keep your mouth shut about that, and what do you do? And you ruin everything. I had him. Almost. You know what he said? I thought you said you weren't old enough to be a mother.

Who? Lucia asks.

Mora hits her again. *And stupid, too? You damn well know. The bitch's father. I had him and you…* one more blow. *I can't take this. If I didn't need you in Spain I'd feed you to the sharks. Get in the closet.*

Lucia is rigid.

I said, she raises the buckled belt again, *Get in the closet. Now!* and down comes the belt, the prong on its back drives into her temple and grabs the skin. Lucia feels the blood. *Sí,* she whimpers as she crawls to the closet. *Claro.*

It is dark, it is narrow, but it is clean, and with room enough to stand when she feels she must stand, and to sleep without her knees against her chest. She has only a strip of light along the floor to watch. Hours pass. Mora moves about on the other side, disturbing the steadiness of the strip of light. Lucia says nothing, even when her mother wants a change of dress. And when she does, she says to her daughter, *You bang on this door for the bathroom, that's it. If I am here... and if I am not, you hold it. You will not ruin my clothes.*

It is dark when the door again opens. Lucia is let into the bathroom.

The light is too bright when Mora hands her a roll and a glass of water.

It is dark when she is awakened and she hears the sounds of two people making noises but not words, sounds she heard from her bedroom in America.

It is light when she hears them again.

The cabin's door opens and closes, opens and closes, but the door to the closet remains.

The motion of the boat changes, motion that had been constant disappears and the lack of it feels like motion. The door opens.

Make yourself presentable. You have blood on you. And throw that bathing suit away. It stinks.

Lucia stands, but she does not stand well, nor does she see.

SPAIN

LIES

Familiar, and not. The Spanish around Lucia, once off the ship and away from the Rock of Gibralter, floods, as does the scent of orange blossoms and the smell of garlic and frying. Watching from the bus the countryside sliding past, she knows, but does not believe what she knows, that she is not being returned to the nuns. But knowing is not always believing. Every meter, every mile, worsens the trembling in her stomach.

Now you listen, Mora instructs, *My mother knows, and my sister Maria, because they are family, but no one else, you hear? No one. You are someone I am kind toward, that's all. You're no relation. Say so, I will beat you bloody and leave you with the Church. They know, but that is it. You will call me Doña Garcia, it is common enough and no one here knows me as anything else, if you even meet any of my people. And you can sometimes call me Señorita Mora, so long as it is when family are the only ones around. Say it.*

Señorita Mora.

You're an idiot. No. What are you supposed to call me?

Doña Garcia.

Verdad.

Lucia returns to the countryside rolling by. As far as she can see, the land is flat. *But I am still Lucia?*

Idiot girl.

But they are not fooled, the many she faces. She is conscious, self-concious, of the white bandage a porter insisted a doctor place against her brow. *I slipped,* she had lied, her eyes on her mother.

She says it again, to the many she faces. *I slipped. On the boat. A giant wave hit us and...*

But they are not fooled.

Only the youngest, Luna, speaks to Lucia, and they begin about the small diamond settled on Luna's finger, a thin gold band buried in her fat knuckle. *You should have been there, the* older says, a bit more loudly than anyone prefers, *My wedding day. There was so much cake! Have you ever seen a wedding? Surely you must have.*

Mora is watching.

Surely you must have. Anyway, she... pointing to Mora, *paid for it all. We were ever so poor, then, back before my Alejandro.* Luna smiles at her husband, who studies them with black eyes, a stare like a picador's lance.

We will become great friends, unless you start to make eyes at my husband! Women do, you know. He is the most handsome man, don't you think?

Lucia does. From the moment she slipped her gloved hand into his, a moment after her mother said, *This is my sister's husband, Lucia. Alejandro. You must call him Señor Senna,* Lucia has thought about him and nothing else.

Later, she leans against the door jamb inside of the kitchen, alone, thankful to be alone, but not beyond the range of hearing her mother addressing a dark, square-bodied woman in black crepe whom Lucia knows, but cannot say, is her grandmother. Mora asks the old woman, *Maria is too good to come, I suppose?*

She is ill.

She is never ill. She is an iron horse, like you.

She is ill.

Of me.

Yes, the old woman says, walking away from her daughter toward the kitchen. Lucia cannot hide, and the old woman looks her full in the face. *Only no good can come of this, you know.*

Lucia drops her eyes. The old woman's shoes are badly tied. She wants to retie them. *I am to do what she wants,* she whispers.

I'm sure she makes sure of that. Look at me. Lucia does. She is not afraid of the old woman. She has had to look into the face of nuns. *Yes, it's there in your chin, plain as my father's nose on me. No good, no good comes.* And she pushes past the girl for the stove.

There are others who talk, and Lucia listens. *I can't believe she's doing this to be charitable. Never a minute of her life,* and *You know where they are staying? Not here with Mother, for the love of God.*

No. Mora's bought a place. She had my son using it, up until she wrote. Anyway, we moved him in with us. Much cheaper, but crowded.

Bet that place cost an arm.

It cost somebody an arm, but wasn't Mora's money.

Can't believe she let you use it.

My Rafa was just married, a new baby, he needed a place, and she wasn't using it. I asked, she named a price.

High?

What do you think? Robbed him with rent.

You are her favorite.

Damn if I know why.

No one speaks to Lucia, for no one knows what she might say.

A TANGLED WEB UPON THE LOOM

Lucia looks past her mother at a thick-waisted man brushing up his mustache with a stubby finger. Mora shoves a part of Lucia's dress into place, tugging a sleeve, pulling into a better place the yellow sash around her middle. *Push up your tetas, for Heaven's sake.*

He doesn't look important.

He is.

And he doesn't look like Señor Alejandro.

Well, there may be reasons for that, for all I know. But it is his brother, and he is important. He is rich, he's got an enormous vineyard and that makes him important, no matter what his chin says.

Lucia pulls in her own chin. A reflex.

Stop looking like an idiot.

I don't want to do this.

What you want and what you get are never the same things as long as you stay stupid. Be smart, girl.

Why should I do this?

Because I said so. Maybe in America you can do what you want, but this is not America, and we do what our mother's tell us.

Lucia wants to run. At least, she thinks, he is not a Moor.

Now you be nice to Señor Sebastiano. Very nice. And you say one word of this to Alejandro, I will cut you and leave you in the street. Not until all is settled.

I do not understand.

Yours is not to understand, but to do as I tell you. And whatever Sebastiano wants, you do it.

Lucia looks at her mother blankly.

She takes the girl's chin between her fingers. *You understand?*

Still blank. Mora pushes Lucia's head back. *Answer me.*

Claro.

Whatever he wants. Mora stands back to study, her eyes on the bodice. *American beef has done you some good. Let's hope you have brains enough to make these do some good.*

Lucia feels tears rising, but not from sadness. Hate. But this is not America, and she understands.

What if he fills me with a baby?

That's the idea, you stupid fish. And the quicker the better.

She does not like the way the fat man looks at her. She often does not like the way most men look at her. They have the eyes an orphan has in a market before a vendor's table. The eyes of unfed hunger readying a thief. But she smiles at him, and smiles again when he offers to buy churros and chocolat. Lucia is about to whisper *sí* when Mora waves her hand.

No, she might get it on her dress. Just coffee.

I insist. I do not like coffee. Churros are the very best with chocolat, I assure you. I have them almost every day, when I can get into town. And when it has been a long time, I get them twice. I adore churros and chocolat. Sebastiano says this with his eyes locked on Lucia, or rather on the spare lace scalloping her bodice. To hide her thoughts, Lucia lowers her eyes, which Sebastiano accepts as her deference. Finding her response agreeable, he purses his lips in the manner he sucks the pit free from plum. *How is my brother?*

Oh, let's talk about him another time. It is Lucia you have come to see. I am her protector. My duty demands I reveal her only to the best.

She is very dark.

In some parts of the country, that is the best.

She has something of the Gitano in her. He squints. *She does look familiar. Have I seen you before, girl?*

Lucia has been looking past them at a crag-faced woman all in black fishing churros from a vat of oil with an ancient wire ladle. His question startles her. Mora, ready to speak for her daughter, raises her fan, flicks it open, then snaps it closed again. *That would be impossible. You have never laid eyes on her.*

No?

Not once in your life. She is from a most excellent family of Navarre, related to the old kings, the most ancient, ancient family. You have the documents. And she has been in America. I was asked by the matriarch to bring her to a good marriage, as they well know I know only the best people, and who better than the Sennas? Had Alejandro not already thrown himself onto a dung heap of a marriage, I would be marrying her to him, and he would not have hesitated.

No, he says, leaning back in the chair and folding his hands over his round stomach, *but I think a young girl would prefer America. I know I would want to be there, even with my estates.*

In this life, in this country, what one wants is not very often what one gets. This is why you should leap, because what you want is exactly what you will get.

Sebastiano examines Lucia again, *Yes,* but she keeps her attentions on others in the shop bending over newspapers and coffee. *I understand you were tutor to a rich man's daughters?*

A General. Lucia is again deflected by Mora from any need to reply. *She is very educated. She speaks decent French, Portuguese, she reads Latin. And she is obedient. You will not have any trouble from her.*

Where were you educated?

Again, Mora. *Toledo. And she has a dowry.*

Sisters of the Immaculate Conception?

Dominican.

I do not suppose my mother would approve of how dark she is, regardless of your dowry.

Your mother lies under a stone in the church. Are you not now your own man?

Sebastiano darkens. *Disrespect? From you?*

I mean no disrespect. Mora smiles. Lucia cannot deny how much more beautiful her mother becomes with such smiles, but the smile does not fool her. All of Mora's smiles, she knows, are for men. *No disrespect at all, but I know women. They have so much more influence than they should. I know what they do to men. I am ready to arrange for you to have Lucia, but I must know that it is on your feet you stand rather than under your mother's thumb. She could persuade, if you want to call it that, when she was alive, but she is no longer alive. We both hope, yes? The power went with her?* Mora casts her eyes upward. *Mine is not unreasonable to demand.*

To expect, but demand? I think that's mine to do.

Then what do you demand?

Even with lowered eyes, Lucia knows what his answer is. She presses her lips together, tight.

She had hoped for at least a better hotel, but the choice had not been hers.

Remember, not a word.

He smells.

132

You'll smell when I have to rip that dress off you and put you back in rags. Besides, I know his family, and what those men prefer, you are already almost too old. In three years he'll forget he's married to you. It will not matter. You breed, and we will have a vineyard at our feet. I am setting the world before you, and all you can do is complain about a bad smell. Mora turns to a window. *Besides,* she thinks, *what he wants is not what matters, and what you're for, bastarda, matters very much to me.*

DEVIATIONS

He continues to smell, and the first night, chaperoned by her mother into a hotel room, a duty Mora quickly abandons once the door is shut. His smell is more than Lucia can stand, and she is sick.

When she finishes washing the foul tastes from her mouth and the cold perspiration from her forehead, she retreats to a large winged chair placed near a still-lighted window, folding herself into as tight a package as she can manage, not so much to cover her nakedness as to keep herself warm. The room is cold, and yet he sweats.

And he stares. He never stops staring, even when he grunts and shoves her closer to the metal headboard that she grips does he look at any other thing than what he has locked his eyes upon. He keeps moving his rubbery lips about, as though each movement was another in a game whose endpoint was a decision. Lucia does not look at him.

This is not going as supposed. You are a virgin, so I suppose it is to be expected. But you must move.

She swallows hard. If there is one thing the street does not allow, it is for any orphaned girl turned loose on them to remain a virgin for long. Regardless whether in his game he reaches a decision, she reaches hers, and she unfolds herself.

That's better, he says.

Mora, having pressed the hand of Sebastiano Senna before he shrugs and walks himself away, the room key back in her hand, takes the elevator to the proper floor, the walk to the proper room. The carpet in the long hall depresses her. A man of his wealth and position should have selected better. She had selected better, but...

She finds Lucia dressed and seated on a made bed. *Surely the animal didn't take you on the floor.*

Lucia shakes her head.

You use the blood like I showed you? Yes? Bueno. Before you put that dress back on, I hope you washed.

The girl nods this time, holding back a desire to say, *Not enough.*

A cab to a train, a train to Málaga, a bus to Nérja, a donkey cart to the foothills below Frigiliana, and then a long climb up a very steep hill to an apartment facing away from the Mediterranean. In Nérja they had passed so many Germans, Russians, the British, some Americans. Lucia in the cart wishes they had stopped to speak to the Americans — they have come to see the wonder of the caves — so that she might ask after her father, or about New York and Philadelphia. But she knows they cannot.

Later you can run off as much as you like, but I am tired. Stop dragging my bags.

Later she runs off, but not far.

In the apartment Mora snores on the bed and Lucia strips herself of the dress that still stinks of Sebastiano Senna. She washes herself in the basin, at the bidet, sits herself in the living room, naked, to dry. Then, exploding from the chair, she washes at the bidet a second time. The tremors of the earlier sickness return and she feels her stomach. Praying is not a thing she does, not since the American sailor took her by the hand at the gate of the orphanage, not even at the school among others who knelt and whispered with vigor, but as the water drips from her bottom and thighs, she begins.

Dios te salve María, llena eres de gracia, el Señor es contigo. Bendita tú eres entre todas las mujeres por el fruto de tu vientre, pero no te bendiga mi vientre.

Hail Mary, full of grace, the Lord is with thee. Blessed art thou among women for the fruit of thy womb, but do not bless my womb.

And then she dresses, and then she leaves. Mora sleeps behind her, and she walks with bare feet toward the sea.

El balcón de Europa, the balcony of Eupope. She crosses from its throat to a rusted cannon still pointed toward the sea. At the rail she looks down where the waves crash and froth around sharp and jagged rocks. Beyond them, along the Mediterranean's emerald edge, runs a narrow strip of blonde sand. There are a few on it, foreigners, for the hour was nearing the end of siesta, and every wise person had long ago found shade. Lucia does not care to hide, for she is used to the bite of the inescapable sun.

The drop from the rail is far. She is certain some have fallen to their ends from where she leans. Their ends, she considers, would have been certain. Had they missed the narrow bit of land, the teeth of the Mediterranean crags would have sliced them to bits.

She lifts one of her feet onto the bottom rail.

But another notices, a young man who also has come to lose himself in the wide majesty of the many-riddles sea. He has noticed Lucia, though she does not notice him, tucked as he is into the crisscrossed shade from a large mimosa at the entrance to the Balcony's court. Her foot lifted to the rail alarms him and he moves out from the shade.

Es mucho bueno, he calls out, *si?*

Lucia laughs without turning. Had not his accent betrayed him, the atrocious Spanish would have. British. In English she replies, *Yes, very much beautiful you is too.*

He stops, curiosity furrowing his brow.

Lucia laughs again. *I speak English.*

He feels surprise. Her shift is simple, her feet bare. She is dark from the incessant sun, and looks like a woman, a girl, who might clean his room. Her English has little accent, American in pronunciation. *You're not from the Colonies, are you?*

No. Lucia shakes her head.

But you had been, once?

I am a princess of Navarre and I have come here to see my kingdom.

I'm somewhat certain this isn't Navarre. Missed it by a rather wide mark. A princess, you say? He maintains that furrowed brow. *I thought the General killed all the princes and princesses of Spain.*

Her eyes shift left, then right, searching. *Even an Englishman should watch his mouth.*

Sorry?

We are in Spain. We say lovely things about the General.

Oh. He is left with nothing further to say, and they stand together for several moments before Lucia turns her back to the repetitious sea and asks him, *Have you come on holiday?*

I have, he says, a smile broadening. *Of a sort. To study the caves. I am to be an archeologist one day. But I don't suppose you know what one is.*

I know everything. I am a princess of Navarre, after all.

He relaxes, laughs at himself. *Bare feet and all?*

Especially with bare feet. It is the fashion among Royals. And holes in our rags.

Well, he says, *you are lacking the requisite holes, so I believe you are putting me on.*

Putting you on? This I do not understand.

You know, pulling the old leg, kidding, making sport of the old sport. Okay, lying. About being a princess.

Oh, yes. Lying. This is also the fashion among princesses of Navarre. And I am very good at lies. Very good.

It is all small talk, feelers in each question, guardedness in each response. Neither desires it to end. But the sun is hot and his skin begins to redden, and she says, *You should be careful of the sun. Have you been here before?*

Here? Nerja?

Spain. To Spain, and yes, here. I mean under this sun. You are pink.

He looks at his exposed forearm, then at the other, somewhat dumbfounded. Lucia finds that endearing. *If only the fat Senna would redden. But he only sweats.*

I have to go. Someone, Lucia turns down her gaze from his forearms, *will be waiting for me.*

Let me walk you back? Perhaps later, we...

There can be no later, she says. *I must go now.*

She starts to leave and he follows. But as when it becomes immediately apparent that he will not forgo the walk together, she stops. *Please, it would not be wise to go with me.*

No? Unwise?

Yes.

I should not be seen... unchaperoned.

Ahh, he says. *But I like you.*

Oh, she says. *But it is a very long walk.* She points to the gleaming houses cascading the front of Frigiliana on the distant mountainside.

Well then, how about a cab?

Mora, awake and at a window, watches Lucia climb the steep road, a young man beside her. Her view of their approach remains unobscured until they reach a corner where an ancient shop blocks a place to walk. They disappear. More moments pass than are needed pass, and she knows what could interrupt Lucia's return. She checks for the time on her wristwatch, then turns toward a bulky wardrobe for a thick belt.

Later, as dark approaches, she opens the wardrobe and speaks to her naked daughter curled inside of it, *Wash yourself, and get your blue dress. It pleases Señor Senna, and he will be here soon. And this time, do not wash him out, even if he wants you a second time.*

A LETTER

In the narrow Seville apartment of Alejandro Senna and his wife, everyone that Lucia knows prefers not to know her, except pale Luna, who often asks when passing near if she might like a second glass of *sangria,* or a slice of *melocoton.* Lucia always with, *No. Gracias.*

They are all related by more than Lucia's thread of opinions about them: Alejandro Senna, too handsome in his Guardia de Sevilla uniform, and about whom Lucia has already fashioned fantasies, erect and vigilant at the head of a narrow, fruit-laden table, silent as Jove, his black eyes following Mora wherever she wanders. By his side is his brother-in-law, Vicenzo, leaning across the table toward his neice, Serena, Luna's eldest. Both of them are sour in the face as the girl pours steaming water into a glass before him. Her grandmother, Señora Dolores, scowls and shoves food at people. She resembles to Lucia's eye a cold pile of dog turd, a dark roll and nothing attractive, more often more silent than a pile, at that moment stopped by Mora and made to listen. Luna, wearing an idiot's smile on her face, repeatedly glances at a cuckoo clock and then at the front door, something done far too often for Lucia not to surmise something has been planned in that unlikeliest of places, Luna's head.

Vicenzo's wife stuffs her mouth with a second slice of melocoton. Their daughter, Emmanuela, sits stiff-legged on a brocaded silk sofa, herself in a crush of *la feria*-styled skirts, eyes wide and flitting from one fearsome creature to the next, her face reflecting a suspicion that at any moment one of them will find fault with her behavior, even though she sits like iron, hands at her side, and will banish her to a room, away from everything.

In a voice too loud, Mora's brother, Vincenzo, shouts at his daughter on the couch, *Chica, come here. I want you to see this.*

The girl obeys, coming up behind him to look over his shoulder. He has begun to tilt sugar from a spoon into the clear hot water, and she hits his elbow, some of the grains scattering on the wood. *Be careful, damn it, or you'll wreck everything.*

The child stifles her response. Serena stands across from him, her eyes fixed on the rain of sugar crystals falling into the water.

Lucia recognizes what he is doing, and without a thought says, in English, *Oh, we did this in class!* The eyes surrounding the experiment turn to her. Lucia reddens, and keeps quiet.

Vincenzo explains, though to no one in particular, *This is called a super-solution. I do this careful, add slow more sugar than the water can support...* his additions slowing, the spoon leveling, *...then, when it is too full of sugar...*

How will you know, Tio?

Because I am a scientist. I will know. His tone allows no argument. *When I tap it, the glass, watch.* But he continues to pour, a few grains, then a few grains, then, the suspense drawing his daughter's attention too much, the girl again bumps his arm, this time causing his elbow to strike and vibrate the table. The sugar in the glass glass falls out of suspension and dumps into a normal pile at the bottom.

La puta de Cristos, Manoli, you wrecked the whole thing. Serena, get me another glass and more water. Damn it, the timing has to be perfect.

Lucia turns away. She remembers that, in her class, no one struck the teacher's elbow, but the sister had to do it three times before success.

Mora is again engaged in speaking at, not to, a pair of young women, two distant Senna cousins. She keeps a pointed finger raised, the rings dancing before the girls' dulled attentions. Lucia cannot recall their names.

Her grandmother — except when eating tortilla from a small plate or when picking among the sweets Mora has brought for something that might satisfy her palate while bringing pain to her teeth — keeps a constant watch on her daughter.

Mora, on the other hand, does not once look across the crowded room at her daughter.

Abandoned abruptly by the two cousins, Mora lifts a plastic cup of *sangria* but does not drink. The hand holding the wine remains locked halfway toward her lips. She appears to Lucia to be thinking. After several moments she looks about, sees Lucia studying her, frowns and snaps her fingers. She gestures, *Come here.*

Lucia goes to her. Mora commands, *My mantilla and purse. They are in my mother's bedroom. Get them.*

We are leaving?

She shoves the girl away. *Idiots. Everywhere, idiots.*

Lucia walks to the room at the back of the apartment, to where things are piled. She is watched, while making her way through the knots of gathered relatives, by her grandmother, who then follows.

What are you doing?

Lucia, startled as she picks up her mother's purse, says, *Mora has asked me to get her things.*

Why?

She is leaving.

No, she is not. Put them down.

She has asked me to...

I said put them down.

Lucia is torn between commandments. Duty is to the matriarch, but her fear of Mora and the woman's belts has power as well. She sets down the purse, but keeps the mantilla over her arm.

I did not see you wear that. There's a comb, on my dresser, yes, that's it. Against the mirror. Good. Give it here. Stoop.

Lucia feels awkward under her grandmother's attention, but seeing the reflection of the mantilla draped over her shoulders pleases her more than she would have suspected. *It is beautiful. Did you make this?*

No. My Isabella made it, before she... anyway, she left it.

Lucia feels what's in the old woman's mention of the lost daughter. *She is the one who is a nun?*

Shrugging, the old woman pats the mantilla.

Lucia admires herself in the mirror. *You're the one who sent this, then? To America?*

Is that such a surprise? I did.

I should not wear this. It is Mora's. Not mine.

The old woman straightens. *It is not Nora's, though I'm certain it was meant for you, not her. It is a horrid pain of old age to know your daughter is a thief who steals from her own daughter. I demand you wear it.*

I cannot. Mora...

Lucia feels herself trembling, but not from a fear of being caught between clashing rocks. Never once has she been called Mora's daughter by Mora's mother.

Stay here. I have another thing for you.

Señora Dolores crosses to a nightstand upon which rests a little casket, and lifts its lid. She removes a white rectangle, a letter, and hands it to Lucia.

Recognizing the handwriting causes the girl to breathe in sharply, and makes her tremble even more. But it is the cancelled stamp and the word *Philadelphia* that calms her. She touches the corner.

The address is to the woman who had handed it to her.

Carefully, slowly, she withdraws two pages. After a momentary glance, Lucia raises her eyes to the old woman, inquiry on both of their faces. *Should I read this? It is to you.*

I do not read. You read it. From America.

She reads the first few lines, surprisingly written in Spanish. Lucia laughs. It is very bad Spanish.

What? Señora Dolores asks her, but the only answer she receives is the girl reading aloud.

Dona Dolores, por favor esta carta a mi hija. Tengo noticias que el va querer leer. Por favor, no le de a mi esposa.

They both then laugh, Lucia's musical, Señora Dolores's voice like that of a rusted hinge.

In English, in much better grammar and spelling, immediately after, is written, *Dear Lucia, My Spanish is really bad. In fact, if it were not for your two languages dictionary I would not be able to write to you at all. I have asked Señora Dolores to please give this letter directly to you. I have news, on the next page, I want you, and only you, to read it. Please, do not give it to my wife.*

Thank you, Edward Radachinski.

She glances down at the torn envelope. Then she reads the second page, all of it in English.

Dear Lucia,

I have sad news, bad news. Our old gentleman has passed away. Dad died in his sleep, in his chair. You know how he always fell asleep there. That's where he went. You may be pleased to know that he said to give you his house. After I bought ours for Mora he said this. Was pretty strong on it. But it's mine in the will, which is good, so my sisters can't say a thing about it. But if you want it, it's yours. I will pay to have you come home.

I do not want Mora to come back with you, but you're still too young to keep a house all by yourself. The Law, I think. I know you'll want your mother. I won't like her back, but I will pay for two tickets, two rooms this time. Enclosed is a hundred dollar bill for your grandmother, to pay for anything you need, including a telephone call so I can know when you are coming home.

I am sorry we have done this to you, but I hope your own house will make up for it. Unless you are happy in Spain. I was. You might be. But if you call me, I will make all of the arrangements to get you back safe.

Be good, Edward Radachinski.

So many responses, so many thoughts, so little space to assess them. Her grandmother stands at her elbow, watching as she folds the letter closed.

There is no money, Lucia says. *In the letter. He, my father, he sent you money.*

Oh. The old woman darkens with concern. *What does the letter say?*

This, Lucia feels worrisome. *If you don't read, who opened this? It's your letter. Didn't anyone read it to you?*

I asked Mora, when it came. It is from America, and I do not read the America words. Alejandro, he has read it too, but not until this morning, when we learned Mora was coming. She bites her lips. *I am not surprised the money is gone. And Alejandro left that out. So did Mora. You are certain that is what it says? There was money?*

There was. Lucia tries to calculate, *There was many, many, thousands pesetas, an American hundred dollars. For you. It is gone.*

Mora. Alejandro would not take it if it was for me, but he said nothing about money. But Mora, she shakes her head, sad, she would.

Well, that is gone. I can't ask her, she will lie and tear up your letter. And you can't ask her, if you do not read. But Alejandro, he can. Should I ask him?

I will ask him. But the letter? This American, he wants something?

Lucia explains what Ned had written, but when she mentions Ned's father, or rather when she uses the word *Abuelo* in her reference, Señora Dolores stops her. *He is not your grandfather. This man who writes can pretend to be your father, but no one can be your grandfather except my husband, and...* she stops herself.

Lucia looks for a long while at the woman's face, hoping to see more of a resemblance to her than what appears. They share cheekbones. She wants to ask about the woman's husband, but she knows already what the old woman will say, because it is what her mother has said of the vanished grandfathers.

If he still lives, he lives in England with another family. He supported the King and had to flee in the trouble. They took all of our money and he made another family. They were terrible times, and he was a coward. He would have been killed by the General, but that would have been noble, to stand up for what is right and noble. I must have sisters and brothers who love the Queen as we love the General.

And, the one time Lucia had asked Mora about whom her father may have been, her mother spat. *Your father was a rapist. I was a child.*

The question Lucia asks her grandmother is, *He wants me to call him in America. Without the money, how will I ever?*

Mora has read the letter, she has taken the money. If you must call America, she must pay for it.

She will call me a liar.

Aren't you a liar? Señora Dolores runs a look over the girl. Lucia is her daughter's daughter, and that encloses every possibility that she is anything other than a liar.

Lucia chooses not to respond, saying instead, *He has written that he has a house. For me. My grandfather's house. Mora was not to know.*

Ahh. Well, she does now.

WITHIN A MOMENT, A GUEST, AND A STORM OF FIRE AND THUNDER

When Lucia, following behind her grandmother, the mantilla removed and again draped over her arm, steps into the party, a knock on the door sounds. People already there, and who had been there long enough to feel time had come to leave, wondered what guest had failed to arrive on time.

Alejandro Senna wears a placid look. He does not care. The cousins and others wear only curiosity. At the knock, Luna has brightened, claps, and she moves to open the door as though she in dancing hops. She sets her hand on the knob and, before turning it to admit the new guest, says across the room to her husband, *You will forgive me, but someone has great news for you, and I thought it best he comes to announce while a party is going on. But he is late, which is only to be expected.*

Alejandro begins to rise, *Who* at his lips, when Luna says, *Sebastiano. Your brother has asked to see you. Please, I must let him in. He has news.*

Alejandro wears a surprised expression. Not since burying their mother has his brother cared to speak with him. Luna is all joy.

It is Mora who drains of color. Lucia flushes, and when the door opens she steps backward to hold herself against the wall. One of her hands feels the empty air where the hallway to the bedrooms begins, and she slips into its shadows. She hears Mora cry out as the door opens.

Sebastiano enters, wearing a tall hat of outmoded style, and a suit to match its inappropriate age. He has been sweating. In his hand is a lilac handkerchief that he uses to mop his eyes, which blink from having entered a shadowed, cooler room contrasting the dusty courtyard he had to cross. As his eyes adjust, he looks for his brother, who is easily spotted, but not before discovering between him and the man a woman he has not expected. *Contessa! It's you? Is our princess here as well? This would be unexpectedly perfect!* He looks about. Lucia pulls herself even deeper away from the room.

From where she hides, she cannot see anyone except the wide back of her grandmother in black. The room is quiet, only the scrape of Alejandro's chair is heard as he shoves it back to stand.

I am glad to see you here, Sebastiano. He looks at the beaming Luna, and he smiles at her a genuine, uncommon smile. *I think my wife has played the little Devil in her plotting and planning. But it is good, very good.*

Yes, yes. I think so too. Very good. I have news, good news, and I wanted to share it with you. I heard you were having a little party, he nods toward Luna, *and once I did, I thought how fun it might be to surprise you. And what I have to surprise you with will be even better. But perhaps I should let your friend the Contessa explain.*

Señora Dolores is the first to question. *The Contessa?*

Certainly, the fat man says, pushing the ends up to his mustache with the tips of two fingers, *as you already know her profession, you know what I have gone and done.*

I haven't the faintest, Bastio.

Sebastiano smiles broadly, sweeping the room with his grin. *Then I shall take the pleasure. I am getting married.*

Lucia finds the doorknob to her grandmother's room but, with her hand on it, does nothing further except listen.

Married? This is... what has Mora to do with this news? Surely, he reddens, *not to Mora?*

Haha, no. The Contessa he smiles toward Morea *would never condescend to marry a fat man like me. But she has found a perfect charm, a delight for my eye. Arranged it all, the match. And the girl is most dutiful. She must be here.*

Alejandro, in a strangled voice, asks, *Mora has done this?*

She has, excellently. Very excellently. All will be perfect, I assure you. She comes from the best family, from the north.

Who does?

The beautiful señorita, of course

What family?

Navarre.

It is a name Señora Dolores has not heard spoken by any member outside of her family in many years, a name not only whose use has remained forbidden, but a name that no one had any desire to employ.

No one except Mora.

Better to have murdered you in your crib. Lucia hears her grandmother cry this, and she thinks it is about her the words are uttered. But Mora knows differently, and she at last speaks.

Yes, mother, it would have been better.

Get out.

Luna intervenes. *Mama, this is a good thing. Sebastiano will be married, and he is here. To see his brother. Please.*

Get out, Señora Dolores repeats, stepping closer toward her other daughter. Mora does not move.

Alejandro watches the anger rise in his mother-in-law, and the paler color of his wife's sister beginning to flush. Sebastiano, confused, asks again about his bride. *Is Lucia not here?*

At Sebastiano's mention of this name Alejandro roars. He shoves away the table, topples his chair as he stands, and pushes past his daughter Serena so hard that she falls. He does nothing to catch her. His hands rise, both, and Mora screams at him, *Touch me and I will gut you.*

Lucia knows, from where she hides in shadow, that already in her mother's hand is the knife she always carries, a knife, Lucia also knows, that already has gutted someone. She claps her hands over her ears and shuts her eyes so tight that nebulae of orange burst with their own lights. Then she waits, waits. Even though deafened by the sweaty palms she presses against her ears she can still hear the cannon-loud reports of muffled anger, the continuing shouts and screams, and she fights a terror that Mora has murdered the beautiful, handsome Capitan.

But the gleam of her knife and the many hands grasping at the enraged Captain of the Guardia Civil is enough to stop him. Mora has fallen back, despite her readiness to slice the man above his belt, or her preference to slice below it. Still, there are shouts, accusations, incriminations, questions, cries of dismay, of disbelief at acts too heinous for even Mora's machinations, and calls, calls for Lucia to come out of the shadows.

Lucia herself has fallen back, crawling crabwise into the room where suit jackets and camphored shawls were dropped, hiding from the shouts of murder and banishment. Even through her hands she understands that all is undone. But there is the letter, and there is the way out, out of ever having to bed again a pig sweating garlic and brandy.

There is then a sound of another in the room. She opens her eyes and it is Vincenzo, Mora's brother, Lucia's uncle, filling the space where galaxies of fire had been raging. Slowly his shape takes shape, and even more slowly the words he speaks become words she hears.

Lucia, Lucia, he says. *Gather your things. And whatever is your mother's. If it were possible, I would bring you to my home. But* he shakes his head, or rather sways it back and forth like a dazed bull long in the ring, *it is not possible. Not possible.*

At Sea, Again

AT SEA, WITH LYRICS

Though most prefer the romantic possibilities of the slow rising and slow falling of a ship's bow, some, especially those who have seen much, prefer an inviting peace at the stern. There, one can see all the way to the lost horizon and imagined traces of what has been left behind. It is there that Lucia stands, watching nothing but the unrolling lace and the shimmering wake. She is not alone, but alone none-the-less.

Where Mora has gone she does not wonder. It is enough, for Lucia, that her mother is not with her.

The hour is far into the afternoon, but not so late as to allow anything but the hazy blue of the sky to dominate the slate waves. The horizons toward which the scar of their wake leads is indistinct, but the separation of air from water remains unmistakable. It grabs her gaze and locks it into a stare, and once it does, it pulls thoughts and desires toward it as though each parcel of remembered Space and Time is tied to a line still affixed to lands left behind.

The thoughts of Lucia, however, are not about the Spanish soil once so much a part of her. Her thoughts and the drift through recollections are for what lies in the physical dimension behind her, yet ahead: the landmarks of soaring New York, the familiarity of newspaper-soured alleys and side streets surrounding a dead, empty house where once operas rang from an old Victrola, where Polish and Spanish had once met to discover English, where she and an old, beloved man together had crooned *In the Still of the Night.*

Where, she wonders, *is the night ever still?* And then she remembers, *Here, on the boat, after the bands go to sleep and the wistful emerge.*

For one crackling moment, Lucia believes she hears Mora's laughter, false as ever, but it passes, and she returns all of her attentions to the water and the wake.

She has not always been thus at the stern. Earlier, Lucia had tried the bow, her hands clasped in a simulation of prayer, her forearms against a biting cold rail, her eyes down on the hypnotic coruscations every now and then flashing off the curling water, and, once, for a long stretch, by a dual trio of dolphins that made everyone also at the bow exclaim and point and clap as though their God had to handed them — and to them only —special notification of his majestic presence.

Not the dolphins but the exclamations disturbed her and made the bow inhospitable, but she did not choose to quit where she sought solitude, not until she heard a young couple — who had begun singing *sotto voce* but had been joined by additional voices badly harmonized — reach the concluding words of the first and only remembered verse of the American anthem... *O say does that star-spangled banner yet wave, o'er the land of the free and the home of the brave...* At that question, Lucia wonders, *Is there ever a place to be brave and walk away free?* She then had decided she wanted no more possibilities which the ever-forward-charging bow might evoke.

Taking care to not stumble from the influence of the rise and fall of the ship's pitching over the waves, she slides a white-gloved palm along the rail, loosing her grip only to pass individuals and couples using the support for themselves, retaking a handhold wherever space allows. Her hands are free when an unexpected shift under her feet causes her to grab the nearest support, which is the back of a solitary man deep in his own ruminations.

She not only presses her weight into his back, but her fingers close around and pull on the fabric of a light seersucker jacket. Regaining composure, she says, *Perdoname.*

Sure. Rough, ain't it?

She does not then know why, but she responds, *No lo sé.*

Huh? No English?

No lo sé.

Too bad. Pretty girl like you. He smiles, and as she turns and walks away to the stern, she too smiles. Lucia does not know his smile continues well after. Nor, when she reaches the rail overlooking the churning waters, does she suspect that he has followed, keeping a fair distance behind so as not to frighten her, though close enough to enjoy her bobbing gate and the swishing back and forth of her long, black, silky ponytail.

Almost American.

The sound is not her mother's voice. It is an imagined sound of her mother's voice, something she often believes she hears but, looking around with a shrinking to her stature, she always discovers the woman nowhere nearby. Lucia does not like the frightful powers of the imagined sound, but it is only imagined, and in more than a few words to herself she chastises the silliness for feeling the fear.

But Lucia feels it nonetheless, every time.

Which she has done again over the trailing froth, in bits and spurts of Spanish, for the language from which she has departed is not yet fully displaced by that toward which she heads. *Possibly,* she has a quick thought, *that's why I didn't answer in English,* which returns her to thoughts about the pleasant-faced man, a man not so young, but not old in the slightest, a man on whom responsibility and duty had sat obviously and well. And he had dark eyes like her own, and they hovered over the gray-blue horizon more than once as she had lost herself at the bow to the pull of the constant horizon indistinct in the haze.

So it is with an unexpected spasm of her muscles that she answers his touch on her shoulder.

Hey, watcha watchin'? Whales?

The need to recompose leaves Lucia staring up at the man's face, her jaw set and lips tight.

Whoa, sorry. Guess I was interruptin' ya. Huh? Sorry. He holds up his hands and steps backward. *Wisht I spoke me some Spanish, but all I know is No way, José, and that ain't gonna get me far. Ya speak at least a little English back there in España?*

And still she shakes her head from side to side.

Well, ya gotta know something to know you hadda say No to my question.

Lucia fights off a smile. He appeals, as a man.

She turns back to the sea, and the man at her side slips his elbows onto the rail.

As in so many seductions, the man speaks and the woman says as little as possible, and when he does, at a loss about knowing anything about her interests that he could use to make her interested, he defaults to what he knows, and that's what is worth knowing about himself, and among those worthy things arrives first the most obvious. *I'm American, case you didn't already get that.*

Lucia knows, swallows a giggle, and he continues. *Bringin' my little girl home* he doesn't see, but Lucia stiffens *after some time on the continent of Europe. Ya know, Paris, Germany, England. She liked England. And Spain, España, too, of course. Lots of olives, and pretty hot, ya ask me. But you people are so easy goin' kinda friendly, bein' Communists and all. Didn't expect that, no sir no way. Anyways, trips done. She needed somethin', after her mama passed on* Lucia, again something he doesn't see, relaxes, though only a little, let's her shoulders fall some *and all. Well, leastways, it'll be better now she's seen things to fill up her head than all the funeral stuff, arrangements and flowers and visitors. They mean well, but they just didn't make nothing better. Not for her, not for me, not even for themselves, I'm pretty sure.*

She almost nods in agreement, but she keeps herself still. *Why talk?* she thinks, saying to the waves *¿Por qué hablar? ¿Qué tengo que decir vale la pena escuchar?*

The man thinks that, though hardly a word she has said means anything to him, she is warming, and he says, *My name is Byron, like the poet, so everybody keeps tellin' me. Don't know the feller, but my mama said it was fittin' for a feller she aimed to have go places, and I've gone a few places. Korea, Japan. And now over there,* he points to the indistinct horizon.

Lucia looks down at her white gloved hands, a decision made. She looks up at his face, and he down at hers, and the thing that happens instantly happens instantly, and she settles a white glove on his wrist. His head droops a little, and she knows, has learned enough to know, he is one gone feller.

A place comes to mind, a place deep in the belly of the ship where the floors shiver and the walls rumble, a place Lucia recalls, a place she had discovered on the last trip across the ocean, a place that had been occupied by a man and a woman, a place she spied into for many minutes, to watch the man and the woman do what a man and a woman wants to do in a private place, a place she again had sought but found empty, a place in which she not so many hours ago had crawled, to never be found by her mother.

The place comes to mind, and Lucia presses her cotton-gloved palm against his seersucker-covered forearm.

She takes his hand and draws him away from the rail. She has a place she wishes he might go, a place for him to forget who he's buried, and a place for her to bury the several whom she wishes dead.

He goes where she leads, and for a half hour, she is older and he is younger, and their ages meld with disregard for any difference in their ages. It is what he least expects for himself, and what she never suspects of herself. But it is good, and it is hers, wholly hers, brave and free.

Later — Ned packing suitcases into the broad trunk of a car newer than the last one in which she had ridden with him — Lucia thinks she sees the man again, a man with a pretty girl holding his hand, both of them at an intersection, both waiting for a safe moment to cross and go, both of them anxious, but only the man looking about as though in search of something he was supposed to bring with them. *But,* she thinks, *he is too short to be Byron.*

AMERICA

Evil succeeds because good men

Ned says little on the return drive toward Philadelphia, his hands at ten and two as always. Mora, however...

You know, kid... he leans toward Lucia, speaking in a guarded whisper, *I am entitled to a sidearm.*

Then he straightens and says, clearly enough to not be mistaken by the woman in the seat behind him, *If I ever see your face after today, mine will be the last face you'll ever see again.*

A house is not a home

Electrolux, the best model, a Jubilee, more than anything needed for the one rug in the house, Its plug remains in the wall, the cord a motionless fabric snake where left. Lucia stands and stares, her arms heavy with books, her legs red and cold from a walk between the bus stop and the house.

What? Where?

She continues to stand and stare at the Electrolux Jubilee, until she hears noises overhead. She thinks, *Ned has forgiven...* but then she sees the sales case on the ottoman, papers and order forms atop the case. *It is not Ned.* She goes into the kitchen, sets down her books, finds the Corningware coffee pot cold in the sink, turns on the tap, the water crashing against the porcelained cast iron sink until she shoves under the tap the pot that needs a washing, then a filling.

There is comfort in the aroma of freshly brewing coffee, from the burbling percolator, from the hiss of lit gas under the pot's bottom, from both taps turned on fully and left running, even from the hands over her ears. But these are not enough. Lucia goes to the old Victrola and starts it, the rotation of the felt-covered platen mesmerizing, but even that is not enough. She kneels to rummage through the old man's records, some old, none new, delighting in the nostalgia of dust and warming tubes, stopping to study a familiar covers until she comes to the heavy bakelite RCA Victor collections.

The simulated leather cover feels so familiar, so memorable, so much so that she can hear the old man's voice sliding under Mario Lanza in a duet of *Che gelida menina* even without the needle dancing on the platter. *Che gelida manina, se la lasci riscaldar. Cercar che giova?* She removes the collection, but the sound of its center is wrong. Wrong. Opening the cover flap, she also sees something wrong. Each platter is broken, some simply, though the first is shattered, the paper sleeve torn. Like someone had set it on the floor and pressed down with a high heel.

A BRICK IN THE WALL

The lobby of the dental fabricator smells of hot plastic, and it burns the nose and throat. Lucia sits on an orange chair, ankles crossed, folded hands on her lap, a plastic smile on her lips, a dull glaze to her eyes. Twice she sees a woman at reception glancing at her, then at the clock.

Still in High School?

Lucia nods.

Little Flower, or that other one?

Hallahan.

Didn't know Hallahan's got a work program. Ya gotta get out before one. Kenya?

Lucia nods again.

The woman squints through her glasses, an expression not dissimilar to one caused by sucking a lemon. *Little Flower's better.*

Too far from my house.

The squint gets tighter. *You ain't one of those Fishtown girls, are ya?*

Lucia shakes her head. *I'm from Spain.*

Well, that explains it. I was thinkin' you was a Spic, but not if you was from Fishtown. Your English is pretty good, not Spic at all. Spain, huh? In Europe?

Lucia lets that pass, especially as she is not wholly sure there is a Spain that is not in Europe. Pretty sure, not wholly sure. And she needs the job.

A door opens and a small, worn man stands in the doorway. *You the one wants to work here? From the school?*

I am, sir. Lucia stands, ready.

Kenya start Monny?

Yes, sir.

Good. S'all I wanna know. Be here. She'll take care a ya. You godda fill out some papers, enya gotta be showned around, but I'll get Betty here for ya, and yas can wander to your heart's content. But I'm busy, so Monny. One, ya got that?

Lucia nods, and grows a smile. *Yes sir.* And the sky overhead cracks, just a little, but enough.

I have the job, she says to Mora, ignoring the man who has become too familiar with the house. Lucia claims little, but that is her cup rolling between his palms. Or, rather, the old man's cup, and it does not belong between his palms.

How much?

Lucia does not respond, except to take the treasured item. She carries it to the sink and scrubs it.

You get check or cash?

Check.

You bring it right here. Claro?

Lucia does not answer.

Every peseta.

I don't get paid in pesetas.

The man says, *She was my kid, I'd slap that mouth.*

NOTHING LIKE A VACUUM, LITTLE LADY

Goldfish in a bowl got more room to swim than we got back here. The vacuum salesman leans with both hands against the window frame, his face close enough to the glass to spread a glaze of fog, his outline slicing the bright white of the winter's day.

I said, Lucia says, *Why are you in my room?*

Ain't your room, kid. What I hear, it's hers.

No it isn't. You can't see my things?

She says, what's yours is hers. And the way I see it, the Hungarian vacuum cleaner says, still not turning, *if it's hers, it's mine. So maybe you should do the math.*

What you mean, hers is yours?

He taps the window glass with the gold ring on his finger. *You're a bright girl, I hear. You tell me.*

Lucia stares at the hand he splays on the window. She turns as cold as the glass. The ring, patterned rather than plain, is familiar. *Where'd you get that?*

He raises his hand, and she sees his face. Needs a shave on what little chin he has, and the tell-tale rivulets of red spreading over his cheeks explains the detectable sweet odor. The odor is never uncommon in the house any more.

Where you think?

You know that was my Dad's ring?

Another thing I hear. You ain't got no Dad, least none you'll ever know. So you know what that makes you? Lucia refuses him his answer. *I hear tell over there in the old country a bastard kid's got no rights, can't even own the shit she dumps in the toilet. That right?*

Again she refuses to answer.

So, like I said, this ain't your room.

This isn't Spain.

Long as she's runnin' the roost, you just one of the chickens. And that makes me... here he grins. She knows the grin. She knows it from men who had cornered her in alleys before she got smart enough to stay out of alleys. She knows it from when she'd gotten on buses, from men leaning against a wall with liquid brown-bag lunches in filthy paws. She knows it. And she knows what's coming next... *the main cock around here. Like I said,* he steps from the window, coming closer, *What's hers is mine. And I'm feeling like some chicken t' put me right as rain. An' about time you and I got better acquainted.*

She'll slice your dick off.

The grin remains. *Only if somebody stops being a little chicken once I turn her into a squealin' little piggy. You sure ain't no little girl. Not age wise, anyway. Ain't like you ain't done it before. An' from stories I been hearin'* he waggles the ring finger *you like keepin' it in the family. 'Sides, who she gonna believe? She ever believe what you say?*

Lucia backs to the stairs. The doorway now frames the salesman.

So how 'bout it? Who's it gonna hurt?

One step farther, one step more, one step too many, one stair too few. She grabs for the handrail, but it is not there.

A FRIEND IN NEED

Aww, honey, what the Hell happened to you? Faris! Faris! Faris, call Julie to come up front. God damn, honey, this happen on the the way here? Faris! You hear me, you call Julie up here.

Lucia poses in embarrassment. Betty comes toward her like smoke from an explosion, all huge fury moving fast. She reaches out to touch Lucia's face, but Lucia pulls back. The swollen lip still hurts, and any touch serves only to increase the pain.

I fell.

How you fell? From the Ben Franklin Bridge? You look more like you was dropped from an airplane.

I fell.

Shit you was.

And try as she might, Lucia cannot stop what falls from her eyes.

First in comes Julie from Accounting, behind her Faris who hired her, then Bill from polishing who has no business being there but comes anyway, and who would stay but Betty says *Get yer weasel face back to the shop*, but him not leaving before asking, *What the Hell kicked you? A mule?* which causes Lucia to cry even harder.

Fifteen minutes later in the breakroom — *verboten*, according to Betty, to all personnel except the poor girl with the bruised face, poorly hidden limp, blackened eye and split lip — the older woman says, *Now, all of it, and you ain't protectin' nobody keeping it to yourself. Please dear Lord and Jesus, don't tell me it happened when you was coming from the school.*

Lucia shakes her head.

Out with it, then. And I'm thinkin' maybe better I send you home instead of...

No.

Lucia's rejection speaks louder than her speaking. Betty sits back in her chair, desperate for one of the cigarettes she has quit smoking. *Somebody home did this? Your mother?*

By hesitating, Lucia confirms. She does not want speculation confirmed. Knows what she has done, so tries a lie. *I fell.*

You said you tripped and fell I mighta believed ya, but ain't one scrape anywheres. You'da tripped, you'da scraped up your knees, or got a rug burn on your hands. You fall, ya get a egg on the noggin', but I seen telltales like these on plenty a women before. My neighborhood got plenty a drunks hate when the Eagle's or the Phillies lose, and they always losin'. Those black eyes're more common than weeds in my grass, come Monday mornin'. Hell you wasn't punched. Or kicked, or somethin' hit ya.

At last, Lucia nods.

She kicked ya?

Lucia continues to nod.

Ain't all she done, is it?

No use, Lucia thinks, *and she's right. Who am I protecting, when there's nobody protecting me?* And so she starts, confesses, good for the soul, explains the fall, describes Mora coming through the front door just in time to see the vacuum salesman over her barely conscious body, how Mora sees him lean down, his face too close to hers, how Mora comes at him, kicking, screaming, fighting, slashing her fingernails at him, him grabbing Mora's arms but unable to stop her legs and booted feet from finding yet again her favorite target, Lucia's face.

Confession may be good for the soul, but does little for the one who must hear it.

Ya ain't goin' home, least not today. I got me a second room, and I'll clear it out, just junk, two seconds and long as ya need it, ya got a room too. Now don't ya go saying no so right off. Something to consider.

Something to consider.

YET ANOTHER SURPRISE

He is okay, he says *Hello* whenever he sees her, but Lucia had never considered anything from or about the man any further than smiling back as she passed. Yet there her pale, droopy neighbor sits on the sofa, tilting forward, hands dangling out of his jacket sleeves and hanging between his awkward knees, his large and mottled forehead furrowed, awaiting an answer.

His question is one that Lucia has never considered him ever considering. And he hadn't begun considering it, until after an early recent evening when Mora had pressed his doorbell to his row home up the street, after Mora had introduced herself — he knew her, everybody on the street knew her, and most on other streets, too, and if they didn't know her, they knew of her — and asked to be permitted entry, after the girl's mother had smiled at his mother, an old woman welded to a Laz-Y-Boy, after being allowed to sit, to take a cup of coffee, to chat about this neighbor, after asking about his job at the Post Office, and after Mora had suggested a most unusual proposal, *I sure you see today my Lucia...*

That is when he had begun considering as hard and as long as he'd ever considered anything, even longer than he had considered the purchase of his first new car. After days of consideration, he decided, and decided so concretely that there was no consequent consideration of Lucia refusing him.

His offer hangs in the air a stink.

He is nice, but I am tired, Lucia thinks. *So tired.* She looks at Mora — arms crossed, legs crossed — then she returns to the droopy gray balding man. Eyes down on the patterned rug, she asks him, *What does your Mama think?*

It is Mora's hand he takes when he prepares to leave, and that of the lurking vacuum cleaner salesman. He does not touch Lucia.

SOMETHING TO CONSIDER

She wants to dance, she wants to cry, she wants to run, she wants to sit on a stonework down by the river, she wants to follow butterflies, she wants to sit so still that dragonflies will land on her knee, she wants the moon more full, she wants to sit with nothing more to contemplate than how pretty the wind chime sings. But above all these things she wants, she wants what she does not know she wants, and that is kindness.

Lucia's job, the droopy man repeats her, is to make sure. Or rather, make certain. And what she is to make certain is the schedule of his household, that dinner be ready and warm by 5:30, that his shoes be waxed and buffed, that she be there wherever there is and whenever he is there, that the pantry be stocked and never without two things: coffee for him in the morning, and marshmallows for his mother, who adores them in the evening. And that she be clean, in the way a woman is to be clean, and to tell him by sleeping on the sofa with a towel when she is not, in the way only a woman I not.

And to be attentive in all things, especially to him, and more especially to his mother, and not to anyone whom he finds distasteful in dress or manner, or unworthy in morals and thought. Like Betty.

He said that? And you're still going to marry him?

Lucia uses the nail of her thumb to pick at a small chip on the rim of her heavy coffee cup. She also bites repeatedly the inside of her cheek, which twists her mouth to the side. Betty takes from her expression that Lucia is thinking about what she has just asked, considering the pros and cons, weighing the benefits against the consequences, but Lucia is not. She is withholding another thing he has said.

Well, girl, ya better think long and hard on that one. Was me, I'd tell him take a flying you-know-what.

Lucia does not know what the *you-know-what* is, but she understands what Betty means. In answer, she lifts and then drops a shoulder.

It's not I want. I must.

What do ya mean, ya must? You ain't...

Lucia shakes her head, loosing a small laugh. *No. But I tell her No, I will not do this, where else will I live?*

Whadda mean, where would ya live? It's your house.

Lucia says nothing.

It's your house.

Lucia still says nothing.

Oh, child, what have ya done?

She make me sign, give it to her.

Make ya? How she make ya?

Again, the shoulders.

Never mind, I can imagine. Mary, sweet Jesus and Joseph.

Mora needs a place to live. I married, she think Stani will sell it, use the money to fix his house, or get a bigger one. And she say she never share the house with Mrs. Kuscinzki, with us. That never work. She right. She need place to live, and she has place to live.

Your mother doesn't need shit. What she does is need to want, and that woman needs to wants everything. Don't mean ya have to give it. Ain't a kid's job to take care a the parent. Her freeloading asshole boyfriend husband whatever should be doing that.

It do not matter.

It does matter. You're being a doormat. What does it matter? Three months under that Polack and ya be dead. Inside, I mean. I seen hunnerts a women die thatta ways, I damn near did, and you're too much to die that a way. Trust me. Ya oughta tell 'em all to go take a flying you-know-what.

Lucia still does not know at what, but she can guess.

Unless ya love him. And ya ain't never going to convince me a that.

Lucia's best thought is to pick again the crack in the heavy old cup.

A LIGHT SHINING OFF A TIDE RUNNING

Lucia says, *We got choice. A work day, or go all of us to Atlantic City. They all say Atlantic City.* And he says, *Well, I can't. And I don't think you should go, and neither does your mother.* And Lucia asks, *Why?* And he says over the meatloaf, *Because. Because you should not be going down to no shore without me, or your mother. Ain't exactly proper.* And she asks him, *Why?* And he says, *Because. It's what I think, that's why. And what your mother thinks. You just shouldn't go without me, and you should know that. I'll take you down to Atlantic City, if that's what you want.* And she thinks, *I have not married yet. And it is not what I want.* But she says, *You not to go anyway, it is only for work people.* And he says, *You're not an employee, you're just a girl helps out, and soon's summer's over you're back to school and you go back to couple hours a week. Which is not* what anyone else thinks. Not anyone at the factory, and Betty has insisted she be along with them, be one of them.

She says, Then I just go work like always. No Atlantic City.

But she lies. Instead she has Betty keep a bathing suit and water sandals — bought with her own money at the Woolworth's down from the factory and never taken home — and a beach towel with *Welcome to Wildwood* that Betty had and says says she can have. No one will know, she will be paid all the same.

Faris says over the loud speaker, *Now ya none a youse is gonna need a dime. All's paid for, so get yer asses out on the bus and if one of youse complains one word we're turnin' this boat around. Today is for fun, and if you sorry asses can't have fun one day in yer lifes ya oughta call yerselfs a sorry lot.* He is smiling, finished, dropping himself in the upfront seat. Betty clutches at Lucia's hand, and she, too, is smiling.

The cities beyond the bridge turn to towns, the towns to suburbs, the suburbs to countryside, and everywhere are long-limbed trees stretching across the narrow road. *You seen Acklantic City, ain't cha?* Adam from Receiving leans over the back of Lucia's seat. *That there's fantastic. I think you'n'me oughta ride the roller coaster together. Just you'n'me. What'cha think? Maybe?*

Lucia bobs her head in a sort of agreement, a sort of acceptance of this news, partly because she already knows about Atlantic City and all the rides from pictures, and partly because she likes Adam from Receiving. Betty tells him to sit back and leave the poor girl alone.

The air changes smells again, this time to salty, if the air can smell salty, and familiar. Lucia recalls the water-pocked muds of the Guadalquivir at low tide. The first salt marshes of the Jersey coast appear, and Lucia presses herself across Betty's lap for a closer inspection. *I'da known ya wanted one, I'da gived ya the window seat.*

They change in the changing room at the edge of the Boardwalk, the smells of wet concrete, urine, coconut tanning oil and roasting peanuts sinking into every nose and cementing the memory of the Atlantic City Boardwalk at summer's end. Then they cross the hot sands, spread towels and blankets, laughing and hooting, Adam from receiving spreading his towel beside Lucia's, using his shoe to hold down the corner of both his and her towels. Faris comes by to collect their wallets and purses, putting everything into a canvas satchel. *Keep some money in yer baybin' suits. Ya needs some more, ya come see me or the Missus, case I'm out swimmin'. One a us'll be watchin' yer stuff.*

I'm goin' in. You comin'?

Lucia shakes her head. Adam is white under his red neck and above his red arms. Lucia is already dark, but less dark where her sleeves fall, and above her knees. *Y'all should dip first, then put on some baby oil. I brung some. Ya go swimmin' after, it washes off and won't do ya no good. I been here before, and ya can get real burnt.*

She's Spanish. She's gonna tan up like toast before she gets to the water. Don't ya worry 'bout nobody but you, Adam Grant. Get off now. We got some layin' out to do.

Lucia thinks, *I would like to like Adam Grant.* Then she lays down beside Betty, squinting at the boy moving toward the water's edge.

Can't believe that boy's gotta be pestery after ya like that. He knows ya are engaged.

Is okay.

I'm sure it is. I'm sure it is.

He finds her sitting on a strip of sewage pipe near where it runs underneath the slow rolling waves, its foam dying on her insteps, dampening the undersides of her calves. *I was wonderin' where ya got off ta.*

Lucia shades her eyes to look up at him. Without asking, Adam sits down.

I was gettin' hungry and was thinkin' maybe you an' me oughta get some funnel cake or pizza or somethin' up on the boardwalk. I'll buy.

Lucia returns to her contemplation of the undulations that shrink to darker lines below the horizon. A plane towing a banner that reads *Visit the Steel Pier* buzzes in the air. *Or we could go there, see the divin' horse and maybe go down in the bell. I never done that, but you can see fish and stuff, all the way down to the bottom of the ocean. Whacha lookin' so hard at?*

Lucia points toward the horizon where a distant trawler crawls through pods of fish.

That boat?

Lucia shakes her head. *More far. My España is there, far way.*

Ya missin' it?

She shakes her head again, stands. *Just another place. Another cage.*

Adam's brow wrinkles. *What's that mean?*

She bolts into a dead run back toward the blankets and towels.

Women. I'll never get 'em.

He dashes after her.

HELL TO PAY

Once it had been a poker that left a riddled scar, more often it had been Mora's left hand — sometimes open, sometimes fisted. This time the woman swings a steel-linked dog's leash. Welts on Lucia's forearms rise swiftly to red.

Lying whore. You think I would not find out? I find everything out. He says you won't do it. You will, or I'll kill you to an inch of your life. She whips the chain down hard, the steel grazing Lucia's cheek and biting her ear, the leather strap handle slapping her on the shoulderblade. Mora pulls back, and with a roundhouse sweep the leash curls around Lucia's neck. Snatching the free end, Mora crosses her hands and pulls.

But Lucia is no longer smaller, no longer thin, no longer lighter, and no longer weaker.

I decided, she says, coughing.

Mora, from where Lucia has pushed her, *You decided? You get to decide? I do this. You will, or you'll be back on the street where you belong.*

Better a street, Lucia says, freeing herself from the leash. She holds it in one hand, Mora's dark eyes afire. Several seconds during which Lucia thinks, and thinks. Then, throwing away what she holds, she says, *I'm taking my things, and I'll go.*

There are thumping footsteps on the stairs. *What the Hell is youse two all up in your faces about this time? Speak in goddamn English at least so a goddam American can goddam understand? Mora! Jesus Christ.* And he is gone in thundering footsteps.

The air is full of breathing. Then, *What things? What things you think is yours? Everything is mine. I buy everything. So you have nothing, you take nothing.* Mora attempts a grab her daughter's blouse, at the tail pulled free from the plaid schoolgirl skirt, but Lucia steps back. Mora scrambles to her feet, turns and goes into the kitchen. Lucia makes herself proper, and Mora returns with a green plastic bag.

Your stuff is garbage, you take it like garbage. What you put in this bag, you take. It lands at Lucia's feet.

It holds much, but Lucia has to remove one sweater and a pair of shoes in order to tie its neck. The bag is heavy, too heavy. She drags it. The bundle thumps on the stairs, twice coming against her legs, but Lucia holds on to the rail, tightly. The vacuum cleaner salesman comes out of his room, shirtless, shoeless, sockless, but with pants. *What the Hell, Lucy?*

She does not look up at him.

Mora is smoking.

The snow fallen before morning the afternoon sun melts, enough for rivulets to run along the curb, gather in depressions turning white to gray. Icicles drip at the gutters, but there is ice enough in the street to make dragging the bag easier.

As if, to Lucia, that matters.

She is on the street, and she knows the street.

BEFORE AND LATER

BEGINNING ALL

One tired old man stands elbow to elbow with other men, some of them also old, most not, all of them looking into the round dead eyes of ancient rifle barrels. *My God,* he whispers, reaching his trembling fingers toward the sleeve of one at his side, *I wasn't even a good Jew.* At the second command he wonders, *What will happen to them?* And then he wonders no more, knows no more, worries no more.

AND IN THE END

Inside a cab Mora holds in her fingers a diamond-studded dog collar, the clasp undone, the leather worn. Her legs are sore from the walk to and back again from a pet cemetery, and from other things. Age, mostly. Her body flows with the aches of age. She watches the ceaseless drizzle pock and streak the window glass. The emptiness of that small parking lot makes the hurts worse, but she blames the weather for turning dreary because she had to enter it.

Against her knee rests an aluminum cane. It is not hers, or rather had not been, but now is. Given by the caretaker of plots. *Go on. Take it. Somebody's left it, if you can believe that.* It is cold, unfriendly. Hers is made of blackthorn, left behind by a wealthy Irishman a decade before she needed it. They tell her it has only become misplaced. She feels certain they have stolen it. Very certain.

She ponders how in America rain falls at every funeral, even at those for dogs, and she wonders if rain at burials is the universal laugh of God. She wants to ask someone, but there is no one to ask except the cab driver, and she considers all servants stupid.

Never in Spain, she says, to no one.

A MIDWORD TO THE READER
FROM THE AUTHOR

Those who have met my wife may have heard some of the stories about her childhood, but many fail to believe, or rather find it hard to accept her stories as, perhaps, honest in their facts. They may do so because the events are, in the old sense of the word, fabulous, more so because they are foreign in ways greater than being of a distant country. They are from a distant — different — culture and sensibility. Most of all, they are from an experience not to be had in America.

A thing about childhood scars: to those who may look on the adult who keeps them, Time and Growth have stretched the surfaces almost to indistinguishable, nearly to gone. For the person scarred, however, they still bleed, they still rage, and they still ache.

I have one at my temple that I cannot find when leaning in towards the mirror, even with intense light pouring over the side of my face. But when I think about it, I remember the day I smashed into a water pipe while running around the perimeter of a house under construction. I remember the wash of blood ruining my shirt, the terrified expression on the babysitter's face. And I recall clearly the searing white hurt resulting from an impractical splash of mercurochrome where rough stitches were more needed.

The memory always returns with pains intact, and always in present tense.

All of my scars, as those on most, are stories now; hurtful as always when returned to the present, yet still their histories get told. It has taken me twenty years to prize out hers. I can only hope I have, in retelling them in these two forms, done it honorably.

With me being an author who steals from everyone, some of the events earlier presented happened to people even my wife does not, nor ever will, know. Many of those have been embellished out of recognition because of my writer's predilection to amplify, if not downright distort, what was actually true. I make no apologies to that, and I truly hope that no one can possibly detect his or her contribution.

This work never was intended as solely a fictional novel. The first part is a novelization of what now will follow. All hereafter had been published and read by followers of this author's internet column, *On Second Thoughts*.

What prompted me to revise that into this novelization came from several sources, or rather I wrote this because of several prompts. First, of those friends who had heard some of my wife's stories — I doubt there's not one who's heard them all — to a person each urged, "Write this down. It's unbelievable." I suppose they were inadvertent in thinking that the act of transcribing from a spoken tale to one in print somehow makes things more believable, but possibly it may. If I had any one chore that taxed me more than another during the conversion, it was making what I had heard from her, and from others, less fabulous.

There is, however, one significant, subsequent event that could lay claim to being the one thing that propelled me into changing the series of articles into a novel.

More than a year after penning *fini* under the *On Second Thoughts* series, me idling with coffee on the back patio one sunny morning here in Mesa, Arizona, when my wife received a telephone call from her mother. There was no reason for the woman to call, just wanted to chat, so I left her to the long-distance conversation. I went over to my shed, then into the house, finally coming out again to meander through our tiny grove of citrus. I could hear one side of their conversation, peppered sometimes with laughter, at different turns in my wandering. And then, suddenly and sharply, nothing.

I had assumed the conversation ended, my wife having wished her aging mother well, following the snapped-shut cell phone with either a cigarette.

I came around an obscuring orange tree to find her indeed smoking, but with a studied, dark, intense countenance, one that I always knew preceded her saying, *Honey, we have to talk.* Being the bold, courageous man that I am, I went straight past her into the house. But also being the loving, attentive husband I am, I renewed both my coffee and hers, got a fresh pack of cigarettes from her hiding place, and returned to where she sat feet up on the settee in study of the dark distance beyond anything visible.

Handing her the coffee I asked, *What's up with your mother?*

Now, before I get to her life-altering response, a few words about what had become altered.

Everything my wife had learned about her Spanish family — with whom she had had no contact for almost twenty-five years — had been tales told by her mother, who had little use for the factual. My wife did not know who her father was, because her mother to this day has refused identifying him. After several trips to Spain, she has gathered enough innuendo and suggestion, and looked into a face that bears so much resemblance to her own, that she has an idea, but no one will confirm it.

Her maternal grandfather did vanish when her mother was eight, but her story was that he had fought for the routed Loyalists in the Spanish civil war, and subsequently had to flee to England. There he supposedly got for himself a new family and a new life without an eye towards looking back.

My wife's grandmother did have a blonde child out of wedlock, and that story came down as something which often occurred to many Spanish women who had to find support from the "occupying" Germans during WWII.

The tales, which even as I heard them smelled of lies, I included in the articles. I had understood that deflection and avoidance of unpleasant realities had been a guiding force and protective shield among her Spanish relations, especially her mother.

I believe that we all make ourselves the heroes of our own stories, and that whatever we present, whoever we are and however we have lived, we have a compulsion to present ourselves in the best of spotlights. Therefore, overlooking this penchant for obfuscation was easy. Seemed a reasonable way to deal with certain inescapable realities. One was my wife's illegitemate birth and her mother's life-long refusal to admit who my wife's father may have been. Another was the poverty settled like a plague on this noble family. They all have an odor of aristocratic about them, but nothing of the avenues that would let them practice the habits of their once-upon-a-time peers. It left them both frustrated and isolated.

After I had handed Manuela her cup of coffee, and after I had asked the innocuous *What's up?*, she said, *After sixty years I just found out I'm a Jew.*

The core element necessary for the stories to become a novel snapped into clarity pretty much about the same time the phrase ended on her lips.

That disappeared Jewish grandfather had been executed by Nazis just prior to the eruption of continental warfare that consumed so many. He died alongside his father, shot, one must presume, in the dead of night in a field outside of Baena. The family was by no means rich, but they had wealth in land and olives, and all of it was confiscated.

All of my own life I have been plagued by the disengaged and often willy-nilly decisions of some bureaucrat who has chosen a course without regard or understanding of the consequences and ramifications affecting people that he or she would never know or meet. I am certain most of us suffer their decisions. It's how modern life, modern politics and modern businesses run. Someone somewhere had said to a some person designed to follow orders, *Go round up the Jews and confiscate their goods. War is coming, and it will be expensive. What you do with them is none of my concern, just get it done.*

Combining that supposition with the real evidences I already had, I knew I had my story.

By the way, kinda wish I knew about the Jewish heritage *before* I penned those *On Second Thoughts* articles, but such is the way of reporting. Won't be the last time I put a pen to paper without all of the facts revealed, but I will do it again with the certainty that I am doing the best I can.

Enjoy the following for what they were.

Charles W. Bechtel
Mesa, Arizona

The Lady from Spain

The "On Second Thoughts" Essays

PROLOGUE: WHERE ONE BEGINS

Where any writer begins a story is rarely, if ever, where one's story begins. This story, the one about a woman now reading in another room from where I write this, will begin at the moment I sensed a desire to tell it.

Her story, though, began far back in the antecedents to that moment, distant in time and place, more distant in years than I can pursue, in places more unreachable than I can ever go. As I sit and look at her I feel almost as much anthropologist as a Leakey holding a skull fragment, as much as a sociologist as Margaret Mead seeing the common behaviors of South Sea islanders studying the face of a child playing in the dirt before her. I feel perhaps at the same reductive pursuit of evidence that Newton must have felt holding a recently fallen apple, or as wondering as Einstein who, lying in his bed, had eyes fixed on the wavering needle of a compass.

I could only wish my talents and mind were as trained, complete, and as strong as theirs, so that I could divine more completely the woman reading a book.

The woman is my wife of twenty years, and she is reading a fantasy novel, the second in a series about the machinations of those who would become kings. Although I have read thousands of books, the one she holds, like the one she has already consumed and set aside, has little about it to attract my interest. I have no love for worlds I cannot travel in.

Unlike me, she has no love for the world we do travel in, and for her these fantastical creations allow an escape from the underhandedness, ugliness, unkindness and cruelty that comes not just through the news, but through her thoughts and memories.

This is not to say she is a sour woman, she's just soured on humanity. She still delights in a field of wild daisies, the unexpected descent of a hummingbird from our orange trees in the back yard, the patterns of cloud shadows rippling over far mountains, the play of our grandchildren and, thankfully, in the quirks of my perspectives on human hypocrisy.

She is a woman whose stories differ so much from those we know that they seem fantastic to those who hear them. Our friends repeatedly have told me I must write them down, though I am truly no biographer.

As said however, this story begins in the moment I considered her bent head. Who is this woman? I am not so naïve as to think that through measuring characteristics of a people can I weigh the character of a person, but taking accounts of both may lead me to necessary whole sight. I intend here to try.

As she approaches sixty years old, her black hair shows little gray. It is long, sometimes drifting forward as she reads until very little of her face shows. Moments ago she tucked it back behind her ear, a movement that may have been what drew my attention from the writing I had been doing. By all accounts, she has a noble profile.

She's a Spaniard, born in Seville midpoint the regime of its long-term dictator Franco. A half dozen years ago, during a visit to her relatives that brought us into contact with a knot of catty thirty-somethings curious to see this American cousin, I overheard one of them whisper, roughly translated, "She's so dark! Surely a gitano." Gitano is Spanish for Gypsy, a disdained race. Not a kind comment.

Her skin is not as dark as people imagine, though it does have the green highlights common to peoples of the Mediterranean rim. Under the incandescent bulb I can see hints of antique celadon in the hollow of her temple and along the shadowed curl of her jaw by her ear. Otherwise she is pale.

The rude stranger probably framed her characterization because of the black eyes and brows she turns on the vain and hypocritical with fierce penetration. Not her dark eyes nor sturdy brows, not her raven's wing hair nor her skin that say to

188

me *Here is a Spanish woman.* It's the mind behind her face, one full of aristocratic training of not just the past century but of two thousand centuries, that says to me she is no common woman.

At the moment this story begins a sudden thought sprang out of the foam of my concentrated ruminations: I know my wife, can now predict what her responses to the world will be, but did I know why she responds in those often unique, certainly exotic ways?

She is a woman of a far different culture than mine. She was raised by overwhelmingly critical and insistent nuns in a Spanish orphanage; I was left to my own education by indifferent Anglicans in a country and at a time when a self-styled, eclectic education was possible. The practices and customs of her region were shaped by invasions and occupation by Africans, Turks and Greeks, Romans, Visigoths and Gauls, by Stoics and Moslems and Catholics; mine rose from the exclusive club of a tiny island rarely invaded and for all intents and purposes, in comparison, indifferent to religious expectations.

She comes from the land of sun and heat and privation, while I came from a land of cold, wind, wet and plenty.

She is a mother to daughters made of her flesh; I am father only to what I make from my imagination. She has three years of standardized education, and I have nineteen.

Much to the amusement of my friends, she smokes rank, dark-odored cigarillos. I tolerate, but hate, cigarette smoking. *(I may take infrequent puffs on expensive cigars when I can get one, but I have never been continuous at that practice.)*

Until she met me, the only travel she had done, excepting the trip to Philadelphia when she was adopted at thirteen, was to foreign houses into which the Church had sought to sell her sometimes for marriage, sometimes slavery.

It's her tales of running away from those enclosures that bring the widest spread to the eyes of our friends. It's those mentions that lead them all to demand I tell her story.

And this is where truly we differ: drop any subject before me and I will have a story to tell, adventures in which I have participated, weird coincidences and happenings that a number of friends call "Chuck Stories." My wife on the other hand has the unusual ability to drop a hint, a phrase or aside carrying just a right amount to make people's eyes bulge and mouths fall agape. Press for more, she just shrugs and give flat facts: I was in Algiers because the nuns thought I might be a suitable wife for a Moor. Do not expect detail, no colors, no crafted shapes to her narrative in which to deliver a punchline. She has no punchlines; she only has punches.

Manuela Maria Iglesias y Serrano, re-surnamed with Ruk, Moore and Bechtel, I am going to tell your story. Friends, stay tuned.

CHAPTER ONE: A NOTION OF STRANGENESS

There is no possibility of excluding myself from her story, for most of what I will have to say of her specifically shall be filtered through my sensibilities. No help against it. No apology regarding it, either.

On my part, you see, ours was love at first sight. Rumored rare as unicorns, this immediacy is, inarguably for me since I experienced it, very real. I am as skeptical as any regarding mysticism, especially romanticized and emotionally-charged mysticism.

However, because the first moment of our mutual awareness returns to both of us with such clarity in regards to its Time and Space, I can't help but express a strong sense of strangeness and remarkability about it.

Though neither of us can attach a date nor time more specific than one afternoon when the weather was warm, we both can be specific as to what occurred that gentle midday. In the town in which we both lived and worked there was an old-fashioned news agency chock-a-block with notions, toys, greeting cards, doodads and newspapers, with a cashier's counter set directly before an always open door. Those making payment waited in a queue for one of two then-maiden sisters to take our money and make our change with nary a smile.

I stood thus with a newspaper, a Pepsi and a bag of corn chips in my hand, head down and eyes scanning the headlines. Manuela came behind me, hands loaded with paraphernalia necessary for her daughters, freshman and sophomore, to achieve a proper start-of-school launch. Ahead of me at the register was a local character, a former jockey and lately stroller of our main street, who dearly loved to tease the somber, humorless and impatient shopkeep. When he left and my attention rose from the page, I spotted something for which I still have a weakness, a neat cadre of Hershey's Special Dark Chocolate bars, novel in those days. I slipped one into my purchases, a thing noticed by the dark, short woman behind me.

As I turned to leave after making my purchases, my eyes took in the sprightly, smiling, black-eyed woman who looked very good in her Jordache jeans. I smiled back, suddenly very aware that I felt very differently than I had moments before.

Manuela says that day she had to refrain from touching my back. I have quite broad shoulders, and though they hold no distinction in my eyes, she found the expanse rather attractive. Her smile had been as instant as it was genuine when I turned to pass.

Who knows what influences such moments? It must be said that at the time we were both acutely aware of the disintegration of relations with the persons to whom we were married. For myself, the wife I then had was a woman better suited to remaining single, and six months after that warm day I agreed with her: our marriage was no marriage.

As for Manuela, hers was far more complicated. There were the two daughters as well as a twenty-three year history with her husband, Louis. She says that she had already begun the mental process of dissolving the day-to-day association with her husband, but actually to do so required resources she hadn't any notion of acquiring.

It's not the catching of each other's smiles that committed us to our futures, but unquestionably the sensations within each of us were like those surrounding conception. The inevitable body of our futures took life at that moment. However, its shape and measures developed in days ahead.

It was not until April of the following year that we collapsed under the weight of its inevitability. That, though, is a story for another time.

What is key here is that from the very start, our communion was remarkable and strange. To be able mutually to recall with such clarity a fragment of common time — how many people have we met, smiled at and forgotten in our lifetimes? — is nothing short of remarkable and strange.

If there can be any two adjectives continually applicable to our lives together, remarkable and strange must be leading them.

We met in departing, fell in love without consciousness, walked away perturbed, met again, denied our feelings, watched each other from across rooms, tried platonic friendliness and failed, and finally we just gave up and said "I must be with you" just like thousands must have said in thousands of places. Two average people, one average story.

Or so I thought. Wasn't long before I got the sense that I was not married to an average Spanish-American woman, an average immigrant from a well-known and not-too-hard-to-understand European country.

Sure, before the clarifying moment about which I am to speak I had already learned of her immigrant status, her being raised by nuns in a Sevillano orphanage, her curious transport into America as the adoptee of a Philadelphian naval couple, but I hadn't understood what these facts actually meant.

Clarity fell on me like a sunburst through dull clouds one afternoon when I turned my rapt attention from whatever dull thing I was doing to what she was doing with a common dish towel.

Manuela had it smoothed out on her lap and begun pressing it into accordion folds with a precision that bespoke of a practiced hand. I asked her what was she doing. She merely smiled and continued. With a twist, another fold and a flick of her wrist, she took the manufactured object into the cradle of one arm and held up to me the most anthropomorphic representation of a living person I had ever seen. The damn thing looked like a real child. Strange and remarkable. But the look on my wife's face said this machination was as loved by her as any child she ever held. Very strange. What she had to say was equally strange, and very remarkable.

"In the orphanage all I had was a rag. This was my doll."

There's a trick of cinema where a long lens shifts, causing the background to recede and the centered object to come forward into sharp focus and complete scrutiny. I felt that suddenly happen: my wife was no longer forty, she was four, a ragged urchin, dirty and unloved, a tossed aside and outside the affection of everyone, yet still able to shower on a dishrag all that a child's heart can muster.

If you've ever known a child's love, you know how enormous and unfettered that is.

I almost cried. I almost cry recreating it here.

How different a child from me she had been. It wasn't a gulf of dissimilarities widening between us at that moment. Rather a gulf of differences long existing between us had become suddenly visible, as though fog filling the chasm beneath our bridge had cleared. The child I had been was in no way similar to the one coddling a doll made from a rag, and I felt a need to pay more attention.

The woman I knew was no longer the woman I knew.

CHAPTER TWO: ON LOOKING UPON THE LADY

A young poet friend, one who died too young to ever truly grasp what he often quoted, favored a saying attributed to an older, more famous poet and teacher, Charles Olsen: *People don't change. They only stand more revealed.*

One evening at the Khyber Pass Pub in Philadelphia, as I leaned on elbows with my hands about a beer, I looked up quizzically at Joe. He had again dragged the pronouncement into our conversation and maybe for the first time I heard it. Or rather I felt it kick another idea across the table like a cue ball against the eight: *So Joe, what reveals them?*

He had no answer, perhaps because he was young. I didn't see him often after that night, but whenever we crossed paths I could see the troubled grasping for an answer shade his forehead. Sorry, Joe. I hope the answer came before you died.

I am now twice the age he was when he passed, and I have begun to see an answer. People are not mannequins draped with layers upon layers of cloth, dummies who might finally stand naked if they would only shed the faddish and fashionable disguises. They are more an infinitely complex clockwork, bodies and minds of mysterious gears, with unsuspected springs of various torsions, affected by sometimes contradicting, sometimes complementing counterweights.

We reveal *them*, not they themselves. Oh, they help. Some spin elaborate stories, others lies; some merely drop a crystalline phrase into an innocuous conversation, the kind of phrase that stumps all further conversation, or slips out of a conversation and later into the center of one's unsuspecting thoughts.

194

To more thoroughly bring someone to stand revealed takes *our* awareness, a good deal of study, much research, and a willingness to let understanding arrive before judgment. To pursue judgment only leads us into unsafe and false security.

Hercules reportedly had to catch a water sprite, a daughter of Poseidon. However much he grasped at her, she dissolved in his fingers and slipped away. Finally he asked her father how might he subdue the nymph. The king of waters replied, "Stand still and she will fall calmly about your knees. Then you may gather up all of her as you may want."

To take hold of all I may want of my wife Manuela, I had to cease reaching for her. Not easy, but possible.

So I sat beside this complex mechanism, this human as unreachable as any, recognizing that she was layered with influences, trainings, habits and expectations that predate not just our companionship, but our lives.

Consider: At any given dinner table with flatware, how a fork gets handled can reveal so much about influences working on a person. I admit to cringing when I see a person grip a fork handle in a fist, thumb pressed against the butt end in the same manner a person nllds a pencil to snap it in half. It's a rare occurrence when I see a person work a fork left-handed, the tines turned down and curving away from the fingers.

How one works a fork speaks about a person's relationship to elegance. It is not enough to call that simple manner *proper*. Instruction about a *proper* way to do anything is an expression of superiority. *Elegance* means a person is self-elevated, not judged inferior or superior.

There is respect not just for those who would witness the use of the fork, which can be achieved, I guess, by 'proper behavior,' but for the materials one has employed, and ultimately for the *experience*, the *beingness*, of using a fork.

As I watch my wife reading her fantasy novel, I see her turn the page with a finger lightly touching the upper right hand corner to lift it, then slide down to halfway along the page's edge, then duck under and turn it. As very simple gesture. And very elegantly done.

Although reading a great number of pages may have led her to this elegant turning, I suspect a different truth. I have observed others reading, many of them with thousands of hours of reading behind them. English majors, book-worms, students. Can't tell you how much more prevalent is the fingerlick, with a dragging down of the corner and a shoving the page over. Inelegant. Look around, you'll see.

The same inherited elegance affects how she holds her cigarette, her coffee cup and her fork, and how she holds her conversations.

Where did the pervasiveness for elegance come from? Is it taught? Who said, *Manuela, hold your cup thus, your cigarette thus?* I believe no one did. But there it is in every move

I think a clue lies in the adjective I chose two paragraphs back: *inherited*. We inherit so much from our cultures that the resultant behavior seems genetic. I realized that if I was to begin understanding Manuela I would have to become familiar with her cultural inheritance.

It would prove a more difficult thing to do than I first thought. She's the Lady from Spain, and to understand her is to undertake Spain.

Being an American descended from a long line of Americans, there's an aspect in my cultural perspective that pigeonholes anyone with traceable immigrant ancestors as inherently *other*. To call it white prejudice is short-sighted and too dismissive to be of any use. The aspect has to be recognized as possibly limiting in scope and potentially denigrating if I think *other* also means *lesser*. I do not.

Every culture has its attachments to elegance, though putting that attachment as most desired often means, in America, making behavior *proper*. And like I said, requiring behavior to be proper has a way of making us miss the point.

The more gestures of Manuela I look into, the more I discover how elegantly she performs them. All of them. A turn of a page, the tap of her cigarette to dislodge the ash, the use of her fork.

I realized that, perhaps, in our first glance at each other which cemented our futures, this attachment to elegance may have become instantly apparent to each. Anyone who does not prize elegance over proper behavior would never be able to see the woman who reads before me. I consider myself most fortunate that, in all I have sought for myself, having inherited a taste for elegance has allowed me to see my wife.

So who was it that set forward this pattern of elegance that leads her to turn a page in so admired a manner? Many, many Spaniards in a land far away. Next discussion: What is the Spain in the Lady from Spain?

CHAPTER THREE: AN ACCUMULATION OF ORIGINS

But what said to Manuela, *go forward elegantly?* Who instructed her not just to hold a fork thusly, but to prefer it?

Though we all know facts are not the truth, just true, they do serve as a place to begin. Here are a few quick facts about Manuela's origin: she was born in Seville, Spain, mid-twentieth century, most likely in what then served as her grandmother's house. She was born to a very young, very angry girl, as a bastard child, for she refused to expose him, and no father came forward. Quickly Manuela was shunted into an orphanage under the dictates of the Roman Catholic Church, within the care of nuns.

The facts in themselves offer speculation as to the effect they had on her training and development, but to understand the facts one must understand Spain. Too often we bring our own recollections and traditions to facts, and therefore misunderstand them. Bastardy, abandonment, the Catholic

Church, orphaning and orphanage all mean something else to Americans than what that means to a Spaniard.

Our system of orphanage, for years, precluded any continual involvement with a child by her mother, father, or family. Lately this has spawned an industry for searching out birth parents. In Spain, this is not the process. Not only is the family allowed contact, it is more than encouraged. It is almost insisted upon.

To be born poor and to be born into poverty is not the same thing in Spain. Poverty is the same the world over: a lack of resource necessary to support growth; those resources being mostly food, clothing, shelter, clean water. To be born poor, in Spain, means that a person has had access to legal rights, social position, educational opportunities and familial connections taken away.

A bastard becomes, if the family chooses, poor in the midst of luxury. Manuela's situation was poor, and because of prejudices within the young, angry girl's immediate family, she was kept very close to poverty.

Poor she accepted; being kept in poverty changed her.

In the orphanage system during those nearly medieval times *(all things change very slowly in the Spanish Catholic Church)* the family is asked to contribute to the welfare of the child through *charity.* We have a notion of charity far removed from its origins. A cursory glance at Wikipedia underscores in an explicit way that Charity was divorced from familial responsibility: *The practice of **charity** means the voluntary giving of help to those in need who are not related to the giver.* This runs counter to another, older notion that *Charity begins at home.* (Americans like to have things both ways.)

Charity, care and char have close ties. We now think of charity as something given to less fortunate to make life better. That's a notion that requires a stratification of citizenry based on fortune, which in very past cultures was a rare case. In most ancient cultures *(and maybe all)* everyone struggled to survive.

Prosperity was measured in the success of not perishing. Charity was the succor and help given to those facing immediate and near death.

We had to take care of those stricken. Furthermore, since death invited pestilence and disease, the dead had to be put into the rapid care of body disposers: the charnal house was the place where a body was either cremated or dusted with lime, to secure quick disintegration. Such places historically were the province of the priesthood.

It's no wonder the Catholic Church ran the orphanage. Their duty, as orphan caretakers, has been to secure the possibility of survival for the child. It was not just their duty; it was the duty of those who created the life as well.

This is why a bond with the family could proceed after a child was given to the orphanage. The sense of *continual responsibility* is inherent in the Spanish system, which it is not in the American system.

Curiously, a man is allowed to refuse a legal responsibility for a bastard child, but this practice depended on ignorance to flourish. No DNA testing. A woman's claim of a father's parentage had to go to court for affirmation. As courts were mostly in the business of protecting fortune, declaring a child fatherless made the child's condition unfortunate. Therefore, responsibility returned to the mother and her family.

Into this Manuela was born.

Unfortunate, with fortune removed. Whatever rights, legal or social, that her mother may have had, Manuela was forever denied.

There's a famous and telling line in Tennessee William's great play, *A Streetcar Named Desire*, in which Blanche, almost witless, declares *I have always depended upon the kindness of strangers*. It is a moment of pure pathos: she has lost even family support for her strangeness.

Manuela was not just given to the Church for her care, she was abandoned into it. The anger and youth of her mother sliced any attachment she had to the baby she bore, and she denied her daughter's existence even in the face of the truth known by her family. This pattern of staunch allegiance to a bald-faced lie consumed her mother, and to this day (she still lives) she can only be seen as a woman wrapped in false fabric. More on this in the future.

Because of this, though, the *responsibility* of Manuela's family was severely crippled. The way in which a family responds is not limited to material offers: orphaned bastard can still be allowed an attachment to family, which brings with it a sense of belonging, even if curtailed and limited.

Manuela lost this. For the rest of her life in the orphanage, up until a few good people came to her aid once she'd become a teenager, she had *always* to depend upon the kindness of strangers. She was always at the mercy of charity, so much so that acts of charity became all she understood as her purpose in life.

There's an object in a cabinet beside me now that has travelled with Manuela since well before I met her. It's a colorful, primitive though carefully produced carving, a thing whittled from a piece of tossed-aside wood. It resembles a small dog. The person who carved it has long faded from contact with her, but he is someone whose care was entrusted to her. The carving was a thank you for helping him survive.

I believe she treasures it above all other things, even photographs of her children, handmade gifts from her grandchildren, and anything I've ever given her. It's a reminder to her that she has a place in the world, that of a care-giver. And that commitment to being the kind stranger upon whom another may depend is her core of humanity, and I, as do so many, love and adore her for it.

But kindness is not her only Spanish-given virtue. Not by a long shot.

CHAPTER FOUR: WHITHER HEAVEN, AND WHY?

San Xavier del Bac glows in most lights, shimmers in the late afternoon of winter, as season which in southern Arizona has little meaning. The adobe Mission stands to the west of an Interstate, well outside the urban sprawl of Tucson, and appears in the distance like a confection as one drives past.

In my mind's eye I have several times attempted to clear away that sprawl, make the power lines vanish, to evaporate the marks of the automobile culture, to sweep away the contrails streaking a robin's-egg blue sky. I have tried to see it as the earliest attendants may have seen it, a gleaming eruption among the honored mountains surrounding the wide valley. Its very existence signifies a division between what the native's God has given, and what the Christian God has promised.

There is nothing about the structure that says it belongs there, even after 225 years. Although made of native earth, it has been caked with decades of white lime mortar. The creative mind, as well as the iconography with which it is decorated, came from a world four thousand miles away, from a people as different from the natives who cultivated and cooked beans as an orange is from an acorn, or as this gringo is from his Spanish wife.

Inside the mission, the artwork has both a familiarity and a strange remove from my daily life. Since the fourteenth century the Catholic Church has had at its core the mortification of the flesh. It adopted that rightly, for the Church was the power during the Black Plague that scored and boiled the flesh of good and bad parishioners alike. San Xavier's Madonna is healthy, but her son is an emaciate, like so many that hang in churches all over the world. In the western wing of the crucifix-patterned building lies, in full view, the mummified remains of an early priest. The air is heavy with incense. For two centuries that essence crusted the ceiling and permeated the plaster walls.

The pews are rigid, unforgiving. There is no reason for the flesh to receive forgiveness; this is a place for the soul. And each is aligned to focus the worshipper on only one thing: the horrors and travails of the mortified, crucified man honored as the son of God.

For me, being in San Xavier stirs a sense of interloping. I am not Catholic, not even Christian, and have no business inside except as a gawker, a tourist. I adore the handiwork of men and women committed to producing Art, and I am fascinated by what lies within and without the mission. But I am indifferent to what it means to the sense of self that I see radiating from the worshippers who have come to pray. It is still a church.

For Manuela, however, there is much about her sense of self in San Xavier. She detests the place, for she feels its purpose is a commitment of criminal enterprise.

We can discuss its abstracted purpose, to provide a replica of Heaven, a place of wealth and wonder for people so poor that a bowl of beans means more than three Mercedes in the driveway. I have had the gaudy over-indulgences of church decoration explained as a visual performance, one that not only delights the senses but which explains the promise of Heaven. For people who have nothing, they will, in time, have a Palace of God just like this Earthly house.

My wife understands this, but she cannot accept it. It revulses her in a way I may never understand, except intellectually, which is the palest form of understanding. Her revulsion is visceral, bodily, for she has known the mortifications of hunger.

As much as the Kingdom of Heaven is promised, the world is given. She sides with the Native American belief that what the world gives enough for us, that it will feed us if we feed it, clothe us if we honor its gifts, and nurture our spirits as much as can any priest echoing the promises.

Being orphaned and put into an institution is different for a child born in our secular, state-run facilities than it is to someone born into a Catholic state. I do not intend to list and ratify the differences. I have to underscore what going hungry to a point past pain means to a child surrounded at the same time by gold and luxury.

One day, thinking of my own flashed memory from when I was three, I asked her what her oldest recollection was. She said, 'begging.'

'What?' I had to ask. She then told me in her flat, direct way, that on every day except Sunday, she and the other female children, who ranged in age from weaned to bleeding, were taken into the streets of old Seville to beg for food and money. They were forbidden to eat any food, or keep any money, because all charity was governed and dispensed by the Church.

If they had eaten before begging it was most often on a heel of bread and a glass of water. Not every day was there food.

Those who know her today cannot picture my wife *sans* her three prized accoutrements: flashing red nails, a cup of heavily-sugared coffee, and a dangling cigarette. What most do not know is these are effects born in childhood, that childhood of starvation.

Her red nails, far too long for normal work, although we've all seen her clean out warehouses without breaking one, are the antidote to having had dirty, broken nails, chewed to the quick nails. To have such long, red nails is an indulgence, a thing reminding her that, like the fictional Oliver, she can have more than what charity allows. Though it took her years finally to go, a trip to the manicurist is an escape from that poverty.

Coffee was the first sweetened treat my wife ever tasted, and it was an instant, is a constant, companion. Coffee banished hunger by delivering deliciousness. It was, for her, what they served in that promised Heaven.

As for the cigarette, she learned before she was eight that any butt end snatched from the gutters and sidewalks, when again lit, would stave off the pains of hunger. To light those cigarettes, she and any friend lucky enough to find and take a usable one would sneak off to where the candle offerings flickered in their ruby glasses. Borrowing was not stealing; they borrowed the light to deflect the abomination of starvation.

She has no use for any practice heralded as honorable that calls for mortification of the flesh. She has seen what a lack of treatment provides: weak bones, crippled growth, stunted ability and in more than one case, transformation into a corpse. To an adult believer, the transformation may signal attainment of Heaven; to a child it means a waxen nothingness has come for you.

'How can the church show all that gold when people are hungry?'

Manuela will never accept that any world promised is better than the world we have been given. And she will continue to despise anyone who withholds plenty from those who most have need of it, the starving.

San Xavier del Bac, as do all churches, come from a world far, too far, away, to be believed.

CHAPTER FIVE: TIME FOR EVERY PURPOSE AND FOR EVERY WORK

Time: how irretrievable a resource, how impossible a concept, how cruel upon us, and how varied the ways of measure.

Time is superior to every event; it can no more be known than the flavor of deep space. The explanation of time alters in every culture.

Time is sliced into meaning by how it is used. Science describes Time as the interval of change between one state and the next. There is the nanosecond, the microsecond, the split second, the second itself, the minute, hour, day, week, month, year, lifetime. And there is eternity.

Time without end. All the time in the world. World and Time enough. The time of our lives. The best of times, the worst of times. A time to live, and a time to die.

Along a small bit of the Delaware River, directly opposite Philadelphia, is a man-made construction of stone, a bulwark defending the bank against an incessant lapping of waves and the crashing wakes of passing ships. It runs the length of one part to the town where I spent my youth. I suspect today it hosts someone sitting on it, who stares into the passing river deep in thought.

The sea wall is a device to stop time, to prevent the change from one state to the eroded next. Those who sit on it soon stop looking at what passes by, and start thinking on what has already passed. Thus Memory displaces Time. That sea wall is, in many ways, for many people, a timeless place.

I had once asked Manuela what was the happiest time of her life. I was not digging for the cheap and deflective answer: *Oh, when I married you*, or *The day my first baby was born*, or *Any waking day is a happy day*.

One usually and quickly gets from Manuela a direct answer, even to questions that others may want to ponder further. It's one of her most admirable traits: she has thought upon what many take for granted, and she's already selected the answer out of the bucket of possibilities.

She said: *"Sitting on the wall at the Med in Barcelona, watching the ships go by, when I was a nine."*

Of course that prompted a *Why?* from me, as well as the attendant questions, *What was it like? How did you feel?* et cetera. To those questions she merely shrugged. For her to know and me to find out, for her to own and me to pluck away. She did give me this: *There was nothing to do. It was fun.*

As usual with Manuela's answers, there was both an instant glimpse and a novel's worth to speculate upon. What, possibly, could a nine year old have to do? *Work*, she said.

Had I no school to attend, as Manuela had not until she came to this country at thirteen, every day would have been filled the same way my summer days were: I fooled around, I walked down to the river, I hung out with local kids, I joined a pick up baseball game, I read a book or I lolled under a shady tree. Work? *At nine?*

If you weren't asleep at the convent, you either prayed or you worked.

They had her rise before dark, since before she could remember, to pray at *Prime*. Every day had its measure, marked by times to pray. These demarcations are known as the *Liturgy of the Hours*, practiced every three hours, roughly, beginning at midnight. The children were exempted from most Dark Hour prayers: *Compline*, *Matins* and *Lauds*.

They did not wash nor brush their hair or teeth. They did not paddle down to the breakfast nook, or sleep an extra five before being called again. There was a wooden rod to prevent dalliance. Before they knew what it was, they had been made to learn a litany of words to be muttered over their filthy hands every morning. Once this was done, they went for buckets, brushes, rags and picking tools, which they then carried inside the church to clean it.

This was done until *Terce*, the mid-morning prayers at 9am. Once *Terce* was completed, they were led onto the streets to beg, fed with the morning's bread and water if it was available. It was the job of the older to supervise the younger.

The older girls, those between seven and eleven, were left on the streets when *Sext*, or the noontime prayers, began. They were to return no sooner than when the sun began to slide down and cast long shadows. The younger children were taken back to the convent to sleep through that national treasure of the Spaniards: *siesta*.

If the children wanted siesta, and often necessary because of the brutal sun, they had to find necessary shade wherever it fell. Since many of these places were unsafe, and you can use your imagination to understand why they were unsafe, you found a place to wander, to do nothing.

Manuela was born and housed for much of her life in Seville. Why, then, was her happiest day in *Barcelona*, at nine?

The nuns would take us places to get adopted or sold, or married off.

At nine? Adopted I understood. Or thought I did. A family wanting children to love and raise came to adopt. It worked similarly in Spain as it does here: the prettiest and brightest go first, the homelier and attitudinally challenged went last.

Manuela was not adopted until she was thirteen, and then by a non-Spaniard. At no time was she considered by her own people.

This was less because of her attitude than her size. She was scrawny, too small. Children in Spain are not adopted to be loved; they are adopted to be worked. They are sold if they have an extra value, such as good size or a learned skill, or were boys. The girls were married off to those who prized their shapes.

At nine? Her response: *As soon as girls bleed, they are married off, usually to the Moors in Africa. The pretty ones, anyway.*

Too thin and scrawny, unskilled at anything besides looking after the younger children, and because of bad food and worse genetics, underdeveloped even at thirteen, Manuela earned the reputation of a runt. In the litters of dogs, breeders selected the runs and snapped their necks. No christened child could be disposed of, so Manuela was paraded on a kind of adoption trade to the bigger cities along the Med.

For an orphan girl in Spain, the measures of Time are set by the day of self-awareness, the moment of menstruation, and the day of disposal, either through adoption, sale or marriage, or simple turnout of those too old.

All days between the marks of Time were days of labor. But there was that one happy day, when Manuela had nothing to do except sit on a wall by the Mediterranean Sea and watch the ships pass by.

She imagined they were going to America.

CHAPTER SIX: HER CROWN OF GLORY

The first Sunday after Easter, past brunch, before lunch in a typical New Jersey diner, the change of shift match the change of services at the local churches. A clamor by the door: a large family barely maintaining cohesiveness is being marched to a table against the back wall. Or rather tables, for three need to be pushed together to accommodate.

In the center of them, unconscious of the attention she receives, the prettiest child — all families have a prettiest child — flounces in her Easter dress, all lace and yellow and confection. She even has the turned-down socks and patent leather shoes.

I watch her, smiling. Manuela watches me watch her, knowing I was thinking of my own granddaughter who must then be skipping ahead of her other grandparents on the way to another table in another restaurant. All little girls are my granddaughters.

I return to my tepid coffee and ask, not giving a thought to the consequence of what I was about to ask, if Manuela remembered her first fancy dress. *Yes*, she said.

Tell me about it' I said. *What do you remember?* She said, in a straightforward manner I've come to expect, *I got it for Easter. That was when I started to bleed. And it was after they shaved my head.*

Huh? My head snapped up and my coffee cup went down.

On any given Sunday you can look around a restaurant and see so many children fresh scrubbed and washed, combed, almost all of the little girls with long beribboned hair. The boys sport anything from a near bald head scraping to ragamuffin long, but the girls wore crowns of glory.

Shaved your head, what for?

Lice, she said. *I hated that dress. I was glad when they took it back.*

I had to ask, *they shaved your head just because of lice? What about shampoo? One of those combs with close teeth, like for cats?* She laughed at me. Like she ever saw a comb. *And they took the dress back?*

Yes, there were other girls, and they didn't have their heads shaved.

All of the elements in what she said had to come together. Her first bleeding, menstruation, her first dress, for Easter service. And the incongruity of the shaved head on a prettied up child.

Manuela claims she was not one of the pretty girls. I asked if that made such a difference in the orphanage, there being so many already down and out, could some facial prettiness make any difference?

Apparently, yes. It was the single blessing, or curse, that a child born into nothing could claim as something. The pretty ones, she assured me, were claimed by the priests. Apparently celibacy among priests was more honored in the breach. Or dishonored in the breaches.

The pretty girls were the first to become women, whether they had bled yet or not. And having experienced what they understood was their future role, they had something to use over the uninformed. I recognized that: in my own youth, the girls who had *done it* always seemed to have an edge up on those who hadn't, though the cost was their eventual unworthiness to boys who seemed to be going places.

The girls I knew who had *done it* were certain to wind up with boys who didn't care they had *done it,* so long as they kept doing it with them. And they were the boys who would become men who eventually wouldn't care what they did.

We suppose, here in America, that we have a more civilized appreciation of womanhood among the young. They are to be kept from things fleshy as long as possible. To fail means to imperil success. The thought that any teen found out as pregnant must be inalterably doomed to a sad life is immediate. What do we know?

We've come to see children as boat anchors to success, barriers to the freedom of movement we so covet. Not all women, but signs of it are everywhere. In my grandmother's day, even my mother's, the notion of a clicking biological clock was unheard of.

That was my first thought, about those children servicing the priesthood: *what if they became pregnant?* Manuela took another sip and fished around for her cigarettes. *So much the better. Easier to marry off. Men wanted women who could show they were fertile.*

This in the heart of Catholic Spain, the Citadel of the Virgin Mother? What the Hell did they value?

I had long known the idea of *virgin* had a corrupted social value in the Roman world of early Christianity. The Levantine states used the word *virgin* to mean any girl of a certain young age, specifically those still in the earliest years of menstruation. Readily marriageable though untested, a virgin birth was rare, and inherently miraculous to the man married to a woman barely out of childhood.

When the notion of Virgin hit the boot of ancient Italy, it met with an already idolatrous cult dedicated to an idea of purity, untouched originality. A virgin to them was not a woman who had not yet been a mother, but one who had not yet been able to be a mother. The Roman Catholic idea of the Virgin Mother took on a whole new meaning. Up on the pedestal that one went.

Not so in Moorish Spain, where the concept of virgin held much of its original, Levantian meaning. Wealth was, and is, measured among men by the number of children he can support. Prudence said a man should only support those he has created himself, which meant women should be sequestered for his use only. Hence the idea of the harem and the full body covering.

In Manuela's Spain, a female child bleeding was converted into a better commodity, more easily sold. And if pretty, so much easier.

But wasn't that like slavery? My idea being that women were thereafter trapped, worse off than a street urchin free to run in the streets. Showed me my priorities.

Meant clean clothes, a safe place to sleep and regular food. I wanted it too, but they shaved my head. Meaning, Manuela was pitched into an unwanted ugliness at her time for prettiness. For the girl prancing down toward our table, that meant attention. For an orphan like Manuela, that meant a chance to escape the cruel requirements of living in an orphanage. It meant the difference between old bread and warm soup.

It meant the difference between beautiful, long combed tresses and lice infestation. Between punishable servitude and rewarded motherhood. It even meant a difference between surviving and prevailing.

My wife now has, and long had, thick, glossy, lengthy, astonishing black hair, uncut. She wouldn't succumb to the modern American woman's predilection for chopping it off to ease child rearing. And since women rarely change hair styles after twenty-five, it's a rare adult woman who today carries on her head a crown of glory such as Manuela's.

I always liked it; suddenly I understood it.

CHAPTER SEVEN: LET IT BE, AS IT IS

> *"When I find myself in times of trouble*
> *Mother Mary comes to me*
> *Speaking words of wisdom, let it be..."*

John Lennon recorded these words in 1969, but they were playing on a woman's I-pod while we waited at the motor vehicle agency in Arizona. The music wasn't loud, but Lennon's plaintive cry is so unmistakable, so much a part of American consciousness, anyway — for people of a certain age — that even a tinny hint reaching us was identifiable.

Far longer than at any other place, Manuela and I had lived in New Jersey, and there we were putting so much behind us. This legal change of address was the final sever to our attachment to decades of history, and it felt funny. Especially for me, since I lived most of my life to date there.

I asked Manuela what the severance meant to her. She shrugged. She'd been in this situation before, when she had first been severed from Spain, but that was different. We began discussing the difference, and much of the difference had to do with knowing what she left. She had been an orphan, divided not only from family but from history, family history, especially that history most members of a family get to witness. In leaving Spain, there was much she did not know about it.

Piecing together events in her life is a bit like matching glass shards swept into a box. One may all reassemble the pieces, but it will never be again a clear window. What we have pieced together can be summed easily: she was born, carried to a Catholic Church, given over to their care, was fed, clothed, housed.

But as said, facts are not the truth. Because of the illegitimacy of her birth, everything she could know of her life as she lived it was kept hidden, made secret.

Some she knows, but much she had to suppose. One thing she had supposed was, *Who had been the family member that carried her to the church? Who wrapped her? Who gave her to strangers? And who had the strength to turn, walk away, sever himself or herself from the future of the small child?*

It took fifteen years and four trips to Spain to learn, but Manuela now knows. The woman who brought her to La Macarena, Seville's magnificent cathedral, was her mother's oldest sister. And her name was Mary.

I am writing after so much transpired, so much had become learned during our four trips to Seville. Much of what I write, and shall write, derives from translated conversations with her Aunt Mary, who will figure in Manuela's story from here on out. That's because she, and pretty much she alone, had never fully severed Manuela's connections.

It's hard, sometimes, to reconcile facts. Since Manuela lived for so many years without facts, especially those kinds of facts about myself that I may easily take for granted, she has now a conditional relationship to facts that I do not. To me, facts — hard, verifiable knowledge — are the coin and canvas of existence. For her they are either conveniences, or inconveniences.

For me, Lennon's words of wisdom serve no one. For me, murder will out, as will anything verifiable. *Actual* is the only real.

But Manuela had a lifetime of filling in her history with what she desired. The kid looking across the glassy Mediterranean at ships sailing to America could have any history, any parentage, any existence other than what she had escaped, even if only for an afternoon.

For her all times were troubled, and the only thing to do with the fog bank of not knowing was to let it be.

We failed that wisdom. When we first began living together, during that time when each of us is a story to be learned and understood, nothing about Manuela made any sense.

Easier to hold hands with an eel than grasp certainty about what she had to say about her past. Everything was always up for revision.

The number of children born to her grandmother shifted with the telling, as did the year she was born, who her father most likely was, what city she called her home. Furthermore, circumstances about her coming to America and all that happened in her first years here had shifted.

It's not exactly that she lied about the facts of her past, it's that with the possibility of anything being an event or circumstance in her past, all possibilities became probabilities, and whatever was convenient to say was sufficient to offer.

This incompatibility between hers and my relation to facts foretold of an inevitable fracture, and I had to prevent it. I detest lying, considering it the most uncivil of all acts. Manuela saw little difference in the value of whether what she said was factual or not. I began to understand in those early years with her that, to her, an untruth is a lie depending on intent, not content.

Many of her untruths were placeholders for what she did not know, and they were offered to me unintentionally disguised as reality. In our first year together even her being born in Spain had to be believed, but had not become authenticated.

We decided to send her back to Spain to get answers. She demurred several times, but I insisted. I saw it as the only thing which could prevent an inevitable fracture that I saw ahead for us. At last she understood, concurred, and accepted what she had to do.

But there was a problem. She had no passport, and no birth certificate, and — worse — no naturalization papers. Getting a child into the US in 1964 was much easier than now, and Manuela, as it turned out, was an illegal alien. This was a frightening prospect: I could lose my beloved, and she could lose her children, to deportation.

When I find myself in times of trouble... let it be. We had to face doing just that. Manuela again had to face losing what reality she had to pursue the reality she had been so long denied. It was not an easy decision, but by then neither of us could let it be.

Ironically it was on a trip to immigration that I got the proof I wanted that she was even Spanish: we were stopped by a family from Columbia for directions to the Customs House in Philadelphia. I understood their Spanish and tried the best I could to help, but it wasn't until Manuela stepped in with her fluent use of the language that she became, for me, an actual honest-to-goodness foreign born woman.

It's not easy living in a world where you don't know what to believe.

It took two years, several visits to Immigration, the assistance of a lawyer, two trips to the Spanish Embassy in New York, and a threat in demanding that all of her past taxes be remitted before some functionary approved the paperwork necessary for her to pass smoothly between her present and future and her past.

And when the broken hearted people living in the world agree there will be an answer, let it be. For though they may be parted there is still a chance that they will see there will be an answer, let it be.

I and her two daughters, her present and her future, saw her off at the airport on a fine, clear day. She trembled, and I do not believe she feared parting from us. There was a fog into which she had to go, and many things that people had let be for far too long.

Obvious in all I've written to date was that an orphan found herself to have family, a history, a place, a reality. To understand her, to understand herself, it is those people and that place, and the times once shrouded in fog, that must to come into the light. Time to *Let it be.*

CHAPTER EIGHT: THEY WOULD BE GIANTS

We all have shadow people in our pasts, those who loom tall but stand indistinct. They roam our memories like old men at parties, not saying much, always the same story when they do, faded as old black and white pictures stored in a candy box.

They are the adults of our childhood, maybe a neighbor, maybe an old friend of your parents back when they had friends, maybe a now-deceased great uncle or aunt. Some of them may pop into our recollections like street signs that the bus we're on passes by, all the colors of their faces drained of brilliance, but somehow still they are still capable of stirring our emotions. *I remember them,* you might say out loud, *back in the day...*

In about ten days from this writing I will be reaching out to shake the hand of one of my shadow people, someone I haven't seen in fifty-five years. One of the most rewarding aspects of the Internet is its ability to allow us to reconnect with those who have faded away. Jerry Truman was my father's close friend during those days when my parents were breaking up our family, and he was a moment of calm when all around us seemed imperiled.

He is the premier Shadow among the ghosts in my memory.

For Manuela, the Queen of Shadows is *Tia Maria,* her mother's eldest sister.

It is an obvious question that arises: how does a child put into an orphanage as an infant remember a woman who was a blood aunt? Again, it is because of a difference between the way an old world institution manages the distresses of life compared to the way we handle them in this new one.

In Spain, it was not acceptable to hand off responsibility because something unfair, unwanted, unmanageable affects one's life.

In our country a most cherished tradition is also an unconsidered one. Every week, sometimes twice a week, we practice something as faithfully as some cultures practiced going to Mass: we put out our trash for collection. We feel compelled to do it, anguish over it when we let a collection day pass without taking out the trash. We worry about our elderly neighbors no longer able to move her can to the curb. We'll do that one cherished thing unasked, and take pride in our selflessness as we drag their containers to the street. We obsess about trash because we don't want to be reminded about it.

216

I lived through the trash strikes that hit New York City, and the outcry over it was far more thunderous than anything I have heard about the failure to prosecute a modern-day lynching in Florida, the mounting threats to birth control rights, even the decimation of our education system. You want to rile up the masses? Don't come for their trash.

I believe it's because we must remove ourselves from the consequence making dirt.

In Spain, where such services are not so simply achieved, they have a different relationship to the unpleasant and its detritus. They learn to live with it. Not in it, with it.

No way around the fact that when Manuela was born she was trashed, put out for someone else to handle. She was the natural result of basic biological forces acting on a young woman, a child herself not fully developed enough to support the complexities a child presented. But it didn't end with Manuela's disposal.

Manuela was the first child born among the children of people whose lives had been wrecked by the Spanish Revolution of 1938. Her grandfather, her mother's father, was on the losing side in the fight, a Loyalist forced to flee his country forever, who had to abandon a house more filled with his children than any three modern American families. Manuela's mother was the youngest of too many. Experience teaches that the youngest of any family is often lost.

Lost people want most to be found. She was found in the most normal way, through attraction to the opposite sex. She was fifteen.

The events surrounding Manuela's birth, the step-by-step story, is lost to this hatred of self-made dirt. No one will talk about it honestly, and what has emerged has been as shadowy as any old family story. We can only conjecture, though with strong evidence, about those early days.

From what has been gathered from those too reluctant to discuss the divisive story of Manuela's birth, my wife was born in her grandparent's home. She suspects otherwise. She believes, and has hints enough, to think she was born at the home of her Aunt Mary, Tia Maria, married and ready to give birth to what would become the first *legitimate* grandchild.

One piece of strong evidence is that someone had to carry the infant girl to the church, *La Iglesia de Macarena*, the most famous in all of Spain, to relinquish her care to women dedicated to the impossibility of motherhood. In whispers and dragged-forth admissions, we believe that someone to be the pregnant Maria.

Manuela will turn sixty years old on the day we meet my shadow person. Her mother and her eldest aunt are still alive, though thousands of miles apart. There is so little love between those sisters that even three thousand miles is not enough separation. They have mutually hated the other for a decade more than half a century.

As said, the orphanage system required support of the family. The child had to be fed, and at a breast, and if there was a flowing breast in the family, it would have been a sin not to provide it for even a bastard offspring.

Usually the wet nurse is the child's mother. But that girl was fifteen, already a ruined sensibility, vain as any teenager and unprepared to shoulder her responsibilities as any lost child. Maria, older, the oldest, understood the rôle and duty, and took upon herself her sister's responsibility.

She took out her sister's trash, so to speak, and kept at it.

What kindness, other than feeding Manuela, keeping the tenuous connection to her Spanish family secure, did this Tia Maria bestow on my wife? Whatever ny may have been, all probably have been lost to this history of animosity that keeps not just her mother and aunt from speaking, but all of Manuela's relatives.

On her first trip to Spain in 1995, Manuela was given a photograph of an eight year old girl standing at the side a woman in a wedding dress. She was told the picture was of Manuela at her youngest aunt's wedding.

She brought it home, put it away, and it lay forgotten until I began asking her the questions making up in this biography. The wedding had been in 1960. Manuela was born in 1952. She was not adopted until her thirteenth birthday, when the American sailor and his wife brought her to the USA. She did not learn of her Spanish family until she was sixteen. All she can remember is being dressed up and taken by an adult lady to a party.

Doing the math, there was only one explanation for her being at that wedding: someone had come to get her. A looming, giant shadow: it could only have been her Tia Maria.

CHAPTER NINE: ALL IN THE MARCH OF TIME

Real history: Manuela's mother, Francesca Serrano, was born into a family of some privilege on March 15, 1933 at her mother's home in Seville, Spain. That following November, a period called by the Spaniards *The Black Two Years* eventually secured a bloody rebellion. The privileged and somewhat well-to-do, including the Serranos, leaned toward democratic and liberal values, while the anarchic and fascist rebels, led by the military, sought authoritarian rule and a socialist state.

In June, 1936, the political and social fabric of Spain ripped. By 1939, cities lay in ruins, families were split forever, the defeated supporters had been forced into exile. Among those fleeing the country was Manuela's maternal grandfather, who left behind a sizeable Catholic family used to condescension, prosperity and inherited respect. A result of his forced abandonment was a sudden poverty foisted on those least capable of managing it. This alone would have been enough to close the mouths of the family.

At the same time Germany was beginning its military wreck of already fragile Monarchist countries. Spain, led by

General Francisco Franco, allied itself with Germany in a calculated effort to prevent the machinery of war from running again in her streets. It was a shrewd but costly move.

Although declared politically neutral, Spain still became an occupied country. Manuela's grandmother, also called Manuela, had mouths to feed, children to house and clothe. She did what many impoverished matrons did during hard times, she sought a benefactor. Hers was a German officer.

The last child born to Manuela Serrano was a blonde, blue-eyed girl of fair complexion and sunny nature. Perhaps because of those blue eyes and pale complexion, her mother named her Aurora. She was born July 4, 1942.

Essentially a bastard. *(My use of essentially will mean something, eventually.)*

Since I have known Manuela we have celebrated her birth as March 31, 1952. Unfortunately this is a clouded issue, since her mother claims she was born on March 22nd, and *two years earlier*. Furthering this cloudiness is a Spanish baptism record that claims her birth as March 22, 1950. These two years decide many critical issues, and she has been wrestling with the effects since.

If Manuela was born in 1952, she'd be approaching her 60th birthday, and she would be little more than a year older than I. If she was born in 1950, she'd be eligible for Social Security, and I'd be married to an even older woman.

To nearly everyone I have known in my life, a birth date has never been an issue. It is a predicate to identity: it establishes when we can drive, what year of school we should be in, the age of consent, the age to drink, to vote, to be eligible for cheap rates at the movies.

Our country openly practices Ageism, and finds no wrong in its discriminations. We live in a community that would have denied my cousin ownership of the house next door because she was seven months shy of fifty-five.

Be all that as it may, there are a few more identifiable dates. In 1960, when Aurora was sixteen, she married a man ten years her senior, Juan Estepa. The following year they bore a child, Mariangela.

Manuela remembers being at the wedding of her aunt and Juan Estepa, and she has a photograph to prove it. She says she was eight, a time post which sets her birth in 1952.

She believes the woman who collected her from the orphanage, who brought her a new dress and allowed her to eat from the desserts, was her eldest aunt, Maria. She remembers being among other children almost her age. Mary's eldest child, the second of the generation of grandchildren to Manuela Serrano, is less than one year junior to my wife.

Returned to the orphanage, no date emerged as a milestone for her until she had well passed her twelfth birthday. She had been several times taken abroad to be married off before then, twice running away and twice brought back to the church. One afternoon she was summoned to get prepared, which meant washed, for a group inspection. Although she thought it was for another marriage lineup among other orphans, the lineup was for house-help to an American woman and her Naval husband.

She remembers the American being tall, although he was not, and grand in his uniform. She also recalls both of them as kind, pleasant, smiling. They had occupied a seaside villa and wanted to help with the orphans, as Americans will, by offering employment. They liked her toughness, no-nonsense attitude. Fact is, she did not lower her eyes as had the other children learned, and the American Navy man saw that as worth having around.

She explains that her actions had been what they were because Ed Rukchinski had the bluest eyes, a thing as rare as sapphires in the dirt of Spain.

She scrubbed their floors, helped with their meals, and ate with them. And not scraps, but 'real' food, the kind Americans ate. She had scrubbed acres of tile for the church weekly, so cleaning those of a small villa was nothing to her.

As enchanted as Manuela was with Ed and his wife Doris, they were as taken with her. Who knows what late-night discussions took place between the husband and his wife on their American pillows, but the upshot of those discussions were that Manuela was to stay with them, to come to America.

She became, at last, adopted. Even more, she became a *de facto* American.

It was a different time than now, completely. Although documents may have been signed with the Church, none have ever come forward. Bringing orphans from abroad without stipulation or government investigation was done for American soldiers on a fairly regular basis since the invasion of Normandy.

Manuela was walked up the gangplank to the steamship Michelangelo hand in hand with Ed and Doris, to be installed in her very first private room. There were no nuns, no floors to be scrubbed, no rags to be washed and put on, no prayers, no punishments. There was only the ocean she'd looked upon, wide as the sky overhead.

About a year after we met, Manuela and I took her eldest daughter to New York City for a meeting with a modeling agency in the southernmost World Trade Center. For whatever reason, we drove to Staten Island and took the ferry. Having parked, we climbed to the observation deck to enjoy the sun, salt air and seawater.

She saw the Statue of Liberty first, although said nothing, leaving her eagle-eyed daughter the passionate exclamation of discovery. I, the English prof, declaimed the Emma Lazarus poem about the huddled masses, the tired and poor, without connecting those words to the woman beside me.

"Hello, Lady. We meet again,' is all she said.

CHAPTER TEN: JUST A PHOTOGRAPH OF SOMEONE
  THAT SHE KNEW

Displayed on a shelf on our back patio is a sketch done by an old employee of a crew I had managed. The sun has bleached the cartoon's colors, though black remains. Names of several have also faded, even the name of the young girl among them for whom I had a fleeting attraction.

Inside the house there's a shrine of sorts made up of my family pictures, photos which Manuela had removed from an album, framed, and put out for display. The oldest photo shows my grandfather, two children at his side and my mother at three on his shoulder. Taken in 1926, it is now cracked and washed out by time and expo-sure, expected in a photo taken 86 years ago,

Manuela has no comparable family shrine, as she possesses only one photo taken prior to 1968.

In that photograph she stands beside her Aunt Aurora, a woman seven years her senior. Aurora is in her wedding dress, a modest white shift with orange blossoms, a ribbon in her hair. Manuela wears sandals strapped to her feet, too large, clumsy for walking. She does not remember problems arising from wearing shoes, only that to have shoes on at all was remarkable.

She wore them for a day. They, with the dress, were returned to the nuns' care after she was returned herself to the orphanage.

The picture stands framed in a dining room hutch, and though it is the solitary relic of her childhood, the photograph does not sit alone. There are many dozens of small photos in miniature frames around it. In fact, the black and white snapshot of her and the Aunt stand pretty much taller than all the rest. The others are smaller because of what they are, why they were taken, and why she has them.

It is a custom in America, mostly to make money from American's fetish for freezing time, especially if it is a time about one's self, of taking individual school pictures marking each year. Everyone has, somewhere, a strangely colored image of him-or herself with hair badly combed, some teeth missing, wearing a sweater or blouse considered at the time the height of fashion but which now looks like a castoff from a clown show.

Surrounding Manuela's sole image are pictures of children she cared for as an adult babysitter, the children of friends she had before she met me, and those of children met through me.

There's Matt in his Midget League football jersey, head buzzed into a crew cut, happy as any unawares dork. He's probably a father to his own eight-year old, worried about getting fired, a rising hairline, or whether he can afford a vacation.

There's young Donna, her missing teeth giving her face the look of a yard with a missing front gate. Skinny and boney at nine, hair the usual rat's nest, freckles spritzed across the bridge of her nose. She's now sadly and badly schizophrenic, unmanageable, susceptible to drugs and known to have lived off her body.

Michael, whereabouts unknown. His face resembles an already aged man, the glare in his eyes saying trouble courts him continually.

There is Chrissie as a fat-faced baby, a kind of Goddaughter to me had there been a christening and had I been there to hand her over to some nameless priest. She, with her parents, has disappeared.

There are several of people we can't remember, snaps of infants hours old. We've discussed them, but all details are gone from our memories. The photos remain because how does one throw out a baby's picture?

There is the most painful of all, Dakota, a beautiful boy with a ringlet of curls about his head. He is two in the picture, a forever two, born into trouble to a woman herself born into trouble. She was a magnet for the angry, the venial, the broken and lame. When last we heard of her, she and her then-boyfriend had been arrested for murder. Dakota was crushed to death by a size twelve boot.

There are five of people we still know well. In each is a smiling, beaming, glowing bride certain of a wonderful future. Of the five, only one remains married. She's an ecstatic mother of two, and curiously as in love with her handsome husband as she was the day they first faced each other's naked bodies.

The other four are divorced. One of those remarried twice more in the ensuing ten years since the first wedding picture. Not married now, she carries a child whose conception precipitated the last divorce.

An inordinate number of pictures show little girls in some dance recital costume, numb flat smiles on the lips, a toe turned awkwardly out, an arm raised overhead. Each posed by some adult wanting her resembling an adult, hair teased into a bouffant, beribboned, cheeks rouged, nails painted and lips already smeared. None today dance in a pattern today. When caught at dancing, they flail arms, swing legs, hump butts and bosoms in uncomfortably close mimic of the sexually engaged.

There are her three grandchildren, the most beautiful, most intelligent, most loved. Sure enough, there is our eldest grandchild, Sky. Her first school photo will haunt the end of her days. The mile-wide grin is genuine, her simplicity and earnestness equally so, but there's something about the two missing teeth either side of the fronts that makes her resemble far too much a child who could chew corn on the cob through a picket fence.

Sixty seven photos, a third of people unknown to me, a quarter of kids who passed through her life like episodes of a favorite tv show never picked up for reruns.

We've moved three times since we met, and every time the pictures get moved with us. They are among the first things she puts into a rightful place. My daughters think of them as Mom's clutter. They cannot know.

I know. Each is a touchstone of emotional attachment. How many passed through that orphanage, here and then gone? I asked her if she ever made friends with any of the girls. She said they wouldn't make friends, because their times together would necessarily be brief. It was not in the interest of the Church to encourage the bonds that create family out of strangers.

I am decidedly childless; never wanted children of my own. However, Manuela brought into my late life *(I was forty)* two beautiful women whom I have since that first meeting called my daughters. They have brought me daughters as well, and they are as much my family as my own blood sisters.

I learned from Manuela that attachments, even if temporary and bound to suffer the failures of memory, are as necessary as dinner. More importantly she has taught me that the accumulation of photos is a result of caring more about those in the photographs than caring about how the photographed care about us.

I've heard that one of the best measures of a person becomes evident in the number of people who attend one's funeral. That may reveal something about us to others.   ·

I think what is revealed about ourselves to ourselves must be in the number of photographs we keep of those we had once attached ourselves, however briefly. Manuela measures up mightily, I think.

CHAPTER ELEVEN: MAN *(AND WOMAN)* LIVES NOT BY
    BREAD ALONE

During the three months prior to this writing Manuela and I dined with a number of couples at a variety of venues, and the several occasions gave us something to discuss: food.

There are few things more enjoyed than well-prepared or well-grown foodstuffs. I began my writing career as a food writer, and though I wasn't good at it then it did start me down the road toward figuring out how to transform this most fleet art into works of permanence. I had become fascinated with cookery and cooking almost three decades before the launch of the Food Channel, and now feel an almost god-fatherly attitude to those discovering what I had already visited.

Although I have never taken food for granted, as an American I had taken the *availability* of food for granted. Divorced in the late fifties when I was a child and jobs were as scarce as they are today, my mother somehow had skirted poverty. Her reduced income translated first into a reduction of food, but we never got to the point where I missed a meal. My sisters and I may have split a can of watered down tomato soup for dinner, but there was soup.

As already pointed out, Manuela was not so fortunate. In the same year that my sister Anne and I wished to boycott watery Campbell's Soup, eight-year old Manuela had to take up discarded cigarette butts filched from the sidewalks and gutters of Seville. Smoking was her way of dulling the pains of hunger.

She avidly smokes to this day. I do not smoke, and desire very much that she quit. However, I have never asked her to quit, nor will I. To do so would have the same psychological punch as would asking a belligerent drunk's daughter to down a shot of whiskey. There are hurts in her memory that will never heal.

My food memory is strong. I can recall my first slice of pizza, the first steamed shrimp, my first barbecued sparerib, my first oyster, first glass of wine, first bite of caviar taken on a wooden paddle.

Manuela does not catalog her firsts. For her, she only remembers her first meal.

Let me clarify and qualify what I mean by *a meal*. A meal requires food taken in ritual. Necessity driven by hunger disqualifies intake from ritual. Under that circumstance, to eat is all. A meal includes proper dress, sufficient tableware, an organized and categorized number of courses, and food preparation in which something, if not everything, had been cooked. A meal requires pomp and circumstance, even if it's so meager as everyone sitting down at a table. It also requires company not so starved that food gets shoved into the gullet without consideration for what it took to bring it to one's mouth.

A tuna sandwich snatched at the desk as one pours over a spreadsheet is not a meal.

The first meal that Manuela recalls was served in New York City on the evening after she passed the Statue of Liberty for the first time. Her adoptive parents, Ed Ruk and his wife Doris, after lodging her with them at the Essex Hotel, had her washed, combed and dressed for dinner. It was a proper thing to do. Her first American meal was to celebrate her new, changed status. She accompanied them to a restaurant called *The Steak House*.

She had no idea what a restaurant was for, no idea what a steak was, no idea even what the letters spelled in the name. Neither Ruk spoke much Spanish, and Manuela understood little English. She does not know what was discussed with the suited man who came to their table, nor what the names were for the foods they ordered for themselves that differed from what they commanded for her. What she remembers is her plate.

It was made of white china with a thin gold rim, upon which were dumped a mountain of mashed potatoes, a hill of steamed green peas and a island of beef that she now understands was a sirloin steak cooked medium rare.

Several years ago we had, with some friends, a conversation about *comfort foods*, the foods to which one turns in order to feel again as small and safe and untroubled as the eight-year old we had once been. I spoke about peanut butter and jelly on white bread. Others described their grandmother's rice pudding. For another, meatloaf. Et cetera. When asked, Manuela said, 'Steak, mashed potatoes and peas.' End of sentence.

Further investigation — prompted by her odd choice — revealed that comfort food was not made so because of flavor or abundance, but rather each became so *because* of the ceremony surrounding it. My peanut butter and jelly on white bread was never served to me at home. I ate it at my grandmother's. Same for my friend's rice pudding and meatloaf.

There was specialness about all of those 'comfort meals.' Once we'd uncovered the nature of ceremony binding our favorites, we easily saw that Manuela's seemingly extravagant choice fit well alongside ours.

We realized that specialness cannot derive from necessity. The specialness of a meal takes flavor and color from Event. By repeating those events we honor them, even though we cannot include the original ceremony. I can no longer eat white bread. Had I a PB&J, the meal would have to include a glass of milk, a sofa under my butt, and an old black and white show on the television.

Once a month Manuela and I dress up for a steak dinner. We never go eat them in diners. To ask a "Hon" waitress to fetch our steaks lacks the care and solemn ceremony that a suited waiter brings *(or should bring)* to the event.

Recently we dined with a particular friend, a former student, that I hadn't seen for fifteen years. Asked what we preferred as cuisine, we tempered our response by the notion she was a vegetarian. *'Indian or Thai would do fine.'*

We dined on neither. We met her and her boyfriend at a restaurant near Hollywood that presented us a 'designer session' about which I may write more in the next column. What made this meal relevant to this topic is the relationship each of us had to the nature of the dinner's specialness. For me it was a chance to see a wonderful, bright former student again. For Manuela, a greeting of yet another far-too-pretty woman who beamed at me. *(I am always forgiven them.)* For my student-friend, it seemed an opportunity to move beyond our teacher-student bond.

The boyfriend, however, stripped eating down to the necessary. He removed all ceremony. A self-styled food savant, he proselytized for 'better' eating. Food did not need be pleasurable, only scientifically fitted to the body. We learned much about the chemistries of food mating to our own. We did not witness much joy in what he ate.

I couldn't ignore the disconnect between the boy who engaged food as an enemy to be managed and the woman beside me who always sees food, any food, as a precious gift never to be dismissed nor dishonored. As we got warned off processed sugars, coffee, chocolates, processed milk and low-fat diets, I detected her polite writhing in her seat.

It is insulting to reduce him to type, but he's a kind we encounter regularly, and always un-comfortably. Though right about reactive agents in what we consumed, he completely missed the ceremonial.

Manuela later noted that he'd shown up in a t-shirt.

CHAPTER TWELVE: SO GLAD TO BE HERE. MAY I GO NOW?

The day after all great transitions in our lives takes place — such as when our first child arrives, when we move into a real house, when we learn we have cancer — the realization that life shall be this from now on will seep into our most exalted feelings.

Prior to coming aboard a ship with the Americans, the most enormous object Manuela had entered was the House of God, Seville's Cathedral de la Macarena. When at last *word* had become reality and she realized her new fate, the adopting Ed and Doris Ruk led her up a gangplank onto the Michelangelo, a cruise ship. Had she ever sneaked up onto the crenellation surrounding La Macarena's steeple, she still would not have looked down from a higher place than the main deck of that ship.

She was thirteen, aware that something prodigious was happening. But she was as completely unprepared for its enormity as any earthbound person would be when climbing into the belly of an alien space ship. For all intents and purposes, as the Michelangelo pulled from the dock, Manuela was leaving the actual world.

I have flown to Europe several times, and it's boring. Stepping onto a plane, strapping into my seat, unbuckling and walking out to a foreign land never felt *transitional*. I could have as easily been hypnotized into believing I'd flown. Nothing changed. Manuela stared into a vast rolling sea for almost a week, had time to dwell in change, to adjust her rhythms and flavors to that of foreigners, especially her new American parents. She had space in which to change herself.

Not knowing the full historic meaning of Lady Liberty for the preceding millions who'd been greeted by her lamp did little to reduce the emotional first glimpse of her green robes, lifted arm and the promise of an education with the book tucked against her breast.

She had been taught reading, but only the Bible. She longed to read more, to understand more, instinctively knowing that it would be have to be in a foreign tongue the New World would be grasped.

After slipping past the Lady, after walking the mesmerizing streets of midtown Manhattan and taken by taxi to the Essex, and after her steak, potatoes and peas dinner, she was put to bed in her own room, asked to dream. What dream could have possibly exceeded the one she had already been walking in? Manuela did not sleep.

Another cab, another train, a subway ride and one more walk from the Philadelphia El stop, Manuela and her new family at last reached the solid set of steps rising to the door of a North Philly row home.

Philadelphia is, and has long been, a city of neighborhoods, most of them demarcated by the uniformity of a foreign language still spoken among those within a half dozen city blocks. Irish brogue and bombast bordered rapid Puerto Rican

Spanish and rough Polish. Chinatown, which meant just about anyone Asian, was nearer to Center City, set apart from the many European enclaves by knots and clots of African Americans.

Many people have written about the immigrant experience in America, and nearly all have expressed the difficulty each has in keeping one foot in the Old World while another seeks purchase in the New.

Mostly wrestle with the survival or disappearance of tradition, the strongest of which was only loving and marrying within the structures of race or social identity. My mother strongly expressed — once I made an aside that Asian women often seemed pretty — her sincere hope that I would marry within my race. She meant not just White, but Anglican. Germans were tolerated, but Italians, Poles, Orientals, Puerto Ricans — even the Irish — were a no-no.

Struggling with the pulls of national heritage was not Manuela's experience though. She felt herself a glass marble among diamonds, a bug among butterflies, bread among cakes. She was not transferred from the familiar flavors, sounds and ways of one home to an enclave of similar villagers; she was a Spaniard dropped among Poles, a Spanish-speaker without more than a handful of usable words.

She discovered, on the other side of the door, that she had not been brought to a house filled with happy and loved children, to be happy and loved herself. Ed, retiring from the Navy, had selected Manuela because of her training at caring for others, for house cleaning and doing laundry. Doris, it turned out, was very sick. Furthermore his Austrian father, an Old Country butcher, owned the row home.

From Manuela's perspective, and not an ill-informed one, she remained the servant she had been in Spain. They gave her chores: to clean, mop, make beds, and especially assist the dying Doris, who had cancer. She didn't know she'd been formally adopted by the Ruks, didn't suppose any permanence to her condition, thinking herself socially-acquired and therefore expendable, returnable.

Her only surprise was that, after Doris Ruk perished less than a month after their return to Philadelphia, she was not made to go back to the Church.

However high her exalted emotions from having been brought to America came to be, they diminished before numerous small terrors of finding a way through her days among so much strangeness.

The Ruks spoke Polish inside the house, and English to her and those they encountered from the outside. The three were kind, and there was a growing fondness in the Grandfather for her — he allowed only her in the kitchen when he cooked, and they often danced in the living room to his collection of 40s and 50s popular music — but they were not otherwise affectionate. None of Ed's married sisters paid her any attention when they visited the father.

There were improvements. The butcher's pantry held a market's-worth of food, and their table was daily piled with what she might have eaten in a year. Every discovery became two-sided: each a delight, for all had that American lavishness not to be found elsewhere, but each was also frightening. How does one take freely what had to be daily begged from people reluctant to give it? Where does one go when none anywhere use a familiar word? Even her name was replaced. They called her Packy.

She was put into Catholic School. The nuns there were no different — except in language and weight — than those back in Seville.

Most of us have at one time or another rediscovered a primary-school chair similar to ones we had once occupied. For giggles, we took a seat, and giggles were had. Imagine being told at fourteen to take that seat daily.

To learn English and sufficient skills to be an American, the high-school aged Manuela was sent to join third-graders, eight year-olds who laughed at her age and odd manners. They mocked her parroted English and roared at her pronunciations.

They ridiculed her for just being among them. Tolerance came easy; she was at least fed.

CHAPTER THIRTEEN: HELLO, MOTHER. PLEASURE TO MEET YOU

There are many conversations in which we have a part that we may only assume. Who has never wanted to turn a curious ear on what transpired between our wife and her sister, or our boyfriend and his buds?

Writing fiction, and the entire art of play-, screen- and script-writing depend on assumed dialogues. The success of most word-related arts turn on the selected words used to voice past action. There's a huge difference between the Godfather saying "Make him an offer he can't refuse" and "I been thinking, how about youse ask him do this for me."

Probably the most used word in America (after 'me') is probably *What?* What you say? What he say? What they say? What they been sayin'? Of the six great questions, answering *What* comes second only to *Who* in satisfying our curiosity.

Not long after Manuela settled into her room and the duties at the Ruk house, a conversation that most likely spread over several evenings took place which would alter her future in inalterable, troubling and sometimes painful ways.

Doris Ruk, Edward's childless wife, had returned to America to wait out her few remaining days. She perished in fewer than thirty days from the landing of the cruise ship *Michelangelo*. The altering conversation may have begun with her still living, but it certainly concluded because of her death.

It regarded the care and raising of Manuela.

The grandfather, Ed Ruk senior, had emigrated with a wife and three daughters from Austria before the First World War,

234

siring his only son shortly after the first days of the next decade. He had training as a butcher, an education that not only secured for him permanent and substantial occupation, but which had its impact on that family's core values. They always ate, and they ate well.

The Ruks were not given to passionate indulgence, carrying with them the Teutonic preference for restrained emotions toward everything except ingestion. Fancy way to say they may not have liked each other, but they loved their meats, cheeses and beer.

Furthermore, the Ruks' mother was from Poland, bringing with her a cultural habit of treating a son like a prince. Between her expectations of Edward to be primary in the family and his father's requirement that the younger work hard and keep his mouth shut, Edward junior developed into a sober but straightforward caregiver, a reliable if not giving man.

It is, perhaps, why he sought an assistant to care for his home: sick Doris could, and would, no longer handle her responsibilities. But when she was gone, both men felt that there was something wrong with keeping the young woman who seemed to adore both of them without giving her something in return that amounted to more than a room, food, and an education.

Though for Manuela these three extravag-ances were plenty, they did not satisfy the White Knight in either man. And they talked about it.

Unknown to Manuela, Ed Ruk the Naval man was well aware of the nature of Manuela's wardship in the Catholic Church. As said, children in Spain are often given *over*, not given *up*, for adoption. This is a distinction with a real difference.

The role of the Church in her case was more similar to the American foster-care system. A child is placed in care, provided for with the best intentions, but not necessarily severed from her family. And as said, there was an expectation that a family surrendering a child to the Church remained responsible to the best of its ability.

As in the American system, anyone wishing to adopt a fostered child needs permission from the birth parent or family in order for it to move forward. A child removed to a foreign power, as Manuela was to America, had to be adopted.

Her release from her Spanish family had been negotiated *with* Ed Ruk, not simply *for* him. He knew her birth-family, and specifically Manuela's birth mother.

After Doris Ruk had passed, there had to have been a conversation between father and son about the mother of the child. Somewhere, at some time, one of the two had to decide that an offer must be made to her mother to come to America and provide the maternal care they both understood was not only the woman's right, but her duty and responsibility.

Manuela supposes, but cannot know since she did not hear any of the conversations, that the stress bringing about this rearrangement came from her new grandfather, Ed Ruk senior. He had had a wife, raised a family, understood the unique linkages between a mother and her children.

In the timeline of her first year in America, Manuela arrived on April 1st. By May Doris had died. Sometime in July Ed junior vanished from the house, "on business." It left Manuela, at last out of the third grade, alone with the man who danced with her in the living room and allowed her to help making the bounties of food that still went to the table.

For Manuela it was a magic time. To help her learn English, the old butcher took her to films, the first and grandest of which was to see Elizabeth Taylor in *Cleopatra*. It was her first glimpse into a world of even more grandeur than New York City, dinner at the Essex, and a never-emptied larder.

It was also a time of singers, mostly men but some women who belted out loudly wonderfully melodic songs. Dean Martin, Frank Sinatra, Mario Lanza, the Platters, Doris Day

236

and Rosemary Clooney. It is from them, and the stars of Hollywood, that slowly the language into which she had been immersed let loose its secrets. She began to understand, as she sang about silhouettes on the shade, what a silhouette was, what a shade was.

She delighted that summer to learn from song and picture what had been repeatedly thrust at her exasperated self for three months of third grade. The patient butcher was strong contrast to the impatient nuns and antagonizing third-graders that hooted when she said a word improperly.

Manuela and Ed senior made sausages, latkes, cruscikis, went out for something called spaghetti, and dined on pizza. Although her grandfather had never been a church-goer he took her to the local Catholic Church, dressing her in a finery she had rarely seen let alone owned. A time of joy and wonder.

Although she remained aware of herself as a servant, she did not find it as hard and as oppressive as she once did.

In August, word came that Ed Ruk junior was back. When the door opened, though, it was not Ed who stepped through first, but a beautiful and very grand woman.

"Manuela, meet your mother," he said.

CHAPTER FOURTEEN: A THUMB IN THE EYE

She was the most beautiful woman I had ever seen, she said, recalling the regal woman who presided over the wedding that Manuela was allowed to attend when she was eight. *Regal, aristocratic, like a queen.*

The young girl she had then been did not know the woman as her mother, can't now recall the woman even addressing her let alone claiming her as family during that wedding. Manuela only carries the image of a Queen among commoners: elegant in dress, fine in jewels, royal in manners. With knowledge she has since gained, Manuela thinks that her mother had a right, of sorts, to parade herself about as though she, and not her young sister, was the bride. Or, at the very least, as mother of the bride.

She paid for it.

At twenty-seven, unmarried, disdainful of her own history — especially of the poverty into which her father's abandonment had thrust them — Francesca Iglesia had somehow acquired funds enough to not just pay for her sister's wedding, but shame them for having not done what it takes to host such a wedding. Her generosity was seen as an arrogant gesture of pride by those who hated her. And there were more enemies made that day.

It is easy to see the 'gift' as from a woman obsessed with the salvation that money promises. Though not to young Manuela, all who were adult enough understood how Francesca had made that money, and each felt shame belonged solely to her. It's an old story, those standing on moral superiority to keep their heads high facing a woman willing to shed those morals in order to keep her nose well above the shit stinks of poverty.

If one considers that Francesca's young biology had already stripped her of any right to superior morality, does the manner she took to earn enough for a wedding feast come as a surprise?

This dichotomy of social standings is, however, the most simplistic views of that day's events. There are other factors at play.

Also at that wedding was a man whose part in Manuela's story had been kept hidden from all except himself and the woman with whom he'd had a child: Manuela's father. Francesca had refused to give up his name, refuses still, although it has come to light since. He was the groom, the man marrying Francesca's younger sister.

Anyone could write bodice-ripping romances with these elements.

It must be understood that Francesca had been the one to reject marriage when she was discovered pregnant. It must also be understood that in Spain, even after the devastations of civil and global wars, occupation and forced poverty, all that most impoverished people had was the sense of dignity derived from upholding tradition and the codes of morality that defined it.

Primary among those traditions was the pre-eminence of the eldest woman, the inviolate authority of that dominant female over the household, especially one in which the primary male figure has abandoned. Unmentioned so far is the matriarch, Francesca's mother, Manuela's grandmother — for whom Manuela was so named. *(For clarity's sake, this Manuela shall be henceforth referred to as 'Señora Iglesia.')*

Matriarchs of her generation negotiated all marriages, often trumping love matches in favor of those which could benefit the family. She had already negotiated for her sons and daughters, not least of which was Mary's, the woman who carried Manuela to the Church. Francesca not only trumped her mother's right to a negotiation by getting pregnant, she demolished her authority by refusing to name, let alone marry, the father. For that crime alone, plunging her thumb into the eye of her mother's right to authority, Francesca had to be hated by her siblings: they could not do the same.

They couldn't because they hadn't the thing to trade for success that Francesca had: the radiant, regal, sexual beauty she paraded at her sister's wedding.

All of these intrigues, however, passed over the head of the young orphan delighted by the festivities. One must wonder, though, at the audacity of the man marrying the virginal younger sister of a woman who not only rejected him, but who bore and abandoned his child. And then to have that child in attendance at the wedding? Too much.

In some societies *primogeniture*, the order of birth, guarantees certain rights and opportunities to the first born of a generation. Matriarchy is passed down to the first female child, but is not passed on until the former family head dies.

Manuela was first born of her generation, and by remaining laws of the country she is the next Matriarch. I shall return to this later, but consider that, if her identity and her position were known at that wedding, how uneasily must have sat the family. Manuela's very existence was a furthered crime of Francesca's, and to have her brought to that wedding was a serious affront.

We do not know whose idea it was to take the child from the church, dress her up in borrowed finery *(a clean dress)* and parade her for the family to see, but it fits the narrative juices perfectly to assess her attendance as put into motion by the one who paid for the party.

At the end of the wedding day, the ignorant bride whisked off by an understandably shame-faced groom, Manuela was taken back to the orphanage, stripped of her clean dress and returned to her status as a bastard child. She had not been fussed over at the wedding, had been completely ignored by all of her family and intentionally distanced from her mother and father, but she had no feelings of ill use. She felt, still feels, honored to have been so singled out for delight.

Manuela would not see her mother again until that late afternoon when the door to her grandfather's row home opened on the beautiful woman Ed Ruk had negotiated into marriage.

Again, there are many conversations of which we share a part but about which we have no knowledge or proof. What Ed Ruk said to Señora Iglesia has never been revealed, though such a conversation must be assumed. Ruk knew the politics of family, and as the world then still honored the rights of family over the individual, he would have approached them in the same manner as negotiating the adoption.

Permission would have been eagerly given, so long as he promised to remove their stain, Francesca's person, to as far away a place as America. As for the effects on the welfare of Manuela, one doubts Señora Iglesia would have cared a fig.

One can even imagine, as Ed left the Matriarch's house, that she and several of her daughters danced at the good news.

What Francesca would have required, though, was not her mother's permission, but the prize she'd always fingered — *money.*

CHAPTER FIFTEEN: ONE THING ON HER MIND

Seven billion humans now live on the Earth, half women. A third or more of that half are mothers, which simple math sets at one billion. Statistically, there are a half billion mothers of daughters which, according to psychologists, means there are a lot of psychotic relationships in the world.

Literature, especially the Western oeuvre, is loaded with mother-daughter novels. Perhaps the earliest most famous of them is *Pride and Prejudice* by Jane Austen. Oh, sure, there's that Mr. Darcy love story, but she's really illuminating a mother seeking enthusiastically and continually how to unload her girls on any man *(so long as he is of good fortune.)*

A famous poet once said to me that women historically have two concerns: 1) which man they will allow to come close, knowing he may either protect or kill her; and 2) how to keep her daughters from making the same mistake. *(She also wrote, 'Men fear most a woman laughing at him, women fear most a man killing her.' I love that poet.)*

People who say *There are two kinds of people...* are at best simplistic generalizers, but my poet friend had a point. With two mothers, two wives, two daughters, three granddaughters, four sisters and four female cousins that I consider immediate family, as well as having one of those plethora things of satellite women whom I adore, I am awe-struck by how some generalizations seem always true. These seem to be among them.

My female associates have invested so much energy, attention, anger, assumption, pain and flight regarding their selection of suitable male company, far more than any man spends in a like occupation. It seems the primary fuss.

Being left-leaning, liberally-minded adults, Manuela and I let our daughters plunge in where angels knew better. They made a pretty fair number of bad choices before they wised up. It's the Modern American Way. We figure experience the best teacher.

Other mother's recoil at the notion that a young woman should be allowed a choice. Several couples we know were paired up by their parents. Surprisingly, they have stable, sane marriages less susceptible to mismanagement. We do not support arranged marriages, and I shudder to imagine who my mother would have arranged for me. (She married three times. Although Dad was cool, she never married well.)

Made in Spain, a most medieval European country that was slow to evolve, Manuela's mother Francesca considered arranging marriages not only a duty, but a legally protected right.

Makes some sense; a marriage contract is a legal document designed to ensure a transfer of property and protect the ownership in perpetuity. A wiser mind should be responsible for its quality, one would think. There are no wise young women (or men.)

I cannot for certain say what ideas occupied Francesca Iglesia Ruk's mind when she entered that Philadelphia row-home and met her marriageable only daughter, but history and tradition have their indications, especially since Francesca was a hidebound traditionalist. One must remember that Francesca was a woman stripped of the benefits of tradition when her father had to flee Spain after the revolution, a consequence that almost wholly formed her obsession with recovering them. Her history says she desired Manuela married, and tradition asked it be done quickly.

I feel I may safely generalize about Western women raising costume as a supremely essential element of their occupation

242

with mate selection. I can't imagine any argument to this, not with three whole industries dedicated to its continuance: *cosmetics, clothing manufacture and retail,* and *fashion.*

A beautiful woman richly attired, well attended and free to make her own choices has become the pinnacle of achievement, or so claims Mass Media. I often joke that I can't wait to see *The Housewives of Fishtown* on television *(or name any inner city poor neighborhood famous for bad teeth, bad manners and wretched fashion sense.)* What makes the joke successful is that no one really wants to emulate them.

I think that Manuela's first impression of Francesca was planned exactly, that through the door had to come the most beautiful woman she had ever seen. The impression was secured by costume.

If any woman of the past half century stands as an emblematic achievement of the aforementioned, she must be Elizabeth Taylor. With her numerous marriages, enormous diamonds and violet eyes *(not to mention those boobs)* she became the It Woman for several generations.

It is a coincidence of no easily dismissed importance that a few weeks prior to meeting 'the most beautiful woman I have ever seen,' Manuela also had her cinematic experience: *Cleopatra,* starring Guess Who. Manuela, a late developer because of impoverished conditions and bad food, thought herself no beauty — her confession, and certainly not my assessment — she couldn't help but elevate her mother even farther into the stars. As is common among the plain among the exalted beauties, she let herself be captivated, even captured by the woman.

As she had no concept of Motherhood, Manuela had no expectation of kindness, tenderness, tutelage nor even generosity from Francesca, who assuredly gave none.

As for Francesca, what had she accepted in accepting marriage that included the burden of motherhood already rejected? Certainly he secured for her American wealth. Some fantasies never die. Middle- to lower-class Europeans still see

America as the Promised Land of Plenty. Her obsession to rise out of poverty and loss overrode any daily reminders of shame, or at least misfortune, in Manuela's presence, which earlier had prevented suitable marriage. She'd learned to swallow her pride years before.

Within weeks of her entering the Ruk household, Edward moved his wife and daughter to a new house. It meant Manuela had to leave her protector, the grandfather, to assume full-time duties as housekeeper, cook, laundress and personal maid to a very demanding woman who considered herself now entitled royalty.

To improve service, Francesca used a little glass bell to summon her daughter whenever assistance was required. Manuela was often belled to retrieve and clean discarded clothing, to prepare tidbits when hunger arose, to draw the bath and wash the woman's back.

Francesca understood that all things must eventually be paid for *(unless they could be secured as gifts, or stolen.)* As payment to her servant daughter, she set about arranging a marriage for the child. Francesca, out of history and tradition, considered Manuela of marriageable age. The girl was, after all, fifteen, the same age her aunt had been when formally engaged.

She used that first year in Ed's new house to investigate, and plan. It caused many a row with Ed Ruk, yet she was firmly set on providing a suitable marriage. For Francesca that meant a union with a wealthy Spanish family.

She settled on a very curious choice.

CHAPTER SIXTEEN: THE PLANS THEY MADE PUT AN
     END TO YOU

In 1488, the fifth daughter of a rather well-known couple was secured by contract as a wife. It was an arrangement made by her parents and one very tough guy. The parents: Spain's Ferdinand and Isabella, of Columbus fame. The tough guy?

King of England Henry VII, father of Henry the Eighth. The woman? Catherine of Aragon, made even more famous as being the wife set aside in favor of a younger woman, Ann Boleyn.

What does not come forward in the above facts is that the woman bound by marriage was not a woman at all, but a child of three. Although it was not for another twelve years, when she turned fifteen, did she meet whom she was to marry, her fate was sealed.

In England, excepting royalty, arranged marriages fell out of favor, or rather out of necessity, because of reforms in economic and property laws. Not so in Spain. Arrangements continued among the gentry and wealthy until quite recently.

As in all countries with marriage contracts, marriages bound people's wealth together. Few Spaniards owned property, and fewer had money. Those with property needed money to maintain them, so arranging for a propitious match — a time consuming but energetic endeavor — was handed over, for the most part, to women. *(To be sure, the final approval remained with the male head of household. He rarely objected once his wife had vetted the bride-prospect.)*

Tradition. For some it's the Holy Touchstone for what can be considered proper. It was for Manuela's mother, Francesca.

What had been lost with the fall of the family, besides money, was a link to its history, which had been aristocratic. One thing is for certain, the *habit* of elegant and privileged living, which the Iglesias had enjoyed, continued well past their moment of loss. This is not uncommon, easily understood, and forgivable. In Charles Dicken's *Great Expectations*, and nearly all of William Faulkner's novels about Mississippi, the retention of dignity rests almost wholly on the maintenance of tradition as embodied in the practices of a former, though vanished, social rank.

However, when desire to retrieve the trappings of status turns to obsession, things can get dicey.

There is hardly a heterosexual woman, and even some homosexual ones, for whom the largest engagement ring and most expensive wedding dress have not become the ultimate objects of bourgeois desire. Even the proposal itself must be so uniquely accomplished as to be worthy of YouTube.

For Francesca Ruk, *nee* Iglesia of Seville, one family's wealth and position had taken hold of her imagination since young. It directed her actions, which ultimately ruined her opportunities. When fifteen, already beautiful in complexion and regal in bearing, much of what Francesca worked hard to exhibit was what she understood as the most marriageable traits. She had chosen the Estepas, owners of vast wine country property, as the only ones worthy of her charms.

In southwestern Spain, Andalucia, the land is sunwashed for most of the year. It is excellent land for growing citrus, sunflowers and especially wine grapes. The most famous Spanish wine is sherry, corrupted by the English from the town-name of *Jerez*, the center of sherry making. To be a sherry maker was tantamount to being royalty, especially since it usually meant being rich. The Estepas were.

The eldest son, Juan, was only a few years older than Francesca, tolerably handsome, and probably dashing in his uniform. Men of his age served, and serve, a mandatory stint in the armed forces.

Wealth does not exempt.

It's too easy to suppose that Francesca had been seduced by the uniform. In a much more likely scenario, Juan was seduced by her. Among the young, beauty trumps every common sense.

Unfortunately for all, Francesca's efforts to unite Iglesia to Estepa were nowhere in the plans of the *matrón* of the Estepa clan. She quashed it.

Perhaps as a result of dashed plans, Francesca's kept her pregnancy secret until it had to be known, and kept the person who got her with child anonymous. *(Francesca still refuses discussion, even 60 years later.)*

What normally would have occurred for Manuela's father should have been his ascendency to *patron* of the winery, but his naval career had seduced him to a greater degree than anyone expected. He desired no parts of the family business.

He very well may have made this clear to Francesca, which may be why she refused, and refuses, to acknowledge his part in her situation. We cannot know, because nobody is talking.

Juan went off to a career at sea. Losing the Estepa attachment altered the course of Francesca's fortunes, but had little effect on her obsession with them.

Juan had a younger brother, Francisco, but he was much younger and not even close to marriageable age. The winery and the wealth, however, eventually fell to him.

Suitable marriage, propitious union, access regained to the trappings of wealth and, more importantly, to the status of Spain's aristocracy were all stripped from Francesca's reach with her daughter's illegitimate birth. These losses insured cauterizing herself forever from attachment to her daughter.

Then the wheel of good fortune rolled her way.

What she saw upon stepping through the door to Ed Ruk's row home was not a long lost daughter, but a found opportunity. She could no longer marry into the reality of her obsession, but she could use Manuela to achieve her reconnection.

In the year following her arrival in America, Francesca set about making plans to achieve her goals. She hoarded every penny that came her way, sold whatever jewelry Ed Ruk bestowed upon her, did what she could. She had found Manuela a job in the city, or rather hounded the nuns until they found her one, the paycheck of which was dutifully turned over to her mother.

To return to Spain a rich American woman required the right appearances. Anything not reflecting her stature as a well-to-do woman was disdained by her. Whatever she did had to cost and show money.

Who can imagine what arose when her plans to return to Spain were discovered by Ed Ruk? Regardless how hot their arguments, Francesca was unmoved. The one concession Ruk secured from her, which he secured without her, was that Manuela be allowed to continue her schooling. He paid for matriculation into the American School in Rota, Spain, in advance of their leaving.

He paid for clothing, for their posh cabins aboard yet another steamship, for appropriate decorations. With bitterness and regret, he saw them off.

For the entire sea voyage Francesca had only one destination. She intended to arrange a marriage for Manuela. The husband? Francisco Estepa, brother to Manuela's father, her blood-uncle.

CHAPTER SEVENTEEN: WHAT IS A MOTHER TO DO?

Any privilege enjoyed by another which should be yours — but isn't — causes unfettered irritation. For a person who thinks every privilege should be hers, to witness any bestowed on another becomes pain. And when the rival is your sixteen year-old daughter, that pain brims with bitterness.

Ed Ruk bought two First Class passages on the *Rafael*, sistership to the cruise liner that brought Manuela and himself to America. For the young girl it was the same ship, though this trip did not include him, nor did it travel to America. The *Rafael* headed to Europe.

Francesca Ruk, determined to marry Manuela into the Estepa family, had lost several of the arguments, but she won the war. Her marriage to Ed Ruk had lasted a bit more than a year, time enough for her to wrangle from her American husband what she needed to return to Spain as a respectable matrón: money, some status, a few jewels.

The First Class passage had been Ruk's idea of proper traveling. What he could not expect was how thoroughly Francesca would assume the role of a First Class passenger, absorbing its benefits and rituals with scarce thought to how little she deserved them. But the entitled rarely consider their worthiness of privileges.

Beauty entitled Francesca to attention; the First Class booking entitled her to a seat at the Captain's table. Together, they entitled her to dance with an attractive gentleman, should one be bold enough to ask.

None of these had Manuela expected, nor did she understand them as part of her ticket. She felt as she had always, that she was adjunct to other's plans, a recipient of whatever may fall from the table of her betters. She still had an orphan's mind, one attuned to the crumbs of generosity, not to gifts of opportunity.

So when a gangly, quiet though handsome man in dinner attire whispered to her, *Would you like to dance?* Manuela did not know what her response ought to be. Flustered, she turned to Francesca, but got from her the expected face of one sucking a lemon. Francesca's cold turning away expressed her displeasure, but not enough to suggest that Manuela refuse the man.

One can only imagine the effect such a moment must have on a street beggar dressed up, for her, elegantly, though in truth she was only dressed sufficiently enough not to embarrass her mother at the Captain's table. The orchestra, small, still swelled the room with sound, playing waltzes for a swirl of gaily-frocked patrons. She rested carefully, appropriately, in the man's arms as they danced, the room itself dancing.

Cynically I would say her night was a film by Disney, but we all get nights like that at some point, so cynicism sounds like cheap humor. And we have all been sixteen, all at some point attended by the kind of looks that reach into the darkest part of our self doubt to sweep it away, even if just for one memorable night.

Perhaps, and again cynically, there is a script for such events that all must follow: walks along the upper deck under stars, whispered nothings that seemed at the time unforgettable and so enlarging to one's place in the Universe, the acute awareness of accidental bumps and intentional touches that thrill with electric pleasure.

His name was Calvin, an American from Iowa, someone a Hollywood script writer would choose for a once-in-a-lifetime role. Nice man, gentle man, innocent man, and in love.

Again, what follows can only be suspected, but there is probable cause. As suddenly as his sea-borne attentions had begun, they ended. Francesca spewed rebukes sharp enough, but they were of the kind and number that Manuela had had to suffer over the past year, so persuading her to give up his attentions was unlikely.

Harsh words, however, could dissuade a man from Iowa. One can only imagine, and must, what she spewed at Calvin in her broken English!

All that Manuela now recalls is two-parted: the specialness of a ship-board romance, however brief, and the consequent venomous treatment of her mother for having happiness co-opted.

Stand at the stern of any ship to watch the loveliness of a churned sea streaming behind like lace on a wedding train, and the one thing you will be sure to notice is how quickly it dissipates to nothing. Thus do shipboard romances. Faint memories of something pleasant only remain.

Memories are good to keep when the cold hard edges of reality cut into your days. On Spanish soil again, Manuela had to sleep beside her mother on a small bed in an apartment barely sizeable to host a couple with a child. But this apartment closed her in with not just her mother but her grandmother, her aunt Aurora, her aunt's husband, and two small children.

Manuela was used to being squeezed into a space, making herself insignificant among so many who considered themselves each more important than the next. Children impose themselves with noise, grandmothers with position, Aurora with motherhood, Juan as head of household. But no one expected herself more forward than Francesca. The crowded quarters often erupted.

Manuela had an escape for a time, by attending the American School in Rota, near Cadiz, a naval base for US servicemen.

She had also found comfort in something she thought lost when she left the house of Ed Ruk's father: unexpected gentle kindliness from Juan. With few words, little conversation but through many gestures, Juan Estepa lifted Manuela from the shadows by offering his arm as the family walked to market, by slipping her an extra bit of sweet cake or melon after an evening meal, by a nudge of his finger into her ribs and then a directed pointing at some folly of her family.

I was in love with Juan. Of course I didn't know who he was. He was just a man to me, and I adored him. As for her mother, she sensed calculation and plans.

There is no grander holiday in the Spanish calendar than Easter. The celebrated resurrection of Christ brings in *La Feria*, a two-week long party celebrated in a carnival of tents on ground that for fifty weeks was barren dirt.

All of Spain prepares for *La Feria*, and no Spanish city does it better than Seville. They have the grandest religious parades wending among the streets of Old City, bullfights in the old *corrida*, and gorgeous circuits of sparkling enameled carriages pulled along by matched teams of the finest Arabian horses at the largest of *La Ferias*. I've lost my ability to breathe amid the superior beauty of Spanish women who wear hand-stitched gowns that imitate, and improve, the multi-layered frilled dresses of the Flamenco-dancing gypsies. Nothing like it in the United States.

These are weeks to flirt, dance, strut, laugh and drink, to preen and parade. They also provide for families to make matches and secure promises.

Men and women prepare hard for *La Feria*, but none labored that year for success as did Francesca. She'd worked her plan for months.

And, oh, what she had in mind.

CHAPTER EIGHTEEN: LOVE AND MARRIAGE, BOTH DIVERTING

A delight of a childlike mind is to disrupt. Who has not watched a drop of water run down a window pane and not reached to divert its natural course? Or played in a running stream without piling rocks to alter the flow?

That simple act can develop into a form of Art. *Trompe l'oeil,* or the art of realistic presentation, works on that principal, as does *Surrealism,* which startles the mind entrenched in expectation by providing the unex-pected at just the right time. Disruption's the power and draw behind LSD. Nothing during its reign over us follows a predictable course.

For some, diversion from natural courses be-comes a fetish, even an obsession. More than one boss, just because he can, has disrupted entire households with a whimsical firing. I knew a teacher who always had students change seats during class, to see what the new mix might provide.

Vague in public persona, shadowy in practice, for fifty years a branch of our military has dedicated itself to providing dislocation and disruption to the human mind, popularly called Psy-Ops. Its personnel develop methods of shattering the brain's lifelong training, to lay a finger against the stream of consciousness of prisoners, to see what pops out.

One word during the Sixties was often prevalent in intellectual discussions: detested *manipulation*. Though it has lost coinage, the idea was wholly repugnant, and the Arts, especially the movies and its allegiance to *cinema verité*, sought triumph over that evil. *(But Madison Avenue was better funded, and the Arts soon succumbed. 'Taxi Driver' lost out to 'Star Wars' as the father of modern films.)*

In our age of 'Do Whatever,' hardly anyone imagines spending a minute, an hour or day, let alone months, plotting, scheming and planning to manipulate events *(except deranged serial killers and trial lawyers)*. The wicked webs we may weave in our practices to deceive are mostly haphazard affairs, accidental constructions that the unfortunate wander in to get stuck.

Our modern sense of manipulation and evil machination is the stuff of conspiracy theorists, though the dedicated methods of people such as Carl Rove and Dick Cheney still scare the commoners. Do we really know any Lady Macbeths these days?

Francesca Ruk, when the shadow of the American Navy man fell onto her path, saw the plan for resurrecting her status, fortune and opportunities in his arrival. It's not that his money or position secured her opportun-ities, but rather they secured what she really wanted: life back in Spain connected to a well-connected family. The one that rejected her earlier.

As Christmas does to Americans, Easter sends Spaniards into flurries of preparation months in advance. Religion and piety are, of course, central to the Easter holiday, but as Christmas is to Americans, for Spaniards it is time to party and parade.

The Spaniards split their parties in two: a mournful, back-whipping homage to the sufferings of Christ, and a more light-hearted applause for his resurrection. The former has its exhibit in medieval showcasing of wooden images of Sorrow, mainly that of Christ, but more those of the Eternal Mother, Mary. She's the Hero of Easter. Statues of Joseph, on the other hand, being a common man, often have a look of surprised bewilderment.

The latter part of the holiday celebrating His Resurrection are full of color, gaiety, parades of finery, exhibitions of plenty and a jovial friendliness towards one's fellow man. Everybody is welcome to every party, no matter whose tent. *(Although some, it must be said, charged admission.)*

In the preparations of *la Feria,* dresses occupy the minds and fingers of nearly all adult women, and they are considered adult as soon as they manifest the distinctions of womanhood, such as menstruation. Thimbles are donned, needles threaded, cloths cut and stitches laid with care. Imagine the dressmaking scene in Cinderella taken to a national female obsession.

With her head bent over hers and Manuela's dress, Francesca considered only what the finest dress would bring: a proposal of marriage for Manuela.

Such a thing is not haphazard in Spain, nor is it left to chance encounters. Especially not to love. Whoever had seduced whom that had brought about her daughter, Francesca learned from dealing with Juan that securing attachment to a good family required more than a handsome face, intense expressions of emotion, or a fine figure. It required negotiation.

Presenting herself as then a rich American wife, revealing herself only in jewels and coiffures — though doing so was rapidly wearing out both her welcome and the lining of her pocketbook — Francesca set herself and her cause before the only person who could decide whether such a match with the Estepas occurred. It was not before the intended husband; it was with his mother.

To the *matrón* of the Estepas, Francheska made suggestions that the fabled wealth of the Americas, which even four hundred years latter still meant streets paved with gold and silver, could be had if only the inheriting son, Francisco, could be made to propose marriage.

Francisco himself had been applied to, perhaps with similar enticements. The object herself, Manuela, was dark and small, and already developing about her was an air of intelligence often unwelcome in wives. A marriage required more inducement. But he saw the benefits in such a match. A wife in Spain, after all, was seen then pretty much the way a dependable car is seen in America.

The only one not consulted, and for good reason, was the eldest brother, Juan. He did not need consulting; his attachment to the Spanish Navy and refusal of the Estepa fields had already transferred inheritance to his younger brother. And, as Francesca well knew, any knowledge of what she proposed would have to prompt him to stop it.

I have met Juan Estepa. He is a man of very few words, and each word he does employ has only *use* as its purpose. There's nothing idle about him in any way. Whether he knew himself as the father of Francesca's child before that *La Feria* is not known, but it is certain he learned of it in time.

Manuela sat in her beautiful gypsy gown aware of several things. Her mother had pressed on her the need to marry, as money had gotten tight and soon they would have nothing to live on. Her family was making louder and more direct noises that their — or rather Francesca's — occupation of the house had become intolerable. And that Juan's brother, the brother to the man Manuela adored and felt herself in love, made attentions that could solve all problems.

So, when he leaned toward her, took her hand and asked what most teenage American girls fantasize having happen to them, she felt impelled to say yes.

Juan, learning of what had just occurred, had his face drain of all color. But not for long: soon white became red, and calm impossible.

CHAPTER NINETEEN: MARRIAGE: ALL HOPES DASHED

Throughout this investigation I've noted distinct differences between the life of my wife, Manuela, and myself. The house I grew up in house was filled with flying ashtrays, hurled butter dishes and verbal daggers that sliced before you knew they were thrown. Not so in my wife's.

A supporting example: Recently her eldest daughter, asked how she managed to stay so calm in situations fraught with anger, said 'My parents divorced when I was sixteen, but I never once heard them argue. Still haven't.'

Not that there weren't arguments between my wife and her then husband. And there have been a couple between us in the past twenty years that were worth watching, and were watched. Unless both people have training enough to hold the tongue until privacy could be had, which I hadn't, differences of opinions will be evident to anyone unlucky enough to be within earshot. *(Happily I never got the habit of tossing objects.)*

I've asked Manuela about this, and she said it is common among Spaniard family members to fight in private and out of sight. Therefore it was a matter of course that, when Francesca's ultimate goal became evident from Francisco Estepa announcing to his and her families the engagement, Juan Estepa only blanched white and then flooded his face with red.

He held his tongue even as people congratulated and tipped wine into glasses for toasts and good cheer. Whatever had been spilled into his glass remained untouched.

Manuela had told me, *I had no idea what was wrong, but I could see Juan was not happy about something. Then he stood up, said something I didn't hear but my mother did, and they went outside. I thought they went for a walk.*

Some walk. So often in this tale have there been intercourses that had no witnesses, but which affected Manuela so deeply. The long walk, and it was long, that Juan and Francesca had taken was one of these *discussions* that many wish had been recorded.

But it wasn't, and has never been revealed.

Francisco eventually bundled up his aging mother and took her home, with nothing said between him and his elder brother, or between Juan and the deciding *matrón*, his mother.

I had zero interest in marrying him. I knew I'd be furniture, a baby maker and locked up in the house while he had a life. But my mother had been insistent that this was our rescue. When you grow up in Spain, even an orphan, there is a strong sense of duty to the family.

It was not a glad and fluttering heart that Manuela had taken to bed, but she had had some contentment knowing her mother was at least happy about the engagement. Until she saw the woman's face when Francesca had returned from the walk.

Snatch meat from a starving dog and teeth will be bared. Beat the dog when you do, and you will make for it enemies of everyone who comes near. To suggest Francesca salivated with the prospect of her fortunes being tied at last, even by proxy, to the Estepas, only to have the meat snatched away by the very man who had turned his back on her, was enough to turn Francesca into a rabid, snarling dog.

That's who, or what, crawled into the bed that Manuela already lay in. The hairs on her own neck rose. She kept her eyes wide, and ears attuned in the dark.

But that evening the anger and violence in the woman's nature was only sensed. She refused to talk to her daughter. It was not until the following morning did Manuela learn anything, and she learned it from her father.

Juan said to her, *You will not be marrying Francisco.* Manuela asked him *Why not?* She was merely curious, not preparing an argument against his pronouncement. He sensed that, and took his usual long hesitation before speaking. *You can do better.*

Blocked from revealing Manuela's parentage by her own machinations, and surely aware that to do so would put both of their asses out on the street, Francesca could only fume and focus her anger on the one who was innocent of any wrongdoing. But Manuela's existence had always been

Francesca bane, and to whom could she direct her bile? Juan? Again, out on ass. My wife bore the brunt.

There's what Manuela knew, what she and others were allowed to know, and there's what no one was ever to discover.

It must be remembered that Juan was not only Manuela's father, but her uncle. He had married Francesca's youngest sister almost a decade before.

Aurora, the younger sister who eventually married him, was an unusual Spaniard, especially among that dark family. She had an occupying-Army German father, was born out of wedlock into a dirt-poor family, and was Francesca's half-sister, all reasons enough to be denied association with the Estepas.

There are many reasons open for speculation on why Juan had rejected Francesca, but his family connections must not be numbered among them.

Juan had already rejected his birthright, had made his own fortune and career with the Spanish Navy, and had no need for or desire to seek permission to marry. He felt he alone owned that decision.

Aurora was a child born to wear daisies in her fair and golden hair. Tall, with a pale complexion, with sweet lips over which even sweeter words flowed, at sixteen she had arrested Juan's heart. Even fifty years since they married, it is easy to see that Juan is still in love with his little *rubia,* his blonde angel.

What rifts and pains any admissions between him and his belovéd would cause. He could not bring Manuela's parentage to light, yet he had to remain firm in his opposition without revealing any reason. That Manuela could do better was sufficient for her; for Francesca, the unmentionable truth was enough. Whatever he said to others is lost to the wind and time.

Unlikely he confessed to his mother and his mother-in-law, Manuela's grandmother, or to his brother. As senior male, therefore head of household, he answered to no one.

There's an old saw, that in Ham and Eggs the chicken is involved, but the pig is committed. In this, the *matronas*, Francesca and his brother were involved, but Manuela was the one committed. Yet, and still, they kept from her the magnificent truth that continued to direct her life and determine her livelihood.

It was Francesca, however, who felt the injury. She had nothing left but to return to the United States, to her rich American Naval husband, to a city she did not know and to a people she would never understand.

She still had her beauty, though now she would employ it with outraged determination. She had in Ed Ruk a resource for money. She thought she could trade on her femininity for support, but didn't realize America not only was *not* Spain, but was changing.

She determined to make her way the best ways she knew: by scheming, conniving and lying. Manuela's ordeal was not yet over.

CHAPTER TWENTY: A FINAL, FUTILE ATTEMPT

On their return, there was no full moon splashing on the dark sea waters, no dances with a gentleman to swell her emotions, no parades in fine dresses. Not this time. They still had First Class rooms, again dined at the Captain's table, and Manuela had eight days of timelessness aboard a cruise ship, but Francesca would allow nothing of frivolity for her daughter.

What she had were orders, commands, instructions and restrictions. Manuela — aware that in some fashion she had destroyed her mother's hopes and caused their retreat to America — remained a dutiful although quietly resentful daughter.

They were met by, but did not return to Ed Ruk. He had bought for them a separate house. In their remove to Spain, the senior Ruk, Ed's father and Manuela's last ally, had succumbed to old age. The two women were friendless, tied to one another by unsupported notions of family, and equally resentful.

The summer of 1970, Manuela looked forward to a final year at school. Old enough to work, she took a job at a corner store not far from home. Dutifully, she turned over every paycheck. Once school started, Manuela found a better job working at a plastics maker.

They say the wisest course of action to take when things turn ugly overhead is to keep the head down, the mouth shut. Instinctively, or perhaps through her years of training as an orphan, Manuela did that.

What Manuela would not realize for half a year was that a third lived with them. A monster in a Seagrams Seven bottle had become resident.

Did Francesca get ever violent when you two argued? I asked with some naivety.

I have the scars to prove it.

Francesca took a Slovakian lover, Miraslav, a married man with children, himself ten years her junior. Soon he was more a member of the household than Manuela. He was not unkind, but an accumulation of assistances with her English, help with her chores, offers to make her coffee, little attentions paid to the girl seeped into Francesca's heart and made there a bitter pool of suspicion. *(She would eventually, continuously and stupidly accuse Manuela with Miraslav fathering her first-born daughter.)*

She set about finding and arranging another marriage for the seventeen year-old, and she found a candidate a few houses down the block.

Many Philadelphia neighborhoods were enclaves of immigrants still coming from Europe with their cuisines and customs as intact as the small icons of saints they'd carefully wrapped for travel. An elder son living with his aging mother was not unusual, not always a sign of some emotional failure about women, but that living condition did often clot displays of amorous affection.

John was a hulking, gloomy older man hardly given to mirth; tall, clumsy and silent, but single. Manuela was instructed by Francesca to show him kindness and attention, to attract him. Reluctantly but dutifully she did.

But with eyes open.

At the end of that summer Francesca arranged for him to take his mother, Manuela and herself to Atlantic City for a week of its Boardwalk rides, dining in restaurants, lying on the sandy beaches. The closed-box of a man opened up some, even making jokes in a flirtatious manner, but Manuela saw John for what he had to be.

The roles for men and women, for sons and mothers, for husbands and wives, were not only more rigid in 1970 than now, they were concreted by centuries of European behavior, and Manuela, like millions of other American girls, saw in matrimony a caging, a jailing, made of steel bars.

But there was little she could do except resent it. Her mother, and John's mother, pressed, and pressed hard. Francesca took Manuela aside in October, fretting that not enough was being done, and instructed Manuela to sleep with him.

She did, and as all first times are, especially with inept and clumsy, emotionally-distant men, it was awful. And it never improved

All an orphan wants was a safe, warm place to sleep, good food, and some better clothes than cast off rags. Marriage offered that, then. She had no expectation of adoration, of love, of laughs and good times, so submitting to John's lumbering attention was not as difficult as one would expect.

By December they were engaged.

But she was becoming an American girl at the foothills of a sexual and feminist revolution. Even though she still lived close to poverty with her mother, by having a job she had a safe place to sleep, food within reach, and clothes without holes. The need to marry had been removed, and slowly the resentment she felt for so many years being at the mercy of other's begrudged generosity rose to the surface of her consciousness. But she had no mother to talk to about these rising feelings, for the mother had ears of stone.

What Manuela did have was a good job, and with it came a friend, Barbara, an older woman who lived alone in a house not far from where Manuela lived.

There was no joy being under a large and emotionless man, and she wanted out. Francesca had become continuously scalding with her accusations of seducing Miraslav. Her bell-ringing had become drunken demands as incessant as her insults.

All this she explained to Barbara, who took it upon herself to cash Manuela's paychecks, so that the girl could keep some of the money she was earning.

A side note about that job. In 1971, minimum was $1.10 an hour; Manuela was making more that $4.00. That summer I made almost $2.00, and plenty grateful for it, for it was enough to set aside money for a year of college. At her wage, she was doing better than most fathers.

Winter weeks drag, and under the press of an engagement, a drunken mother, schoolwork and a job, as well as the on-again-off-again love affair between her mother and Miraslav, the weeks crawled. Manuela had been a child of sun-loaded streets, and the winter of '71 was harsh, dreary, wet and cold.

In a dark February, all collided. For the first time in her life, though, Manuela had no need of support, no need of handouts or kindnesses from people positioning themselves as her superiors. She was young in America, working, capable of befriending. In a word, she'd become independent.

So when next her whiskeyed mother struck her with a many-ringed hand, she flew. First to her American father, Ed Ruk, asking that he take her in. She was not used to asking for anything, having spent a lifetime being told to be grateful for anything that came.

He turned her away, calling inappropriate an adult man living with a young girl. She saw herself as his daughter, and he did not. All she could feel, walking out of his house and back to Francesca's, was betrayed. Having dared to hope, she felt the first true pain of her life.

What to do? What to do? She asked this repeatedly with each step back to the only home she'd ever had. The only thing Manuela understood was, she had to do something.

CHAPTER TWENTY-ONE: STEPPING TOWARD THE BETTER UNKNOWNS

Earlier that day she knocked on the blank-faced door of her fiance's row home. John answered and invited her in, perhaps disturbed by the solemnity of Manuela's expression. Sometimes the air carries our messages before us, no need for words, but she had words. When she finished, John asked for the ring back. She was only too glad to oblige: he had let it slip, in asking for it back, that it had been one he'd purchased for another girl who'd refused his proposal.

No woman tolerates second place, even in the heart of a man she has no desire to keep. She dropped it into his palm, and truly the air then carried all that needed to be said, and she left without adding anything further.

What words she weighed, and she weighed each one of them, were for her mother. She already knew the fury they would engender, but she underestimated the woman's ability to land a backhand while drunk. The blow was quick, direct, furious, and it left a scar on Manuela's temple. It stunned, but it did not deter her from what she intended.

Francheska wore a large ring, encrusted with sharp-edged stones. We may forget that a woman's ring is made of faceted rocks and chiseled metals, but once it slams against our face, we remember quickly. But what Manuela remembered was her objective: *to be shed of them all.*

Her friend from work, Barbara, had listened to what Manuela protested against. The woman lived alone, not far from the house where the ladies from Spain resided, and her house had plenty of space that went unused. She had many times offered it to the girl, but Manuela always had shaken her head at the suggestion.

But as the rivulet of blood seeped from her wound and down past her ear, the wisdom of refusing Barbara's offer dissipated like pipe smoke in a high wind.

Manuela made no reply, even though Francesca's battering by insult continued well past the blow. She turned her back on her mother, who struck at her again, to climb the steps to her room. Manuela tossed what she had within reach into a pair of plastic garbage bags while her mother stood at the doorway still screaming. Finally the girl put on her coat, wrapped her head in a scarf, grabbed a bag, each too heavy for her but she managed them despite their bulk, and she dragged them and herself downstairs.

Then out through the door, down the steps and onto the snow-choked sidewalk. Francesca did not follow her into the cold, but she sent insults and prognostications for a sad, wretched life for her daughter at Manuela's disappearing back.

Anger may propel a body, but only determination will keep the body moving. With each step the anger gave way to a sense of freedom, and independence. Such emotions are always companioned with fear, but it's an elated fear, trembling that differs from what one feels under the repeated blows of nuns, priests, strangers and family.

She had no plan except to continue. Barbara took her in with no questions, fed her, listened, and gave that most benevolent gift of strangers, protection from one's past.

She had school to complete, work to attend, and decisions to make. The shelter and comfort Barbara offered allowed her to manage all of it, and she graduated with excellent grades.

An undercurrent theme running among these many pages now confessed has been that my wife and I may share many similarities, but there are very distinct differences. They arise mostly in how dissimilar our cultural environments were.

For many who separate from family, it usually has to be done with explosions, like seeds flung out of a pod to find way. The best defense against the injuries, either real or blown in our imaginations, is to allow no further offense. Leaving our homes in angry shouts, we treated our former attachments as thoroughly severed. We cut off all communication, allow no further exchanges, consider dead those who have been so unkind when kindness was all that was wanted.

I quit my family for more than three years, returning with great reluctance only through the manipulation and actions of my sisters when my mother fell ill. There was no sense of familial duty, no emotional glue that bound us together. Mine was a cold family, undemonstrative. I was not ready, but reconnected anyway.

Manuela managed her future differently than I had. She kept the avenues open. Francesca, her lover Miraslav, and her estranged adopted father Ed attended her graduation.

To Francesca's credit she maintained her relationship with her young Slovak lover for many years, until he decided that his future was best with his wife and children. Manuela met a young, tall, fair haired and blue-eyed man. Being an enlisted airman, he took her to California, leaving Francesca in Philadelphia.

Ed Ruk died young. Surprisingly, he'd left everything to Manuela, including the house he'd bought for his new family. Manuela and Louis drove back east to reclaim the property, only to discover that Ed's sisters, who'd never accepted his foreign gypsies as family, had cleared everything from the property: furniture, pictures, papers and savings.

Tennessee Williams penned a line that ripples daily through the American culture, and many who repeat it miss the irony of what he wrote. At the end of "A Streetcar Named

Desire" Blanche, stripped of everything except what fantasies she could manage, mentally unbalanced, is helped off stage by literal men in white coats. Their hands on her elbows, Blanche pauses and looks back at what lay strewn, figuratively, behind her. She says, 'I have always depended upon the kindness of strangers.'

What the play underscores is that she could always rely on the unkindness of her kind, her family.

Perhaps, as Williams reports, that is always the way of all things. We are sent into grim, gray futures because of our ejection by those who claim to, or at least should, love us.

All that I have reported about Manuela's life lies far, far in past years. So much has passed, so greatly have things changed, that she feels herself almost a wholly different woman from the one who'd dragged garbage bags through the snow.

Not one author would ever suppose that we completely shed ourselves of the tracks we've made, whether its crumbs dropped as we go, churned wakes behind our transports, or footsteps in the snow. All of them are always clear and distinct in our minds. When we think on them they emerge in present tense like magic ink-marks asked to reveal themselves.

We cannot help but look back over what has brought us to our present days, but wisdom, especially that kind that derives from those experiences, let us know we do not have to keep walking in them.

EPILOGUE: LAST WORDS ABOUT A LIFE

Perhaps a twenty-year antipathy toward my mother-in-law has affected my portrait of Francesca. Truth be told, I have only spoken to her three times since I met my wife. That, I suppose, makes her the best of mother-in-laws. The last time we graced each other with our bare, naked dislike, we only said *Hello* to the other.

My wife, Manuela, has been the light of my life, and people who know us have identified us as among those legendary couples who remain holding hands well into old age. We joke, publicly jibe the other, ridicule each other's shortcomings as other couples do, but there is never malice or any desire to lessen our statures before others. We do not want our statures lowered in each other's eyes, and work had to keep respect for the other ahead of our affection. It's been a breathless twenty plus years together, and we can't imagine anything less than twice twenty more.

My common dislike for her mother probably has been furthered by how much I truly like my wife. I've written this part of her story, and it is only the first third of her life thus far, at the urging of many friends and co-workers who have found her and her stories as remarkable as I have found them.

I could share more stories, but they would only underscore or — worse — repeat what has already been established. I've already repeated some things too often in this telling, but then it was an organic presentation developed each week of publication, which is unlike most works.

Usually an author works everything out in a complete first draft, re-envisions what he's done, re-addresses things that never worked, tosses out things too well loved, removes the natural quirks of his writing style *(such as my Pennsylvanian Dutch tendency to invert clauses)* and then submits it for publication.

And then an editor hacks it apart, makes it really work, then gets authorial approval for her hack job, then publishes.

I skipped a few steps. So sue me.

So I am faced with a haunting that follows many authors: a work that has a billion things I would fix is already in the public realm. Oh well.

I can only hope that the essences of Manuela's story have served to entertain, and possibly instructed.

TRANSLATIONS

There are several words and phrases used in this book whose context may not reveal the meaning. Regardless of this, here follows usable translations, preceded by the page number upon which the phrases are first found:

3 — Nada digno de perdurar que no pueden sobrevivir a su pérdida. *Nothing worth keeping that cannot survive its loss.*

Note: This line and other references to this poem, *Primer Aniversario*, come from the published edition of Lorca, Federico García, *Antología Poéetica*. Barcelona, España: Ediciones Orbis, S.A., 1982, pg 33, print edition.

Primero Anivesario	First Anniversary
La niña va por mi frente.	The girl crowns my brow.
¡Oh, qué antiguo sentimiento!	Oh, this agéd heartnote!
¿De qué me sirve, pregunto,	Might you serve me, I beg,
la tinta, el papel y el verso?	ink, paper, and verse?
Carne tuya me parece,	I feel your flesh,
rojo lirio, junco fresco.	your red lily, my cooled reed.
Morena de la luna llena.	Gypsy dark, moon rounded.
¿Qué quieres de mi deseo?	Shall you adore my desire?

The translation is by Charles W. Bechtel.

sí, quatro	*yes, four*
imposible	*impossible*

4 — Mi pequeño mono. *My little monkey*
Patio del las Naranjas. *Courtyard of the Oranges*

5 — *see poem translation above*

6 — la rubia *the blonde*

9 — Guardia Civil *Spain's national police, once considered corrupt and given to excessive force and violence.*
Alemana *Of German nationality, culture or tribal citizenship*
Raus! *German for "Get a move on, now!"*

10 — caricoles *edible snails, often served in brown butter and garlic sauce*

11 — Salé *The command to go, leave.*

12 — Rubia, y eso explica lo que creo *A blonde, which pretty much explains what I think.*

14 — Cabron *Literally, a man who tolerates or cannot stop his wife sleeping with another man. One of the worst insults to a Spanish male*

Tia Maria *Aunt Mary*

16 — Claro *Understood, as in "That's clear and I agree with you."*

20 — Dolorosa of the Passion *Reflecting the complete sadness of the Crucifixion, usually in the expression on images of Christ's mother, Mary.*

La Macarena *The carved stature of Mary paraded out of the main cathedral in Spain beginning Maundy Thursday and ending Good Friday. Considered the most revered of objects by the Catholic people of Seville.*

21 — Nazarenos *Hooded parade personnel walking to honor the icons of Christianity: Christ, Mary and Joseph. They precede the floats, carrying lit candelabra whose melted wax covers and affixes the hand to a long staff.*

22 — Gitanos   *Gypsies, a people distrusted and disliked in Spain as in most European countries. Being disenfranchised from society, they form their own, and often have little respect for the laws of those who would not include them.*

25 — La Cocina de Tres Gitanas   *The kitchen of three gypsy women.*

27 — Señorita, chica   *The former a term of respect for a young woman, the latter a more common, familiar term akin to the English "girl."*

Donde está mi hermana   *Where is my sister?*

28 — Las Ramblas   *A fashionable walkway of Barcellona, popular with tourists who like vendor shopping, and a haven for buskers and pickpockets*

La Feria   *The carnival fair that lasts for two weeks in Seville. Families and businesses set up tent locals in a reserved field, and invite as many who will come to celebrate. A well-attended La feria concession is considered a great honor.*

29 — bucaro   *a clay water jug in which water cools from the condensation process*

Meriende   *a late afternoon meal following siesta, the national celebration of the nap.*

32 — Puerta del la Macarena   *The celebrated arch that leads to the Basilica of the Macarena , which houses the image of the Virgen de la Esperanza Macarena.*

33 — Para los pobres y los pequeños bebés   *For the poor children and little babies*

Jetzt (German)   *Now!*

34 — Nehmen Sie sie nach oben, und zu tun, was du willst
(German)   *Take them upstairs, and do what you will.*

38 — si, si, mucho mas, mucho mucho mas   *Yes, yes, [thank you] very much. Thank you very, very much.*

40 — ¡Cállate!   *Shut up!*
Bien, lo haré. *Well, I will.*

46 — Parque de Maria Luisa   *The Sevillano park grounds built and owned by la Reina Maria Luisa, Spains last prominent female monarch.*

47 — abuela   *Grandmother*

48 — Guadalquivir   *Seville's, and Spain's, main waterway. A river.*

49 — Tor del Oro   *Tower of Gold, built in medieval times to guard the merchant ships on the Guadalquivir, used to accept the incoming gold from the New World brought by Spanish plunderers.*

64 — el toro y el matador *bull and bullfighter*

bandarillos   *short barbed spears thrust into the shoulders of bulls to lower the head and to prevent sideways movements of the horns. Figuratively an annoyance.*

Sophia, agua fria. Ahora.   *Sophy, bring cold water now.*

65 — tercia del muerte   *the curved sword thrust down by the matador in between the shoulders of a bull in the ring that is supposed to reach the heart and kill swiftly.*

68 — un salvaje   *the savage (an insult)*

Gitana sucio *filthy gypsy (another insult)*

69 — Pobrecita   *poor girl (in the pitying sense)*

Delicioso   *delicious*

76 — Dios Mio   *My God!*

82 — Catorce   *Fourteen (the number)*

85 — picador   *In the bullfight, one of a pair of horsemen who lower lances to slice the neck muscles of the bull, further limiting its head movements.*

87 — El capitan   *The captain (in this case, of the ship)*

88 — Policia   *with the police, a policeman*

   de la barca   *of or with the boat.*

91 — Imposible! Sus ojos son azul!   *That is impossible! His eyes are blue!*

   No es mi abuelo   *He is not my grandfather*

93 — Abuelita   *Making fun of Lucia, the grandfather refers to her as the little grandmother.*

106 — Puestaté péra pequeña, la loba esta aquí.   *(Roughly) Mind your station, puppy, the Big Dog is here.*

116 — supongo   *I guess*
   yo sé   *I know*

117 — Qué? Qué estás haciendo   *What? What are you doing?*

   Puta! Gitana!   *(Insults:) You whore. You gypsy.*

   Su puta católica está aquí. Yo la tengo.   *Here's your catholic whore. I have her.*

118 — Para estó, tres días   *For this [transgression], three days*

119 — requin   *shark (French)*

   tiburón   *shark (Spanish)*

   Tenga cuidado con los tiburones   *Be wary of the sharks*

   Ahora, aqui   *Now, here [where Mora points]*

125 — Verdad.   *In truth*

127 — tetas   *bosom, breasts*

136 — sangria   *wine into which fruits and sometimes a carbonated water are added, considered a refreshing summer drink.*

Melocoton   *a peach*

137 — La puta de Cristos, Manoli   *You whore of Christ! (Manoli is the diminutive of Manuela)*

139 — tortilla   *a pan-fried cake made of potatoes and eggs, sometimes garlic, peppers, fried onions or the like are added for additional flavor. A poor food that keeps well, that farmer's and laborers could carry to their labors for a filling lunch.*

139 — Dona Dolores, por favor esta carta a mi hija. Tengo noticias que el va querer leer. Por favor, no le de a mi esposa.   *(The heading to Ned's letter is written in bad Spanish:) Dona Dolores, please this letter to my daughter. I have news that will want to read. Please do not give my wife.*

150 — Perdonamé   *Forgive me (more as in "excuse me.")*

No lo sé   *I don't know [what you are saying.]*

152 — ¿Por qué hablar? ¿Qué tengo que decir vale la pena escuchar?   *Why talk? What I have to say worth listening to?*

158 — Che gelida menina   *(Italian, a song title) Are you cold, child?*

Che gelida manina, se la lasci riscaldar. Cercar che giova?   *Are you cold, child [young woman]? Let me warm you. Why bother looking [elsewhere.] (This song's lyrics have sexual overtones.)*

Books by Charles W. Bechtel
The Drew Nolan Series, in order

**A Hole
in the Water**
Book one

**Hell's
Cold Furies**
Book two

**When the Ball
Drops Foul**
Book three

**Running
Before Thunder**
Book four

**And Then
You Don't**
Book five

**A Hypocrisy
of Oaths**
Book six

All of the **Drew Nolan** stories
are available as Trade Paperbacks from
Amazon.com, and as e-book editions
from various sellers.

**The Odor
of Orchids**
a novel

**Book
of Days**
a novel

**On
Second Thoughts**
collected essays

**The Lady
from Spain**
a novel

**Sound Words
Seen**
selected poems

**The Long and the
Short**
selected stories

Follow the Author on Facebook:
https://www.facebook.com/charlesbechtelauthor

also

the Author's Website at
www.charlesbechtel.com